MURDER AT THE MASKED BALL

THE KITTY WORTHINGTON MYSTERIES, BOOK 3

MAGDA ALEXANDER

HEARTS AFIRE PUBLISHING

To Derek, one of the finest young men I know

CHAPTER ONE

WORTHINGTON HOUSE, MAYFAIR, LONDON,
JULY 1923

"*L*ORD PELLEGRINE IS ENGAGED to Lady Mary Darby-Murton," Mother said with a heavy sigh as she read the society column of *The Tell-All*, London's premier gossip rag.

"I sincerely hope she resembles his horse."

"Kitty!"

I gazed at her from my perch on the sofa where I'd been perusing today's post. "It's a compliment, Mother. Lord Pellegrine deems his horse the most beautiful creature he's ever beheld. At least that's what he told me at one of our at-homes."

Mother stamped her finger on the engagement announcement. "This could have been you."

"Not likely. I don't ride horses." Ever since I fell off my pony as a little girl, I'd eschewed all equine endeavors.

She turned toward me. "But you wouldn't have to, dear-

1

est. Lord Pellegrine would have never asked such a thing of you."

"Really, Mother?" I pierced her with a glance. "I've heard otherwise." Rumor had it Lady Mary Darby-Murton, after a strong push from her mama to do whatever was necessary to obtain a proposal, had slipped away with Lord Pellegrine to his stable where he'd vigorously entertained her on his stallion. My imagination did not reach quite that far as I had no experience of the amorous congress between men and women. I mean, how did one even go about such a thing?

Her face flushed pink. "That rumor is not true. It can't possibly be true."

I arched a quizzing brow. "And yet, they're engaged."

"Well, if not Lord Pellegrine, someone else," she asserted. "You've had many proposals. More than any other debutante this season. And you've turned down everyone." And with that reproof, she resumed addressing invitations to our next supper party.

Poor thing was frustrated she hadn't secured a titled spouse for me. Never mind I wasn't interested in such a thing. But Mother firmly believed the acquisition of a husband was the ultimate achievement of any properly brought-up young lady, and her mind would not be changed.

One would think one victory would be enough. After all, my sister Margaret was now engaged to the Duke of Wynchcombe. But in all truth, Mother couldn't take credit for that triumph. Margaret had met Sebastian at Oxford, where they'd subsequently fallen in love.

I rose from the couch and put my arms around her. "Dearest, you know I have no wish to marry. At least not at this time."

"Nonsense. Every woman desires marriage to a gentleman."

"Not me." I kissed her cheek and returned to my seat where I'd been reading the latest spate of letters I'd received, every one of them asking for my help in looking into one matter or another. After our last investigation into the murder of an aristocrat, the papers had been full of praise for me, as well as my family and friends, for our work in identifying the murderer. As a result, people thought I was in the detective business and were writing notes begging for my help.

She put down her pen and glanced askance at me. "And what pray tell do you wish to do instead?"

"Excellent question." She had cause to worry. All three of my siblings had achieved their life's goals. Ned, the oldest, was a partner in Father's investment firm, Worthington & Son. Next in line Richard had decamped to Egypt and become an archeologist. And Margaret was attending Oxford while furthering the cause of women's issues. I, however, had not settled on any particular interest. The only thing I seemed to excel at was solving murders, and that couldn't be a vocation. After all, one simply could not count on a murder to come along every week. But there were other matters I could investigate. The letters were proof of that. "I could become a lady detective. I'm rather good at figuring things out."

"That's not an occupation for a lady, Kitty," she huffed.

"Maybe it should be."

She studied me with careful thought. "You're not seriously considering such a thing."

"Ummm," was my only answer, for I was indeed thinking about it.

"Young women of gentle birth do not involve themselves in tawdry matters."

"I've already helped solve two murders, Mother. Doesn't get much tawdrier than that." Never mind she only knew the half of what I'd done. If she ever discovered my forays into the seedier side of town, she'd be horrified.

"But you had help. Your brother and sister, your friends. And those investigations were conducted for good reasons."

"Well, these are good reasons, as well." I waved one of the letters at her.

"What do you mean?"

"For the last two weeks, I've been getting requests to look into certain matters. Lost objects, missing persons." I didn't mention the ones that asked me to investigate circumstances involving blackmail or an errant husband, for she would definitely frown on those.

"It would be beyond the pale for you to become a lady detective. I forbid it." And with that, she returned to her invitations, putting paid to our discussion.

I loved my mother, and I honestly sought to follow her wishes. But I was of age, having turned twenty-one in May, and I had the dowry Father had settled on me. So, I could carry out such an endeavor with or without her approval.

But the thing of it was I couldn't simply hang out a shingle. I needed to have some instruction as to how to go on. Books would help. The lending library would almost certainly have some I could borrow. But I would need more than that, ideally personal instruction from someone who'd worked in the field. Maybe a retired inspector who would be willing to tutor me. But how to find one?

Inspector Crawford would be of no help as he would side with Mother on the issue. Chief Inspector Bolton might be more approachable, though. After all, I'd helped him solve a murder which had raised his standing at Scotland Yard. The least he could do was recommend someone. I would write and ask for a recommendation. With any luck, I could have an answer by tomorrow.

But before I could act on my decision, my sister Margaret sailed into Mother's personal parlor, windblown from the blustery day, and promptly buzzed Mother's cheek. "Hello, dearest."

Mother offered my sibling her sweetest smile. "How was the clinic?"

A strong advocate of women's issues, Margaret volunteered at a women's health center which served those of modest means. As she did not have the medical expertise to treat those who sought its services, she performed the never-ending administrative tasks which needed doing as well as engaged in community outreach.

"Busy, as always. It's all we can do to keep up with the flow of patients." Straightening, she put a hand to her back as if it ached. "Just wish we could do more."

"Maybe Kitty could help."

I could see the wheels turning in Mother's head. Keep Kitty busy with the women's clinic, and she won't think about becoming a lady detective. "I don't think I'd be much good since I faint at the sight of blood."

"Thank you for the offer," Margaret said, "but we need money more than volunteers so we can build additional health centers." Unfortunately, the government refused to permit any access to birth control information through government-funded programs. That left the work of family planning to private clinics, such as the one at which Margaret volunteered. Since there was only one in all of London, the demand was much higher than the clinic could meet.

"We could hold a fundraiser," I suggested. Excited about the idea, I jumped to my feet. "Mother could advise us since she has a great deal of expertise in that area." She was the chair of the Ladies Benevolent Society, after all, and had planned many an event.

"Of course. Anything I can do to help," Mother responded.

"That's a grand suggestion, Kitty." Margaret pressed my hand. "But the timing is not right. It'll take at least two months to organize such a thing. By that time, everyone will have left town. It would be better to hold it next year."

"But you'll be busy with your wedding plans then, dear," Mother reminded her.

After Sebastian proposed, they'd decided on a June date for their wedding. Sebastian had flat out stated that he couldn't wait for Margaret to become his wife longer than that, an incredibly romantic thing for him to say.

"We'll figure something out," Margaret said. "Speaking of Sebastian, I must dash. He's picking me up in half an hour, and I desperately need a wash. We're going to the Royal Botanic Gardens. Apparently, they have a new bloom."

"A new bloom at the Royal Botanic Gardens? Will wonders never cease?" I teased.

"Oh, stop. It's a rare orchid from Borneo, or some such place."

"What will you wear, dearest?" Mother asked, always cognizant of the face one must present in public.

Margaret scrunched her brow. "I hadn't given it much thought. Something brown, I think, to camouflage the dirt." Unlike Mother, Margaret had never given two figs about clothes.

"I wish you'd allow me to refresh your wardrobe, dear," Mother said. "Your gowns are at least two years old."

"I don't need new outfits, Mother, to study at Oxford. As a matter of fact, they frown on ostentatious fashion."

"You will be back for supper?" Mother asked, seemingly giving up on her argument. But it was bound to be a temporary reprieve for she was a strong proponent of dressing well.

"Of course. We'll stop at Wynchcombe House and collect Lily on the way back. Now I simply must bathe." And with a wave of her hand, she was gone.

Mother's knitted brow evidenced her disappointment. "Most gentlemen take their fiancées to the theatre or the opera."

"Either would bore them to tears. Sebastian loves nature, and Margaret loves Sebastian."

"But they will be seen, and there she'll be wearing a gown years out of date. The thought is not to be borne."

She had a point. Fashions had changed drastically from two seasons ago. Skirts were shorter for one, and for another, they were better tailored. "You must give her a reason to obtain a new wardrobe, Mother."

"Being engaged to a duke is not enough?"

"Not when the duke is Sebastian. She could be wearing sackcloth and ashes, and he would not notice."

"But the world would."

"So, take a different tack."

"Such as?"

"Margaret is passionate about women's causes—health, equality, and, of course, suffrage. As hard as she works, she can't do it all on her own. Funds are needed to build more clinics. But society ladies are not going to donate money to someone dressed in unfashionable attire. Obnoxious, I know. But they don't want to be seen with someone who's garbed in outdated clothes. Once she's seen in the latest thing, socialites will happily attend any events she sponsors as they will want to claim they're friends with the Duchess of Wynchcombe. So, explain she'll get better results if she dresses in style. I'm sure you'll be able to extend those orders not only to tea frocks, but ball gowns and anything else."

Mother's gaze softened. "How very clever you are, Kitty."

7

"Thank you, Mother." I took the compliment in stride. "I got it from you. And Father, of course. But mostly from you."

"Ummmm. Before I get a cavity from all the sugar you're pouring over me, why don't you get some rest? You want to look your best for supper tonight."

Mother had originally held at-homes every Tuesday to encourage admirers. Many gentlemen had attended, and many had proposed. All of which I turned down. Not one to go down in defeat, she'd recently changed her strategy to holding supper parties twice a week. And she always made sure to include an eligible bachelor with a title attached to his name.

Suspicious, I narrowed my gaze. "Who did you invite, Mother?"

"Lord Marlowe and Lady Emma. And her mother, of course. Lord Rutledge. The Winthrops. They're clients of your father's."

She loved to seat fourteen to dinner whenever we entertained, and she was a stickler for even numbers. Once you added our family, Sebastian, his sister, Lily, and me, it left her one gentleman shy. "And someone else."

"Lord Hollingsworth."

The newest aristocrat in town. He'd been absent through most of the season as he'd been adventuring somewhere in the South Seas. As busy as I'd been last month in my quest to discover a murderer, I'd barely caught a glimpse of him. But he was handsome and definitely of marriageable age. And, if memory served me right, Lord Hollingsworth was a marquis. "I didn't know we were acquainted with him."

"Lord Rutledge suggested we invite him. Apparently, he's looking for someone to manage his finances."

A perfectly reasonable explanation, which I didn't believe for a second. Mother had a scheme up her sleeve.

CHAPTER TWO

SUPPER AT WORTHINGTON HOUSE

OUR SUPPERS TENDED TO BE CASUAL GATHERINGS, even when we invited guests. Thus, no greeting line was created. The usual custom was for arrivals to be announced by our butler, Carlton, as they made their way into the drawing room where cocktails were being served. After their entrance, Father would greet them and inquire as to what they wanted to drink. If they were unknown to the other invitees, he would introduce them, offering a tidbit about who they were as they strolled about the room.

Tonight was no different. Since most of our guests knew one another, no special introductions needed to be made, the only exception being Father's clients who were quickly absorbed into the group.

Lord Hollingsworth, however, was a different matter. Since Mother and I hadn't been formally introduced and he was a member of the nobility, we stood next to Father so we could officially make his acquaintance.

While Father and Mother engaged him in polite conversation, I had a chance to observe the marquis.

He was tall, dark-haired, impossibly fit. In his mid-thirties would be my guess. Where Inspector Crawford's eyes were dark, his were a bright blue which struck a bright contrast against the healthy glow of his skin. He probably spent every moment he could outdoors, much as Sebastian did. His hands were not the smooth ones of an aristocrat. They were rough, calloused, strong which spoke of manual labor. A scar marred his right one. But rather than detract from him, it enhanced his masculinity. Everything about his persona revealed a man who led a full, adventurous life.

When he stood in front of me, I extended my hand. "So very nice to meet you, Lord Hollingsworth."

Doing what was expected, he bent over and kissed it. "The pleasure is all mine, Miss Worthington."

"What would you like to drink?" Father asked now that the niceties had been observed.

"Whiskey, neat, if you will," Lord Hollingsworth replied with a grin.

It took but a few seconds for Carlton to comply with his request.

Having officially met him, I wandered back to Lady Emma. Marlowe had made some inane remark she'd taken objection to, and I wanted to prevent a skirmish from breaking out. But I couldn't avoid Lord Hollingsworth altogether. Mother had arranged the table seating for maximum matchmaking capabilities, which meant during supper I was seated next to him.

"You're an explorer, milord?" I asked after the soup course was served. The topic should keep him busy talking with only an occasional nod or a 'how marvelous' from me.

"I am. I just returned from the South Seas," he replied.

"How marvelous."

His piercing gaze drilled into me. "Do you really find it so when I have yet to tell you about it?"

Clearly, he would not be content with polite conversation which meant I would need to employ my full faculties. "Well, I have my imagination. And I can very well envision how wondrous your adventures must have been." He could not possibly find objection to that.

But then, the devil challenged me. "What do you envision, Miss Worthington?" he asked with a spark of humor.

Fiddlesticks! Geography had never been my strong suit. "Well, there's the Pacific Ocean. The southern Pacific Ocean." The South Seas had to be located there, didn't they? Or was it an it?

His mouth quivered with repressed humor. "As opposed to the northern Pacific Ocean?"

"Yes, of course. And then there are the islands. Australia, New Zealand."

He waited until the next course was served before commenting, "Well, I suppose they could be called islands. They would refer to themselves as countries, though. Anything else?"

He had a point. That had been unbelievably silly of me. Vowing to do better, I countered with, "The Hawaiian Islands?" I couldn't be faulted for referring to them as such. They were definitely islands. It was built into its name.

This time his grin was on full display. "Very good, Miss Worthington."

I stiffened. "You're mocking me, Lord Hollingsworth. Something I do not appreciate."

To my surprise, he admitted it. "My apologies. I promise not to do so if you promise not to make inane remarks."

My face heated up. To be caught out was extremely

embarrassing. Most people did not notice when I offered nothing but small talk. Obviously, he was cut from a different cloth. "Very well." I accepted his *mea culpa* with grace. He was a guest after all.

"I do enjoy the adventures, as you've guessed," he offered by way of an olive branch. "The peoples and cultures are of particular interest to me."

"Why those two areas?" I asked, now fully immersed in the subject.

The footmen served the entree, delaying his response. But at the first opportunity, he explained, "I find them endlessly fascinating. They can be quite different from us, and yet, at the same time, they're the same."

"How so?"

"Well, Miss Worthington, everyone has basic needs, such as food, clothing, shelter. They also have a desire to belong. That's where love and friendship come in. Finally, most people want to be appreciated for who they are, what they've accomplished."

I took certain things for granted—the roof over my head, the food I ate, the very clothes I wore. But I'd always appreciated the love of my family. And recently, I'd come to value the friends I'd made. Without them, we wouldn't have been able to solve two murders. "I never thought about it quite that way. But you're right. How very clever of you."

"Thank you, but I can't take credit for the theory. It's been well documented. Of course, we go about it in different ways. For example, in British high society, women value marriage. Men do as well, but their reasonings are quite different."

"Ladies perceive marriage as a status symbol." As I was well aware.

He leaned slightly back as he pondered my words. "I believe you underestimate them, Miss Worthington. Yes, they see marriage as a status symbol, especially if they secure a husband with a title and a fortune. But they also need it to be safe. The food, clothing, shelter aspects. Men, on the other hand, don't need all that. They already have the title, the estate, and the money that goes along with it. They seek a wife to ensure their lineage."

"That's not so in other cultures?"

"It depends on their customs. Some are patriarchal in nature; others are female-centric. The purpose of marriage in many other places revolves around property and physical needs. Property is offered to the female's family to compensate for the loss of a daughter who would have been of service to them, and the male gains a wife so she can satisfy his physical needs. Sexual, of course, but also someone who will cook, clean, and care for him."

How very refreshing to hear a man discuss the subject of sex out in the open as that subject was deemed taboo in our society. And heaven forbid it be discussed in front of an unmarried woman. Clearly, Lord Hollingsworth did not adhere to the rules.

"What about children?"

"They're valued as well since families depend on offspring to share labor responsibilities. But it's not the prime impetus for marriage in many cases."

"That's fascinating. I can see why you love it so." I sliced into the Beef Bourguignon and took a bite before asking, "How do you determine the best time to travel?"

He sipped from the burgundy wine before he answered. "Our trips usually take us to places in the southern hemisphere. When it's spring in the north, it's winter in that part of the world. So we arrange them to enjoy its warmer weather."

"But you just returned from a trip, and it's summer now. Were you traveling during their winter?"

His brief hesitation made me wonder, but then he responded readily enough. "No. We departed England last September, crossed the Atlantic, then traversed Panama through its canal. By this time it was October which was spring in the Southern Hemisphere. Unfortunately, en route we got caught up in a typhoon. By necessity we needed to stop for repairs. That put our journey back a month. We did not arrive at the Polynesian islands until November, but it still gave us five months to explore them. My crew loved every moment. It's quite a beautiful part of the world, much of it unspoiled by civilization."

"You make me want to travel there."

He arched a brow. "What's stopping you?"

A spark of laughter escaped me. "Oh, Lord Hollingsworth, I'm barely allowed out of my home without a chaperone. A trip halfway around the world would be impossible."

"You must break free of your confines, Miss Worthington. Only then will you truly live."

"A noble sentiment." And one I was trying to achieve in my own way. "Tell me about your return trip."

"We stopped in Tahiti where we spent a month cataloguing our finds and making necessary repairs. By the time we began our journey back to England, it was May. As we crossed the Pacific, it became late spring once more."

"How marv—" Noting his mocking brow, I changed course. "Who travels with you?"

"The Hollingsworth expeditions include a full contingent of explorers. Some specialize in botany. Others in the geography of the places. We have a cartographer as well who creates maps and another who specializes in cuisines. Our chef is the only woman on the ship. One very clever individual is a zoology expert who has a special way with animals. Finally, we have a historian as well as interpreters who are proficient in the native languages."

"That seems a daunting task. Do you go on these expeditions every year?"

He laughed. "No. More like every two, sometimes three. It takes time and money to raise funds for our travels and organize the trips. And sometimes circumstances have forced delays on us."

"Such as the Great War?"

"Yes. We didn't conduct any expeditions during those years as most of the crew and scientists volunteered their efforts to it."

"Including you?"

A shadow crossed over his face. "Yes."

I addressed my Charlotte Russe to give him time to regain his bearings. Only when his somber mood had lifted did I resume our conversation. "Do you share your knowledge of everything you've learned with the world?"

"We do. When we return to England, we write expedition reports for the Royal Geographical Society and hold lectures there. They're usually very well attended. We also bring back objects, plants, what have you from the places we've visited. We pay for everything we bring back. Quite generously, I might add."

"That's good to hear. What do you with them?"

"We either sell, donate them, or auction them off. Sometimes, we have requests from individuals interested in a particular item. The proceeds help fund our next trip. By the way, I'm in discussions with your father's firm to handle those proceeds, as well as my own fortune. I want to keep everything above board."

"Worthington & Son has an excellent reputation."

"Lord Rutledge highly recommends the enterprise. Others do as well. I've checked."

"Sebastian would love to discuss the flora of the place with whoever your botany expert is. That's his passion. Well, other than my sister, Margaret, of course."

He gazed in their direction. "They're well suited."

"You can tell from a mere glance?" It was my turn to challenge him.

Amusement sparkled in his eyes. "And a discussion at the Royal Botanic Gardens. They were there this afternoon."

"Oh, yes, he was eager to see a rare orchid."

"We brought it back from Palau. A miracle it survived the journey, but then we have an excellent botanist."

"Goodness! I'm impressed."

"Are you really?" His tone changed into something else. Something more intimate.

An alarm rang in my head, causing me to hesitate. "Y-yes?"

"Then maybe you'd like to become an investor. We're always looking for sponsors for our expeditions."

I laughed so hard it drew Mother's attention.

"What do you find so amusing?" he asked, seemingly curious more than anything else.

"I mistook your interest, that's all."

He quirked a brow even as his lips turned upward in a smile. "I've heard about your horde of admirers, Miss Worthington. Rest assured. You won't be adding me to the list as I'm not looking to marry. I enjoy my freedom too much."

"Well then, we are alike in that respect, Lord Hollingsworth, for neither am I."

The rest of the evening we continued to discuss his adventures in the South Seas without my fearing a proposal.

CHAPTER THREE

TEA AND SYMPATHY

*L*ADY CLINTON'S AFTERNOON TEAS were a weekly ritual to which ladies were invited, some hailing from the nobility, others merely well-off. Those with a title attached to their names always positioned themselves in an exclusive enclave separate from the nouveau riche, lest the odor of the common folk adhere to them. Ridiculous, if you asked me, as we both breathed the same air.

The Worthingtons rightfully belonged to the latter faction as Father made his substantial fortune investing in trade. But with my sister's recent engagement to Sebastian, the Duke of Wynchcombe, the situation had changed. Were the Worthingtons to be honored with a spot in the nobility camp or be snubbed along with the rest of the *hoi polloi*?

On our way to the tea, I'd predicted the titled ladies would clutch Margaret to their respective bosoms. Figuratively speaking, of course, as none would dare make such a public display of affection. It just wasn't done, don't you know?

In the past, Margaret had roundly ignored the whole pretentious mob. But Mother had now convinced her to look favorably upon them, at least in public, since these women could contribute to her causes. Acting on my suggestion, she'd also talked Margaret into ordering a new wardrobe arguing that ladies of the nobility prized appearances above just about anything else. Margaret, seeing the wisdom of her words, had ordered an entire slew of gowns, the first of which had been delivered this morning. As we marched into Lady Clinton's drawing room, she set herself the task of seeding the ground, if you will, so that next year when she held a fundraiser, her efforts would bear fruit.

My prediction proved to be true, for it took no time for Margaret to be swept up by the nobility clique.

"Oh, Miss Worthington, what a gorgeous frock."

"You must come sit by me, for I must hear all about your engagement."

"When is the wedding to be?"

I sought to provide interference for she was truly being swarmed. But before I could do so, Lady Clinton pulled me aside, an ingratiating smile in full display. She wanted something from me.

"My dear Miss Worthington, I understand you were deeply involved in the resolution of our latest murder mystery. You must tell me all about it."

Unable to deny it for the papers had blasted the news all over their front pages, I dodged the inquiry by sticking to the truth. "I'm sorry, Lady Clinton, but I'm under strict orders from Scotland Yard not to discuss the case. I'm sure you understand."

"But—"

Eager to provide whatever help I could to my family, I

glanced their way. But Mother had the situation well in hand, so I opted to leave them to it and seek my own escape. Gazing about the room for a lifeline, I found it in the person of my dearest friend. "Oh, there's Lady Emma. I promised her the recipe of my new face lotion. If you will excuse me, milady." And then, offering the briefest of curtsies, I rushed off.

But when I reached Lady Emma, I noticed she appeared somewhat peeved.

"Is something wrong?" I asked taking a seat next to her on the settee.

"Look at them." She nodded to the ladies twittering away at Mother and Margaret. "Two weeks ago, they couldn't be bothered with your sister. I doubt they even knew her name. But now that she's engaged to the Duke of Wynchcombe, they all want to become bosom bows." She snorted with disgust. "Toadies, every last one of them."

Exactly as I'd predicted. "I fear it's the way of the world. Margaret managed to do what many of them have not. She got herself engaged to a duke. Not because he's one, but because they're in love, something that most of them won't ever know."

Her furrowed brow communicated her disdain. "And Margaret approves of this?"

"She's planning to hold a fundraiser to create more women's clinics. Many of those ladies have very deep pockets." I nodded toward the swarm. "If she offers a few smiles here and there, she has much to gain."

She turned back to me with a frown. "When is she planning this event? The season is almost done."

"Next year."

Everything about her drooped. "I wish I could be here to help."

Well, that got my attention. "Why wouldn't you be?"

The corners of her mouth edged downward. "I haven't acquired a husband. Nor do I have the faintest expectation of gaining one as I didn't take."

"Why would you want one?" I was of the firm belief a woman did not need a spouse, at least not before she could draw some enjoyment from life.

A bitter laugh escaped her. "Kitty, I'm not like you. My family is not wealthy. We're barely making do as it is. Since I didn't manage to attach a gentleman, I will be kept home next year so my sister Gloriana can be brought out."

This was horrible. Not only for her sake, but my own selfish reason, for she'd made the season much more bearable than it would have been. I couldn't imagine being deprived of her company next year. Something would need to be done. I pressed her hands. "Try not to worry. We'll find a solution."

"Such as?"

"I don't know. I'll think of something."

"Please do. I've enjoyed this season so much, and all because of you and the investigation." Poor thing was looking downright miserable. All her spark had gone missing.

I had to cheer her up. "The murder investigation was fun?" I teased.

Her common sense emerged as I hoped it would. "Well, not the reason for it, of course. But I've treasured the camaraderie among friends." Her mouth flattened. "Well, except for Lord Marlowe. He can be downright insufferable."

"Right." I suspected she was drawn to the earl. Unfortunately, the last thing he desired was a wife as he was not finished sowing his wild oats. Or so he'd told me at a ball. Giving her time to collect herself, I glanced around the space. That's when I noticed someone I hadn't seen before, a strange occurrence for Lady Clinton tended to invite the same guests every week. "Who is that lady on the opposite side of the room? Tall, chestnut hair, two-tone color eyes, a bird's nest on her head." Why some ladies chose that particular decoration for their hats was beyond me. "Do you know?"

Lady Emma peered into the far-off distance. "That's Abigail Morgan. Her brother, Archibald, is Lord Wakefield's heir. Strange that she's been invited. She's neither nobility, nor that well-to-do." The two requirements to gain an invitation to Lady Clinton's teas. "At least from what I've heard."

"Maybe she accompanied someone?"

"I doubt it. She's seated by herself."

Apparently, since Miss Morgan was neither fish nor fowl, no one had welcomed her to a group. She sat all alone eating her scone, drinking her tea, while calmly gazing around the room. She was self-possessed, I had to give her that.

I was just about to suggest we go greet the woman when a footman approached with a full complement of scones, crumpets, and assorted pastries, as well as the ubiquitous pot of tea. By the time we'd refreshed ourselves, Lady Freshfield had joined Miss Morgan. Maybe the older maven had taken pity on her.

"Lady Wakefield is back in town," Lady Emma remarked.

My gaze bounced back to her. "Really?" I was surprised to say the least. Months ago, Lady Wakefield had withdrawn to her country estate, ostensibly to rest from the hectic social season, but in reality, to escape her husband's physical abuse. Her return to London was not good news. "Why would she put herself in harm's way again?"

"I don't believe she had a choice. Lord Wakefield is eager for an heir, and that can't be done if they're leading separate lives."

Their union had produced no issue, something for which Lord Wakefield blamed his wife. He often "disciplined" her when her courses came due, as it was proof she was not expecting.

"Do you think Newcastle knows?"

"I suspect he does. He's quite attuned to the comings and goings of Lady Wakefield."

Newcastle was in love with her, something I'd learned early in the season. "Do you know why he didn't marry her?" I'd asked Ned since he was friends with Newcastle, but it was something they'd never discussed as their friendship ensued from recent years. But Lady Emma was remarkably knowledgeable about British high society, so she might very well be cognizant of the details.

"They met about six years ago during her one and only season. From all accounts, they were instantly smitten with one another. But at that time, Newcastle was a mere mister, not an earl, and not exactly flush with money. Her family's finances were such that it was imperative she marry well. Generations of spendthrifts and gamblers had wasted whatever fortune they had. So his offer of marriage was turned down."

"That's horrible." So many young women were brought to the marriage mart and paraded around like prize mares to attract the attention of gentlemen in possession of sizable fortunes. Some might be old and less than desirable, but that made no matter to families. The important thing was the size of the gentleman's purse and how much could be obtained to replenish the family coffers.

"By this point, the Great War had started. Feeling he could be of more use in the battlefield than in London nursing a broken heart, he enlisted. He was injured but miraculously did not suffer any serious harm."

"Thank heaven for that."

"Yes, indeed. Unfortunately, the same could not be said of his cousin, the heir to the title. He was killed during one of the last battles of the war. When his father found out, he suffered an apoplexy. He lingered for some time but eventually passed away, making Newcastle the new earl. But by then it was too late for him to claim her as his bride. She had already wed Lord Wakefield. He thought a young girl would be the most likely to bear fruit."

"And yet, it hasn't."

"He blames her, which is so unfair. After all, he was married before and there was no issue there, either. He won't be satisfied until she's with child. And, as things stand, that's not likely to happen." She gazed at me, a worried look in her eyes. "I'm afraid of what may happen to Lady Wakefield."

"That he'll abuse her again?" That was my fear as well.

"Or worse."

Dread curled up my spine. "What do you mean?"

"His first wife fell down the stairs. It was ruled an accident, but rumor had it she was pushed."

I'd heard the same, but I'd attributed it to just that. A rumor. But Lady Emma was intimating something else, something much darker. "You think he'd do the same to Lady Wakefield?" The thought was not to be borne. "He wouldn't!"

She scoffed. "Wouldn't he? I wouldn't put anything past that man."

CHAPTER FOUR

VISIT TO THE MODISTE

*W*E ARRIVED HOME to discover invitations to that most exclusive of events—the Duchess of Brightwell's Midsummer Masquerade Ball—waiting for us. Mother had not-so-secretly envied those who received one in the past, for it signaled they were among the crème de la crème of society. But, of course, since we were not nobility, an invitation had never been issued. This year, however, Margaret's engagement to Sebastian seemingly had made us worthy enough for that honor. Needless to say, Mother was in alt.

"We must visit Angelique's right away," she said, all atwitter, "before everyone gets the march on us. I must send her a note immediately."

Before she rushed off, I asked the obvious, "Wouldn't it be better to call, Mother? She might not read your note until later in the day or maybe even tomorrow."

"Telephone her?" Mother believed the contraption to be

the devil's tool, a relic of her Victorian upbringing, and one she refused to use unless absolutely necessary.

"I can do it if you wish," Margaret volunteered.

"Yes, that would be best." Mother turned only to swivel back. "Right away, mind you."

"Of course, Mother."

And off Mother went in search of Cook for Father had sent word he was bringing a client to supper. Although Cook was always happy to accommodate her wishes, Mother was ever mindful of the respect due her, especially since she was one of the best ones in all of Mayfair.

After Margaret picked up the stick telephone in the hallway, it took a few minutes to be connected to the modiste, but she eventually got through. Apparently, Angelique's services were already being requested for the masquerade ball. But thanks to our steady patronage, and, more importantly, our timely payment of bills, an appointment was arranged for the next day.

"Well, that's taken care of," Margaret said. "One less thing to worry about."

"Will the fittings interfere with your time at the clinic?"

"More than likely, but there are others who can take my place."

"Not as efficiently as you, I'm willing to guess."

"It is what it is, Kitty." She heaved out a sigh. "It seems awfully silly to worry about what to wear to a ball."

"But it will be time well spent. Hopefully, it will encourage those with means to contribute to your causes."

"That's the only reason I'm willing to attend. Well, that and Mother's happiness."

"It has made her happy, hasn't it?" There wasn't much either of us wouldn't do for Mother. After the loss of our sister Emily to the Spanish Flu several years ago, it had taken her months to recuperate. So, if our attending a ball made her happy, we would do it with a full heart.

"What are you going to wear?" Margaret asked as we climbed the stairs so we could change out of our afternoon frocks.

"I'm thinking of a Spanish flamenco dancer costume. I love those flouncy dresses."

She scrunched her nose. "Difficult to manage at a ball."

"A modified version then. What about you?"

She followed me into my room where we both took a seat on my bed. "Boadicea, I think."

The warrior queen of the Isceni tribe. "Yes, that would suit you. Do you think Sebastian will attend?" If she had received an invitation, he must have as well.

"I doubt it. He's still in mourning." Even though his deceased relative had treated Sebastian and Lily abominably, etiquette required a six-month mourning period to be observed. But it would not last forever. By December, they'd be free to participate in balls and such. In the meantime, they were able to attend private gatherings such as suppers at our home as well as hold a few of their own.

She blew out a breath. "I'm not exactly thrilled about attending the ball, especially since Sebastian won't be there." A small smile lit her lips. "With his sense of humor, he would have made it such fun." Sebastian and Margaret were well matched as they shared the same goals, but he faced life in a lighter frame of mind while Margaret took things more seriously.

"But if you don't attend, it would disappoint Mother, and as the future Duchess of Wynchcombe, you must show your face."

She arched a brow. "Even if it's covered with blue paint?"

"You wouldn't!"

"Oh, wouldn't I?"

I couldn't tell if she was teasing or speaking the truth.

* * *

THE NEXT MORNING Angelique's was busier than Victoria Station at the height of summer when holiday seekers took to the railways to trade the stifling heat of London for the cooler breezes of Brighton. Every fitting and consultation room buzzed with activity. Not a surprise for she was one of the best modistes in town. Not only was she contending with those who needed costumes for the masquerade ball, but regular clients as well. Those who hadn't secured matrimonial prospects were desperately trying to gild the lily and those who had, well, they needed to impress.

Upon our arrival, we were shown to one of the larger consultation rooms. And, of course, we were attended by Angelique herself. Not only was she a talented modiste, but an astute businesswoman who knew how to keep her favored clients happy. And that included her personal touch.

"So, Mrs. Worthington, Misses Worthington, would you like to review our costume pattern books?" Angelique pointed to a stack which rested on a small table. "Or are you already decided on your preferences? We'll be glad to accommodate anything you have in mind."

"Why don't you discuss Margaret and Kitty's choices with them first?" Mother asked. "They already know what they'd like. In the meantime, I'll review these." She patted the books with a gleam in her eye.

"Very well." Angelique gave her an indulgent smile before turning to us. "So, ladies, what will it be?"

"Umm, you go first, Kitty," Margaret said eying the books. "I want to get some ideas from these." She pulled up a chair and joined Mother at the table. So much for her not being excited about this event.

The ultimate professional, Angelique somehow managed to keep a straight face.

I described my ideas for the Spanish flamenco costume. "Magnifique, Miss Worthington. You certainly have the right coloring for a Spanish *señorita*. What about a wig? We can arrange it for you, if you wish."

"Oh, I don't think so. If the weather turns sultry, it will be awfully hot. Maybe just a satin rose to pin on my hair?"

"It shall be so, then. We already have your measurements, so it should take no time at all to create your costume."

"Wonderful."

Having taken care of my needs, she turned to Margaret. "So Miss Worthington, have you decided?"

Margaret pointed to an outfit. "Boadicea."

The modiste studied the drawing. "Oh, yes. A female warrior. That would suit you very well. That's what you are. You fight for all women, *n'est-ce pas?*"

"I try, madame," Margaret answered.

"You more than try, Miss Worthington, you succeed. That's more than can be said for many others. As you say in England, talk is cheap, but actions speak loudest."

"Thank you."

"Let's see, for your dress, you'd like a maroon tunic, over a pair of pants, and a cloak, black I think. For your armor, a breastplate, a choker, a tasset belt, and leather gauntlets. Is that correct?"

"And a sword and a sheath."

"Margaret!" Mother exclaimed. "You don't intend to march into the Duchess of Brightwell's ball carrying a weapon?"

"I wouldn't be the first. Plenty of gentlemen do."

"But they are men, dear. Ladies do not carry such things."

"This lady does, Mother." Going by her stubborn expression, she would not be dissuaded.

As Mother must have realized, because she gave in. "Very well, dear."

"Now that your daughters are settled, Mrs. Worthington, have you found something you like?"

She pointed to one of the costumes in the book. "This one, please."

We rushed over to glance over her shoulder. She'd chosen a long, flowing gown with bell-cut sleeves, its square-cut neckline encrusted with dark jewels. The dress a medieval lady would have worn centuries ago.

"What a wonderful choice, Mother. You'll look splendid in it."

She colored with pleasure. "You think so, Kitty?"

"Absolutely. Don't you agree, Margaret?"

"I do. But we must add a crown." She turned to the modiste. "Would that be possible, madame?"

"Most *certainement*, mademoiselle."

"There you go, Mother. You'll look absolutely regal in it."

Mother scrunched her mouth. "You'll have to excuse my daughters, Angelique. They like to dump the butter sauce over me."

"Maybe so, madame, but in this instance, they're right. You will resemble the queen you are deep within."

"Oh." Mother grew even more flustered. Though she totally deserved every compliment she received, she'd never been able to accept them. It came from her upbringing. As a pastor's daughter, she'd never been allowed to shine. She soon regained her composure, however, and got to the business at hand. "When will the costumes be ready, madame?"

"In but a few days, Mrs. Worthington. You shall have them by next week."

"Splendid," Mother said. "I knew we could depend on you."

"Merci," A smiling Angelique responded.

We emerged from the fitting room to discover a familiar face reviewing pattern books in the reception area.

"Lady Wakefield!" I said drawing her attention.

She curtsied. "Misses Worthington, Mrs. Worthington, what a pleasure to see you."

"The pleasure is ours; I assure you." Mother responded for the three of us. "You've recuperated from your illness?" Mother's way of allowing Lady Wakefield to save face. At one of the balls we'd attended, we'd seen the damage her husband had inflicted on her. Shortly after which, she'd left town.

"Yes. I . . . regained my health and thought I'd return."

"You must come to tea, Lady Wakefield," Mother suggested. "So, we can properly visit."

What Mother left unsaid was that she was worried about her, as we all were, for I'd shared the news of Lady Wake-field's return with Margaret and her. More than anything else, she wanted Lady Wakefield to know she could depend on us whatever her need.

But before Lady Wakefield could answer, the shop's front door blew open and Lily breezed in. Sebastian's sister sparkled with confidence, a stark difference from the young woman we'd first met who'd been afraid of her own shadow.

"Kitty, Margaret, Mrs. Worthington! How very pleasant to see you."

After introductions were made all around, my smiling Mother asked, "Ordering more gowns, dear?"

"How did you know?" That tinkling laughter of hers rang out. "It's naughty of me, I know. But I get such pleasure from having a closet filled with new frocks, even if most of them are either black or lavender. Angelique is a genius at designing different styles."

"How splendid." None of us would even think of finding fault with her as she'd come to us with only five gowns to her name, all sadly out of date. During Lily's short stay with us, we'd learned to love her as a sister and, in Mother's case, a daughter. Now that her brother Sebastian had inherited the Wynchcombe fortune, along with the title, he was eager to indulge the sister who'd suffered from neglect for so long.

"Lady Lily. Angelique is ready for you," a shop attendant announced.

Lily scrunched her brow. "No time for a coze, I'm afraid, and I so wanted one." Because of the mourning period, Lily could not attend any large event, so she depended on our small gatherings to socialize. As busy as we were, there simply weren't enough of them to satisfy any of us.

Giving a little hop, she clapped. "I know. Why don't you come tomorrow for luncheon? And of course, Lady Wakefield, you are included in the invitation. We shall have a jolly old time. Just us ladies as Sebastian will be off to Parliament. You must come too, Mrs. Worthington."

"Thank you, dear. That's very kind of you, but I have a meeting of the Ladies Benevolent Society."

"Lady Lily, this way, please," the shop attendant repeated in an insistent tone. A polite reminder that Angelique was waiting for her.

"And we must have Lady Emma as well," Lily said. "I'll telephone her, shall I?"

"Splendid," I agreed. Lady Emma would happily round out the group.

The shop attendant cleared her throat.

"I better go," Lily said. With a wave of her hand, she disappeared into the consultation room.

"What a delightful young lady," Lady Wakefield said.

"She is that and more," I agreed. "Until tomorrow?"

Lady Wakefield nodded but didn't say a word.

I couldn't help but feel there was something worrying her. Maybe tomorrow I would find out.

CHAPTER FIVE

A LUNCHEON AT WYNCHCOMBE HOUSE

THE NEXT DAY WE GATHERED AT WYNCHCOMBE HOUSE, an imposing Georgian-style mansion which stood three stories high with wings flaring on both sides. While the structure itself was magnificent, the furniture tended to be on the stodgy side, reflecting a style of several hundred years before. But that was slowly changing. With Sebastian's approval, Lily had enthusiastically thrown herself into the task of refurbishing some of the rooms on the ground floor. Upon our arrival, she proceeded to give us a partial tour.

I was truly awed by her efforts. She'd replaced the ornate, baroque-style furnishings with more delicate Queen Anne pieces. Not only that, but she'd papered the walls with fresh new designs and hung drapes to match. The rooms, which now reflected Sebastian's and Lily's vibrant youth, were absolutely charming.

"Gorgeous," I said. "What a wonderful eye for style you have."

"Thank you, Kitty. Your mother was a great help." That statement did not surprise me. After Sebastian and Lily had taken possession of Wynchcombe House, Mother had not only shown Lily the best furniture warehouses in London but lent Lily her expertise. It was good to learn her efforts were appreciated.

Lady Wakefield turned to my sister. "Did you assist as well, Miss Worthington?" Not a strange question. Since Margaret was engaged to Sebastian, it would be natural for her to be involved in the redecoration efforts.

"Oh, heavens, no. I don't have the flair dear Lily has, so I'm glad to leave it to her." As busy as Margaret was with her social causes, she was more than willing to delegate the task of redecorating Wynchcombe House to Lily. It wasn't selfish of her, as it provided Lily with the creative outlet she sorely needed. Having grown up practically neglected, Lily often felt she lacked worth. So, she was never happier than when she succeeded at a task.

"Thank you for your vote of confidence, Margaret," Lily said. "I truly appreciate it."

"You're doing all of us a favor. And remember, it's your home as well." Margaret shared a loving gaze with her future sister-in-law.

"Shall we enjoy our luncheon now?" Lily asked with a smile.

"Oh, yes." Margaret declared. "I, for one, am famished." A chorus of voices agreed with her.

With Lily leading the way, we proceeded to the dining room to enjoy a repast comprised of cucumber soup, an entree of ham with red wine and almonds, and a raspberry meringue for dessert. After the luncheon had been thoroughly enjoyed, we retired to the drawing room for coffee, tea, and a much anticipated coze.

Before long, we decided to eschew the *Miss this* and *Lady that* and call each other by our first names. Except for Lady Wakefield, of course, for she was a married woman.

"I'm sorry to have missed the March for Women, but I would love to help in your next effort," Lady Wakefield said.

"Well, Margaret's newest venture, the women's health clinic, is looking for sponsors," Lily suggested.

Poor Lady Wakefield grew red-faced. "I'll see what I can do." Rumor had it her husband kept her on a very tight leash, dishing out money only for matters which reflected well upon him, such as his wife's wardrobe. That explained yesterday's visit to the modiste.

Aware of Lady Wakefield's state of finances, Margaret jumped in to take away the sting. "I plan to hold a fundraiser next year. You could help me organize it."

"I will be more than glad to do so." Lady Wakefield regained her smile, making her appear years younger.

But she really was, wasn't she? If she'd made her debut six years ago, she couldn't be more than twenty-four. It was her husband's dastardly treatment of her that made her seem older than she was.

"Now tell me about this venture of yours," Lady Wakefield said.

Margaret took a deep breath before she went on to explain. "As you may or may not know, the mortality of women during childbirth is very high, especially among the working class. Some of it stems from lack of health care and poor nutrition, but much comes from bearing child after child in short periods of time. Their bodies simply give out."

Lady Wakefield suddenly grew somber. "Makes perfect sense. Childbirth can be a . . . grievous experience."

Something of which she had no personal knowledge. Still,

it evidenced proof of her kindness that she could sympathize with the plight of other women.

"The Women's Clinic provides family planning counseling to married women. We offer condoms and fit those who choose with devices to prevent conception." This information was not new to Lily, Lady Emma, or me as Margaret had taken it upon herself to provide a clear explanation of the services the clinic provided. Something all three of us appreciated, as we did not wish to remain ignorant of such a basic part of life.

"But there is only one clinic in all of London," Margaret continued. "As you can imagine, the need is greater than we can serve. I'm hoping next year's fundraiser will help us build more clinics and add additional staff."

"That is such a worthwhile effort," Lily said. "We'll all be glad to help in every way we can. Won't we, ladies?"

Everyone answered in the affirmative, except for poor Emma, who was looking downright glum.

After our conversation at Lady Clinton's tea, a notion had taken root in my mind which would hopefully help her out of her predicament. And this was the perfect opportunity to take her aside and discuss my idea. But before I could do so, a commotion occurred outside the drawing room. It was soon followed by the entrance of three gorgeous men—Sebastian, and Lords Newcastle and Marlowe.

"Oh, ho. What do we have here?" Sebastian asked, a grin on his face.

"As if you didn't know," Lily teased.

"We hurried back just so we could join you, ladies." After Sebastian kissed his sister on the cheek, he strolled toward Margaret whose blushes told of her pleasure at seeing him. "Milady."

"I'm not."

"You are mine." He kissed her cheek as well. Anyone with

a working eyesight could see how these two felt about each other.

"Have you eaten?" Lily asked.

"No. We're famished. I already asked Temple to deliver sandwiches and refreshments." He then stood up to his full height and grabbed his lapels. In an oratory fashion, he proclaimed, "You'll be glad to know we succeeded at the House of Lords."

"Did you really?" Lily asked. "What did you do?"

"It took some arm-twisting, but we managed to convince the Labour Leader to introduce a bill extending suffrage to all women over the age of twenty-one."

"How marvelous!" Margaret exclaimed.

Several months ago, she'd spent weeks planning a women's suffrage march which garnered much attention but no new legislation. But now Sebastian had managed exactly what she desired because he was a duke and a man. The power of a title and gender could not have been made more clear. It was good that he was on the side of social justice as many other peers were not.

"Unfortunately, it will come to naught as this term is soon coming to a close. But the important thing is that it will be considered. We'll try again next year."

Before he could expound on the subject, two footmen arrived with trays stacked high with food and drinks which they set on a table. After helping themselves, the gentlemen arranged themselves around the room—Sebastian next to Margaret, Marlowe close to Lily. Newcastle chose a seat near Lady Wakefield.

"So how were you ladies entertaining yourselves?" Sebastian asked while satisfying his hunger.

"We were discussing women's clinics," Lily said, "and Margaret's plans to raise funds next year for them."

"A noble endeavor," Sebastian said. "Anything I can do to help?"

"Oh, don't worry," Margaret answered with a crooked smile. "You will."

"Margaret, I meant to ask," Lady Emma said. "You only counsel married women?"

"Yes." My sister's gaiety dissipated. "We are prevented from doing more by law."

"So, what are unmarried women supposed to do?"

The men all stopped eating and stared at us.

"Unfortunately, we're not allowed to serve their needs," Margaret explained. "The best we can do is advise them to abstain from sexual congress."

"I say," Lord Marlowe exclaimed, a peeved look on his face, "are we supposed to discuss such a thing in mixed company? It puts a fellow off his feed."

"Oh, stow it, Marlowe," Lady Emma spit out. "What are single ladies supposed to do? Keep their legs closed?"

"Well . . . I'm only saying—"

"I know what you're saying. You'd prefer your wife to be ignorant of copulation and how babies are made."

His face turned bright red. "I would explain things to her, of course."

"How very noble of you." She came to her feet. "I'm leaving. Thank you, Lily, for a lovely luncheon." And then, her eyes brimming over with tears, Emma rushed out.

Once she cleared the room, Sebastian turned to his friend. "You can be such an ass sometimes, Marlowe."

"What did I do?" The chastised lord asked, a troubled look on his face. He honestly had no idea what he'd done wrong.

Leaving the tension in the room behind, I dashed after Emma and caught her by the front door where she'd already donned her outer garments. "How are you getting home?"

"I'll take a taxicab. I have funds." She hitched up her chin. "I'm not as poor as all that."

"Let me ask Neville to drive you home. Please."

"All right." I accompanied her down the mansion's front steps to my Rolls. After giving her address to our chauffeur, I silently watched as she rode away. Her state of melancholy was such I feared she would revert to that creature I first met, rooted and potted along the wallflower wall. She'd made great strides since then and had become a dear friend, but I feared this change of her circumstances might cause her to turn bitter, a fate she did not deserve. I vowed to do something about her fortunes. One way or another, Lady Emma would shine brightly again. I returned to the drawing room to find a somber crowd.

"I should apologize," Marlowe said. "This is all my fault."

"She's upset, Lord Marlowe, but not at you. Well, not entirely." He had been rather an ass.

"What's bothering her?"

"She won't return next season. Her sister will take her place." I did not provide any more details. They knew enough about her family's finances to guess.

"I'm sorry. Truly, I am." Poor Marlowe looked downright miserable. Served him right, the fool.

"I know you are."

"I should go. I have some business matters to attend to at home." Whether it was true or not, he soon made his way out.

Margaret and Sebastian did not remain in the drawing room for long. After excusing themselves, they made a beeline for the conservatory, where supposedly he had a new plant to show her. What they really wanted was some privacy and who could blame them? Certainly, not I.

Lady Wakefield and Lord Newcastle were engaged in a conversation which appeared private in nature as they were speaking in low tones. Leaving them to it, I joined Lily to talk about one of her favorite subjects—fashion.

Not long after Sebastian and Margaret's departure, however, Lady Wakefield took her leave. Lord Newcastle escorted her out.

With Lily and I the only ones left, I took the opportunity to offer her much deserved praise. "You did a splendid job today. Did you enjoy playing hostess?"

"I did. But I can't help feeling I have some ways to go. Otherwise, I would have avoided all talk of next season."

"How were you to know Lady Emma's circumstances? She hasn't made it public knowledge."

"But you knew."

"Because she brought it up at Lady Clinton's tea. Otherwise, I'd be as much in the dark as you."

Just then Sebastian and Margaret returned, with their hair in disarray. One guess what they'd been doing.

"How was the plant?"

"Promising," Sebastian said. "With any luck, it will turn into a full bloom."

"That's wonderful." No idea what plant he was talking about, but if he was excited, it was a good thing.

"Will you be attending the Royal Geographical Society lecture?" I asked.

"Yes, of course. Looking forward to it. It promises to be a corker."

He would think so, but then he was a scientist at heart. A lecture about an expedition to the South Seas was bound to excite his intellect.

"Lord Hollingsworth invited Kitty to attend as his special guest," Margaret said, an amused expression on her face.

I knew what she was thinking, but she was wrong. "He's more interested in my making a donation for his next adventure than anything else."

'I wouldn't bet on that being the only reason," she said, a smirk firmly planted on her lips.

"He doesn't desire a wife, Margaret. He enjoys his freedom too much."

She arched a brow. "Until he sees a reason to change his mind."

CHAPTER SIX

THE ROYAL GEOGRAPHICAL SOCIETY

I'D EXPECTED TO BE BORED, but Lord Hollingsworth's presentation turned out to be anything but. An amusing speaker, he not only spoke knowledgeably about his subject but infused the lecture with a great deal of humor. Seemingly, the audience agreed for he received enthusiastic applause.

Immediately after its conclusion, Margaret and Sebastian excused themselves to hunt down the expedition's botanist. Apparently, Sebastian had met him at the Royal Botanic Gardens and was eager to further the acquaintance.

I didn't find myself alone for long as Lord Hollingsworth headed toward me as soon as he stepped off the stage. A surprise, for he had more notable people who were clamoring for his attention. "Did you enjoy it?" he asked.

"I did."

"You sound surprised."

My face flushed with chagrin over being caught out. "I

was. I thought it'd be deadly dull. But you managed to inform and entertain at the same time. You have a rare gift as an orator." And that was the honest truth.

His eyes crinkled with humor. "Which particular part did you enjoy the most?"

I raised a brow. "Are you testing me to see if I was listening?"

"Not that so much as to find out what amuses young ladies."

"Oh, planning on entertaining many young ladies?"

The smile never left his lips. "Perhaps."

I threw back my head and laughed. That's when I saw him —Inspector Crawford. Who was supposed to be on secondment in Yorkshire investigating a case. Instead, he was right here in London. And from the looks of the lady hanging on to his arm, in the company of a dark-haired woman impressively attired in a long-sleeved black dress. Its simple lines and below-the-waist belt would have fooled someone else, but not me. I knew a Chanel when I saw one.

She'd rouged her lips and cheeks, applied mascara to her lashes, not in an ostentatious way, but to enhance her features. To complete the look, she'd donned a necklace, which I was willing to bet was comprised of perfectly matched pearls. She was older than him by at least a decade. And breathtakingly beautiful.

"Miss Worthington," Lord Hollingsworth recalled me to him. "Do you know the lady?" He must have noticed the direction of my gaze.

"No. She's striking. Is she not?"

"Indeed." A measuring look surfaced in his eyes. He was probably trying to determine how to approach her for a contribution. As well as she was dressed and adorned, she certainly spoke of money.

"Miss Worthington." The voice that regularly haunted my dreams spoke close by.

I raised my gaze to him while willing my heart to cease its sudden, mad rhythm. "Inspector Crawford. You've returned from Yorkshire, I see." Somehow, he'd left his companion behind.

"Yes. I concluded the case."

"How splendid."

I felt more than heard Lord Hollingsworth's amusement. For someone who hardly knew me, he was remarkably attuned. But then he studied people on his travels so he would be particularly sensitive to a person's moods.

"May I introduce Detective Inspector Robert Crawford, milord. He investigates crimes for Scotland Yard."

They'd barely exchanged pleasantries when the woman in the Chanel sidled up to the inspector and curled a hand around his elbow. "Robert, won't you introduce me to your friend?"

"Lord Hollingsworth, you know."

Did she? How very curious. Hollingsworth hadn't mentioned it. He'd only asked if I knew her.

"And this is Miss Catherine Worthington."

The woman's gaze assessed me, but she was wise enough not to reveal her thoughts. "I've heard much of you, Miss Worthington."

"All good things, I hope." I said, glancing at Inspector Crawford.

"Oh, not from him, dear. He's a clam when it comes to his friends. I read about your exploits in the papers. Well done." This time there was clear admiration in her eyes.

"Thank you."

"Catherine, may I introduce Lady Cookson."

"A pleasure, milady." Unsure if she would shake my hand, I offered a nod which she returned.

"May I have a private word, Hollingsworth?" Lady Cookson asked. "There's a matter I wish to discuss with you."

"Of course, ma'am."

"If you will excuse us." She traded Inspector Crawford's elbow for Lord Hollingsworth's and drew him away.

As I watched them wander off, I remarked, "They must be friends."

"It certainly seems that way." Well, he was as silent about Lady Cookson as he apparently was about me. After a cursory glance in their direction, he returned his gaze to me.

Searching for something to talk about that wouldn't reveal my foul mood, I settled upon a subject bound to garner a reply, "So the case was concluded satisfactorily?"

"Yes. I returned last night." And then he added, as a non sequitur, "Lady Cookson needed an escort to the lecture."

"So, you volunteered for the task."

A brief hesitation. "Yes."

I gritted my teeth. How very noble of him.

Having apparently finished his conversation with Lady Cookson, Lord Hollingsworth returned to my side. "I apologize, but I must attend to . . ." He waved his hand at the crowd.

"I understand." After all, one of the objects of the lecture was to recruit sponsors for his next expedition. He would never have so many wealthy individuals likely to contribute in one place as right now.

"May I call on you?" he asked.

I felt more than saw Inspector Crawford stiffen. Apparently, he did not approve. I could have explained the reason behind Hollingsworth's request was that he wanted a donation. But right now I had no wish to ease the inspector's concern. "Of course. I'll be free tomorrow afternoon. Say, two o'clock?"

"I shall be there. A pleasure meeting you, Inspector Crawford." And with a nod he was gone.

"Interesting fellow," Inspector Crawford commented.

"He is that. Tell me about your case."

"A child was kidnapped. The nursery maid's intended was to blame. We recovered the boy unharmed."

I let out a small laugh. "I'm sure it wasn't as simple as all that."

"It wasn't." His unsmiling gaze drilled into me. "How did you meet Lord Hollingsworth?"

What was this all about? He'd never once inquired about my admirers. Not that Hollingsworth was one. Well, if he could summarize a case in three sentences, I could do the same. "He came to supper last week. Told me about his expeditions. When I expressed an interest, he invited me to the lecture."

He quirked a brow. "Is that all there is?"

"What more could there be, Inspector?" I asked, wide-eyed. If he thought to obtain more information from me, he was sorely mistaken.

I sensed he had more to say about Hollingsworth. But before he could do so, Margaret and Sebastian chose that moment to return. From the sour expression on Margaret's face, things had not gone well with the botanist.

"It was rude of Mister Geckhart to refuse your request." Fury blazed in her eyes.

"I admit I was disappointed," Sebastian responded in a much calmer tone.

"What happened?" I asked.

Margaret turned to me. "Sebastian expressed an interest in studying the plants the botanist brought back from his travels. But he was refused."

"Now, Megs. Geckhart had a point. Those plants traveled thousands of miles and were kept alive through extraordinary measures. It won't do to have them trampled by people. The slightest miscalculation might very well kill them off."

"But you're a botany expert. You would know how to take care."

"We must trust Geckhart to know best, dear. It's not like I'll never see them. Most are bound for the Royal Botanical Gardens."

Margaret shrugged. "I guess I'll just have to accept it." Her frown told me she was not happy to concede the point.

"Thank you," Sebastian said. One could easily see he was the peacekeeper of the two and Margaret the firebrand.

While their contretemps was going on, Inspector Crawford had simply stood back, wisely staying out of the fray. I, however, couldn't help but make a comment.

"Where are the other plants bound?" I asked. "Maybe you could inspect those."

"A private collector who made a specific request," Sebastian said. "Paid handsomely for them too."

"Do you know who it is?"

"I didn't ask," Sebastian explained. "It would have been rude."

Apparently, there was a code of honor among botanists. Who expected such a thing? But the subject piqued my curiosity. "People collect plants?"

"If they're rare enough."

Margaret pressed a hand to her brow. "All this cigarette smoke is giving me a headache."

My sister could handle the occasional gentleman enjoying a cigar. But with so many around us lighting up, it'd proven too much for her.

She shot a pleading glance toward Sebastian. "Do you think we could leave?"

"Of course," Sebastian said, a look of concern on his face.

I would have liked to say goodbye to Lord Hollingsworth, but he'd disappeared into the crowd.

"Are you coming with us?" Margaret asked noticing my search. "Or do you wish to stay?"

"I'll come with you. Lord Hollingsworth will be calling tomorrow. I'll talk to him, then."

All I got from her was an enigmatic look.

"Goodnight, Inspector Crawford."

Bowing, he said goodnight to the three of us. "Misses Worthington. Your Grace."

I didn't expect more than that, not in the public space. Still, I wished he would have done or said something more.

We climbed into Sebastian's Hispano Suiza, the new motorcar he'd recently acquired. Although he'd grown up the heir to a dukedom, his grandfather had barely provided the necessities of life, so he'd never owned a vehicle before. I was very glad he was finally able to own one. Once he set the automobile in motion, I remained silent in the back while he and Margaret conversed in the front.

Unfortunately, Margaret noticed. "You're awfully quiet, Kitty."

"I'm enjoying the night air." I wasn't. I was quietly seething over Inspector Crawford's behavior. But I refused to let my feelings show for Margaret would immediately determine the cause of my upset. As soon as we arrived home, I rushed upstairs to my room. Only by exerting the strongest willpower did I stop myself from slamming the door.

Free to give way to my anger, I tossed my purse and gloves on the bed before I took to pacing the floor. After a two-week absence, during which he'd neither telephoned nor written, Inspector Crawford had returned to London with me being none the wiser. The last time we spoke, he'd intimated it was the start of something between us. And then he'd gone away, seconded to a case. He could have found a way to communicate. After all, Yorkshire was not on the other side of the world.

But he'd done nothing.

And now he'd returned with a woman on his arm. Older than him, but immensely beautiful and more than likely rich. Was she responsible for his exclusive address at Eaton Square and his fine clothes from Savile Row? Heaven knew his inspector's salary would not cover such luxuries. It wouldn't be the first time a wealthy woman kept a younger man. And then he had the audacity to question me about Lord Hollingsworth. What right did he have to do such a thing?

"Oomph." I kicked off my shoes and threw myself on the bed to glare at the ceiling. But after a few minutes, I gave up as no answer was to be found there. What I needed was a long, hot soak in the tub. That always calmed my nerves. By the time I crawled into bed, I'd come to a decision. Let him enjoy Lady Cookson and the riches she more than likely bestowed upon him. I was well and truly done with the inspector.

CHAPTER SEVEN

KITTY VISITS THE LENDING LIBRARY

*T*HE DAY AFTER THE LECTURE, Hollingsworth called as promised and spent the entire hour amusing Mother and me. She was so taken with the tales of his delightful adventures that she invited him to supper the next day. An odd thing for it meant there would be an extra gentleman at her carefully arranged seating. A catastrophe not to be wished on any hostess. But I need not have worried. As she later explained, Lord Rutledge had cried off as an out-of-town matter had suddenly cropped up that needed his attention. So, Lord Hollingsworth's acceptance prevented a disaster. Or so she said.

The thing of it was, though, she could have asked Ned to make up the numbers, as he hadn't been included in her original arrangements. Clearly, the real reason she'd invited Hollingsworth was to encourage a connection between him and me, something that was bound to fail as neither of us was interested in marriage.

While Hollingsworth had proven quite adept at dancing attendance on me, Inspector Crawford had neither called nor written since his return. But then, why should he? After all, nothing had been settled between us. I was disappointed for I would have liked to have heard about the Yorkshire case. True, the papers had reported every detail that had been made public. The nanny had fallen in love with a man who'd schemed to kidnap the child so they could demand a ransom. Inspector Crawford had obtained not only a confession but discovered the child's location. And the child had been found unharmed. But it was dull reading about it. It would have been much more fascinating to hear it directly from the inspector. Even if I no longer had an interest in him.

I heaved out a deep sigh. Maybe if I told myself that enough times, I would come to believe it one day.

But I couldn't sit around moping. I needed to get on with my life. And that meant learning everything there was to know about criminal investigations.

I'd sent a note to Chief Inspector Bolton asking for a referral of someone to teach me the ropes. He recommended a retired Scotland Yard Inspector by the name of Owen Clapham. Upon receipt of Inspector Bolton's reply, I'd immediately sent off a letter to Mister Clapham explaining my need and asking him to call upon me at his earliest convenience.

While I waited for his response, I decided to visit the lending library to borrow whatever materials could be found. Of course, I couldn't step out of the house without a chaperone. Betsy, my red-haired sprite of a maid, was my usual choice. But I hesitated to ask her as she was feeling under the weather.

"Are you sure you're well enough to attend me today, Betsy?"

"Absolutely. I'm right as rain, Miss." Then she let out a prodigious sneeze, followed by a hacking cough.

"No, I don't think so. I'll go it alone."

"Oh, Miss."

The look of disappointment on her face almost made me change my mind, but I stood fast. "Go down to the kitchen and ask Cook for one of her remedies."

A look of horror rolled over her face. Even her freckles paled. "Those taste horrible."

"That means it's working. Go on. Take yourself to bed the rest of the day. If you're still feeling poorly tomorrow, I'll ask Dr. Crawley to examine you."

"Yes, Miss." Shoulders drooping, she dragged her feet leaving my bedroom. Poor thing. More than likely she was suffering from only a cold, but it was too easy for that to turn into something more serious. If she didn't improve, our physician would provide her with the treatment she needed.

After she left, I checked the hallway to make sure the coast was clear, and then I sneaked out of the house. What Mother didn't know wouldn't come back to haunt me.

The visit to the lending library proved fruitful as I found several books. It was when I exited it laden with *The Basics of Criminal Investigation*, *Fingermarks*, and the popular—it'd been checked out exactly once—*Forensic Studies of Blood Patterns* that I experienced a shock—Lady Wakefield and Lord Newcastle emerging from the hotel across the street.

I watched in silence as he helped her into a cab, kissing her hand as he did, before hailing another one for himself. What on earth were they doing? There could have been a perfectly reasonable explanation for their rendezvous, I told myself. But that gesture, that kiss, had not seemed innocent. It was the caress of a man deeply in love.

"Miss Worthington?" A male voice called out my name, breaking into my reverie.

I turned to find its owner. A mature gentleman in a bowler hat wearing a clean, pressed suit. Graying hair and a weather-worn face marked him in his early sixties. Nothing old about his eyes, though. They were bright button brown. "Yes?"

"I'm Owen Clapham. Detective Chief Inspector Bolton recommended me to you."

"Oh, yes." I glanced at him confused. "How did you know where I was?"

"I didn't. I was coming to the lending library to explore their books on investigative techniques so I could suggest some to you." He pointed to the ones I held in my arms. "But I see you've gotten ahead of me."

"Yes." I clutched the heavy tomes to my chest lest they slip away. "I was eager to get started."

"Those are excellent guides, but two are a might advanced. You would benefit from something more basic."

"Oh." He was more than likely right.

He nodded toward the other side the street. "I couldn't help but notice your interest in the couple that just left The Majestic. Friends of yours?"

How very observant of him. But then he was a detective. There was probably little that he missed. "They might be."

"Would you like to know what they were doing there? I can find out for you." His question did not seem impertinent. More than likely he'd done something similar a thousand times before. But it would not do.

"No. I would not." I was very firm about it.

He hitched a brow. "Knowledge is power, Miss Worthington."

"What they were doing is their business, not mine."

He nodded. "I apologize. I didn't mean to offend."

"None taken." It would not do to start off on the wrong foot, however, so I opted for a more amiable approach. "Shall we adjourn to a more private place?" I suggested. "A tearoom, perhaps."

"Of course."

Maddie's Tea Shoppe was located nearby. Once we'd settled into one of their tables I said, "I did not mean to be rude, Inspector Clapham. It's just they are my friends and I was—"

"Surprised."

"Yes, but there could very well be a perfectly reasonable explanation for their being at that hotel." Although a very improper one did spring to mind.

"Of course."

He was placating me. I could tell by the tone of his voice. But it would not do to get upset at him.

A server approached, and we gave her our order. When she departed, he asked, "Why do you wish to learn about investigative techniques, Miss Worthington?"

"Well, I've been involved in two murder investigations," I said by way of an opening gambit, curious to know how he would respond.

He didn't disappoint. "And been quite successful. The newspapers sing your praises, and so does Chief Inspector Bolton."

"It was not only me. My family and friends helped. But it seems I do have a talent for this, so I would like to pursue it."

"As a career?"

"Maybe. Although Mother would absolutely frown on that." I shared a smile with him. "But you see, I've received several requests."

Threading his hands, he leaned forward. "Such as?"

"Finding lost objects, locating family members. Some requests involve blackmail or spying on an errant husband. Those last two things, however, I have no interest in investigating."

"The errant husband?" He frowned. "That's a tricky matter indeed. It can get quite messy."

"Exactly. I do not wish to involve myself in those kinds of family dynamics. But locating lost objects or missing relatives does appeal to me. I would like to be more methodical about future investigations. Do you think you could help me?"

He nodded. "I believe I could. Give me a day to come up with a reading list for you." He pointed to the books I'd placed on the table. "If I may make a suggestion."

"Of course."

"Keep *The Basics of Criminal Investigation* but return the other two."

"Very well. I'll do so. How do you recommend we go about this?"

"We would meet at your convenience. I suggest twice a week." He retrieved what appeared to be an appointment book from the depths of his coat. "Maybe Tuesdays and Thursdays for an hour or two. I'll suggest you read certain passages in the *Basics* book so we can discuss them when we meet. If that is too hectic a schedule, we can meet only one day."

"Twice a week is fine." I retrieved my own journal, a catch-all of sorts in which I not only noted dates but wrote observations and sketched as well. I flipped pages to the current month. "Thursday. I'm free at ten in the morning. Is that amenable to you? We could meet at my home. We have a splendid library."

"That will do very well." He wrote the time and date in his appointment book before pointing to the *Basics* tome. "I recommend you read the first chapter before we meet. It will give you an idea as to what to expect."

"I shall do so. Thursday it is." I paused while the server arrived with our lovely spread of scones and pastries and, of course, a pot of tea. Once she'd left us to it, I prompted him to open up, "Chief Inspector Bolton told me very little about you. I'd love to hear more."

"I was an Inspector at Scotland Yard for thirty years, a police officer before that. Retired a year ago." He laughed, seemingly to himself. "Retirement is not what I thought it would be. I have no family, so I find myself at loose ends."

"You like to remain occupied," I said, in between bites of a blueberry lemon scone.

"Yes. I set up as a private detective but find little business coming my way."

"Maybe I could refer some of my more troublesome inquiries to you."

He tilted his head. "Do most of them come from women?"

"Almost all." I hadn't realized that until now. I was surprised to say the least.

"Ladies find it difficult to engage me in an investigation. My guess is they would prefer to hire another woman. That's why they've come to you. Plus, they trust you since you're from their own class. Lady detectives are practically nonexistent. If you are serious in pursuing this interest, you would be doing them a service."

"I see." Maybe my idea of setting up a lady detective business was not so far-fetched after all. Something to think about, that was for certain.

While we enjoyed our tea, we continued our conversation, with me asking questions and him telling me about his more colorful cases. By the end, I felt he would do. He was knowledgeable, down to earth, and straightforward.

I was a little hesitant about bringing up the next subject, but it was something I needed to do. "Now, if we could discuss your fees."

He proposed a perfectly reasonable daily fee, plus additional expenses for incidentals.

"Incidentals?"

"Travel expenses and such."

"Oh, yes, of course."

He cleared his throat. "It is normal in these circumstances to offer an advance."

"I'll be glad to do so. Do you have a certain amount in mind?"

"Twenty pounds."

I wrinkled my nose. "Doesn't seem enough. How about I make it fifty?"

"Oh, no, Miss Worthington. I'd be tempted to run home to Brighton."

I laughed, as he intended me to do. "I'll have it for you at our first session. Will that do?"

"Of course."

He accompanied me to the kerb and remained with me until I climbed into a cab. "Until Thursday, Mister Clapham?"

He doffed his hat. "Until then. It's been a sincere pleasure, Miss Worthington." I believed he meant it.

But when I gazed back through the rear window of the cab, I spotted him crossing the street and entering The Majestic, in direct opposition of my wishes. I had no doubt he would enquire into Lady Wakefield and Lord Newcastle's rendezvous. Whatever he found, I prayed it wouldn't hurt them.

CHAPTER EIGHT

MURDER MOST FOUL

$\mathcal{B}$Y THE TIME THE MIDSUMMER MASKED BALL ARRIVED, I was more than ready to be done with it. And with the entire season as well. But, of course, I couldn't dampen Mother's enthusiasm. Not as excited as she was to attend the most highly coveted event of the season. So that night, I slipped into my Spanish *señorita* costume, pinned a silk rose on my hair, and plastered a smile on my face.

Margaret was already in the drawing room, garbed in her tunic and pants, breast plate, belt, gauntlets, and carrying a spear. A surprise for she'd chosen a different weapon at the modiste.

"That's a fearsome looking thing. I thought you wanted a sword."

A devilish grin popped up on her face. "I changed my mind. I've been practicing. Want to see?" Excited did not begin to describe her. I wondered if she would feel the same after hours of wearing the cumbersome costume.

But right now, I needed to meet the moment. "Of course."

She flourished the weapon this way and that, missing an expensive vase by a whisker, and ended her demonstration with a deadly forward thrust.

Heavens! She'd truly thrown herself into the role of warrior queen. "Remind me never to get on your bad side, dear sister."

"I can do other maneuvers as well. May I show you?"

I doubted the furniture would survive further flourishes. Thankfully, before I could say nay, the door opened and Father strolled in holding Mother's hand aloft, much as a courtier of old would have done. "Behold Queen Mildred."

"Oh, shush, Edward," Mother chided. But going by her high color, she was pleased, as well she should be, for she appeared truly regal. Her burgundy full-length gown was cut in the courtly tradition of the late Middle Ages, its bell-cut sleeves and square-cut neckline trimmed with a fleur-de-lis pattern. Her long dark hair, streaked here and there with silver, flowed down her back nearly to her waist while a golden crown encrusted with dark jewels sparkled from the top of her head.

"Mother, you look magnificent."

"You think so, Kitty?"

"Oh, yes. Don't you think so, Margaret?"

"Absolutely."

Not to be left out of the praise, Father kissed Mother's hand and gazed deeply into her eyes. "I'll count the minutes until you come home, my dear."

Mother's face turned pink with pleasure. But then the mantel clock chimed the hour intruding into the reverie. "My goodness, look at the time. We better go."

Father accompanied us down the stairs, handed us into the Rolls, and waved us goodbye as we rolled away.

"What is he planning to do?" I asked.

"Probably spend the evening reading *The Financial Times*," Mother said with a soft smile. "His idea of entertainment."

Margaret and I both laughed for she was absolutely right. My brother Ned and he were much alike in that respect for they spent hours studying the financial news, scrying them, if you will, for nuggets of information. But then, that's why they were so very successful.

Two hundred guests were expected at the masquerade ball, all properly masked of course. Although a costume was not required, most ladies had chosen to wear them in the past. This year would prove no different if Angelique's busy salon was anything to go by. Most of the gentlemen, however, usually opted for a simpler disguise, made up of a loose, dark cloak over evening formal wear.

Upon our arrival, we easily made our way past the front doors of Brightwell Mansion. Grander than other Mayfair residences. it stood four-stories high and sat on an acre of land with lushly landscaped gardens. But it was the inside that truly raised it above all others. The ground floor consisted of the ballroom on the east side and grand drawing and dining rooms on the west. The size of those two was reportedly so large they could each easily hold over a hundred guests. In the center of it all a grand staircase rose upward to an impressive balcony which looked down on all sides. The magnificence of it all took our breath away.

As soon as we made our way into the mansion, we were guided toward a long line of guests waiting to make their entrance into the ballroom. It would probably take some time to make it to the front, but we didn't mind. Not only were we able to observe the magnificence of Brightwell Mansion but take note of what guests had chosen to wear.

Pirates with cutlasses, shepherdesses with crooks. An Arabian princess whose costume revealed more than concealed her flesh was deep in conversation with a knight in shining armor. One particular pairing caught my eye— a lady dressed as a French courtesan and a gentleman attired as a cavalier with a plumed hat. While her costume was truly outlandish with the towering wig and the pannier skirt, his seemed rather simple in comparison. But they were so tall, they towered just about everyone.

It took twenty minutes or so to reach the entrance to the ballroom where an official-looking fellow, dressed all in white with gold braiding and epaulets, collected our invitations and noted something on them. The time of arrival perhaps. How very curious. After he read our names, we moved forward to greet our hosts both of whom were dressed in formal wear rather than costumes.

The Duchess of Brightwell surprised me for she was nothing like what I'd thought she'd be. From her reputation as a revered social hostess, I expected a tall, commanding figure, but she was of diminutive stature. Tiny in fact. Her husband, at least a foot taller, towered over her. Not only that, while the Duke of Brightwell appeared to be in perfect health, she did not. Her complexion wore the pallor of an ill person, and her voice quivered when she addressed us.

"Mrs. Worthington, how delightful to finally meet you." She said all the proper words but there was no feeling behind them.

After a moment's hesitation, Mother curtsied. She must have made the same observations I had. "Your Grace. The pleasure is all mine, I assure you."

"And these are your daughters?" The hand the duchess waved toward us trembled.

"Yes, may I present Margaret, my eldest, and Catherine."

From somewhere the duchess retrieved a piece of linen

and used it to dab her lip. "I've heard much about you, ladies. I'm so glad you could attend."

Margaret and I curtsied in unison. Well, I curtsied, Margaret dipped. There was only so much she could do with the armor she was wearing.

Just as we rose, a scream rang out. As all heads turned toward the sound, an austerely dressed gentleman came rushing toward the duke and duchess.

"Hughes," the duke exclaimed. "What the devil's the matter?"

"I'm afraid an unfortunate accident has occurred, your Grace."

"What kind of accident?" The duke barked out.

"A guest has . . . suffered a collapse."

"Well, show her to a room and allow her to rest. No sense interrupting the festivities."

"It's more serious than that, I'm afraid." Hughes was so flustered he forgot to add the honorific.

"Well, spit it out, man," the duke ordered. "No sense shilly-shallying."

"It's Lord Wakefield."

Even before he said the next words, I knew.

"He's dead."

"Dead?" The duchess crumpled into her husband's side as she raised a trembling hand to her throat. "Are you sure?"

"He took a tumble down the family stairs."

Took a tumble hinted at an accidental fall. But was it really? Or was this Mister Hughes' way of breaking the news? Regardless of how Lord Wakefield had died, though, action needed to be taken. I glanced at my watch to note the time—10:17—before turning to the footmen who stood by the open doors. "Close them. No one comes in or goes out. Your Grace," I addressed the duke, "you must send for the police."

"But it could have been an accident, or he could have suffered from physical distress," he answered while attempting to cope with his wife's collapse.

"Whatever the cause, Scotland Yard will need to investigate. Trust me. I have experience with this sort of thing."

He took but a second to weigh my statement. "Yes. Of course." He turned to Hughes. "Go telephone the police."

"Nobody can leave," I said. "Not the guests, not the staff. Do you understand?"

"Yes. Yes."

"The police will ask for the names of your guests as well as your staff."

"Hughes can handle all that. Now, if you'll excuse me. My wife. She needs her rest." The look he bestowed upon his duchess showed care, love, and, above it all, worry.

"Of course. But the police will want to speak to you tonight."

"I shall make myself available to them. Come, my dear." Practically carrying his wife, the duke negotiated the crowded ballroom with the guests making space for them.

They had no sooner wandered off than Hughes returned. "The police are on their way."

I glanced at my watch again. I would have no more than fifteen minutes to get the lay of the land before they arrived.

"Mister Hughes, is it?"

He bowed. "At your service, Miss—"

"Worthington. I'm here with my mother and sister." I pointed to them.

"Ma'am. Miss." He acknowledged them with a nod.

"Could you take me to where Lord Wakefield is located?" I couldn't bring myself to refer to him as the deceased.

"Yes, of course."

I glanced toward Mother, as my heart filled with regret she would not get to enjoy the ball. "I'm sorry to desert you."

"Oh, child," Mother said. "Go do what you need to do. Don't worry about us."

I had to be satisfied with that as I trailed Mister Hughes through the ballroom. Not that I would have needed him. A throng had already gathered in the back of the space. Ghouls and gossips, all of them. But then, such was human nature.

"The guests need to be kept away lest they muck up the evidence. Can you ask your staff to secure the area?"

"Of course."

Thankfully, a couple of footmen were standing nearby. After he gave them their orders, they were soon standing sentinel.

"Don't let anyone through, except for the police," I told them. "They should be here soon enough."

"Yes, miss."

And then Hughes led me to where Lord Wakefield lay, sprawled face up at the bottom of a somewhat secluded set of stairs in the back of the ballroom. But the thing that garnered most of my attention was the pungent scent of the blood that had pooled beneath him. I swallowed back the bile that rose in my throat. But it was not enough to ward my growing faintness or the edges of my vision dimming. I turned away before I passed out.

"Miss Worthington," Hughes called out seemingly from a distance.

By sheer will, I held on. "Whiskey, please."

Hughes was efficient, if nothing else, for it took but a few seconds for him to put a tumbler in my hand. In one deep pull, I swallowed it back. My stomach protested the vile assault for it was not accustomed to spirits, but it did its job and the faintness soon retreated.

"Better?" Mister Hughes asked.

"Yes, much."

"Here."

He slid a chair that had been lining the wall under me, and I gratefully dropped into it. Avoiding the sight of the very dead Lord Wakefield, I focused on what was important —gathering the facts. "Where does this stairway lead?"

"The family floor."

"Can you please explain?"

"The family space is reserved for intimate gatherings. It contains a private drawing room, a small library, the duke's study, the duchess's private parlor, and the family's dining room. And, of course, the necessaries as well."

Necessaries, an old-fashioned term for bathrooms. "Who knows that floor exists?"

"Well, the family, of course, but also close friends. The more public rooms, such as the ballroom, are used for larger events."

"Such as the Midsummer Masquerade Ball." I said more to myself than to him. "The police will need a list of anyone who's visited that floor in the last few years."

"It shall be done. We keep meticulous records."

My gaze bounced up. "Really?"

"The Duke of Brightwell holds an admiral's rank." He permitted himself a small smile. "Shipshape and all that."

Goodness! And I'd given orders to him. It was the measure of the man he hadn't dismissed me outright, but actually listened to me.

Mister Hughes cleared his throat. "Should we place a sheet or a blanket over Lord Wakefield?"

"No. It might interfere with the evidence. He shouldn't be touched in any way."

"Too late, Miss Worthington." Lady Wakefield said from my right. "I already have and so did Newcastle."

"Where did you come from? No one is supposed to get through." Most especially the widow and a man widely known to be in love with her.

"That was my doing, Miss Worthington," Mister Hughes said. "I showed them to the receiving room."

The place where guests shed their outer garments before they are greeted by the family. Made sense it was near the stairs.

"I thought Lady Wakefield could use the privacy," Mister Hughes said.

A noble thought. Unfortunately, it had left them alone with the body of her late husband. They could have very well tampered with the evidence.

"I apologize if I erred."

"What's done is done. No sense crying over spilt milk." I looked around for Newcastle since she'd mentioned him, but he was nowhere nearby. "Where did Lord Newcastle go?"

"I sent him away," Lady Wakefield said.

"Away where?"

"To the ballroom. He had nothing to do with what happened tonight. I did not want him implicated."

Wishful thinking for he was already implicated. How had he ended up inspecting the body alongside Lady Wakefield? A question I would need to ask. I took a good look at her and did not like what I saw. "Could I speak to you in private in the receiving room? Might as well put it to use once more."

She nodded. "Of course."

Once we entered the room, I wasted no time. The police would be here before long. "Your face is bruised. What happened?"

She could not meet my eyes. "I fell at home."

"I don't believe you. You must tell the truth. The police will find out anyway."

When she remained silent, I asked, "What were you doing with Newcastle?"

"He . . . I."

I heaved a sigh in frustration. "Please don't make me drag

the entire story out of you. Don't you understand? There is no time. What happened? The truth, please."

"Wakefield . . . struck me. I thought with enough maquillage and a mask it would be enough to hide the bruise, but Newcastle noticed. As you can imagine, he was furious and concerned for me. He led me to the family library on the first floor so I could repair the damage. Wakefield found us. There was a row. Newcastle struck him down."

I gasped. "Is that how he fell down the stairs?"

"No! We were still in the library, nowhere near the staircase. Wakefield was woozy but alive. I urged Newcastle to leave. Told him I would take care of Wakefield. He did. But when I tried to help my husband, he refused me. He came to his feet, wobbled a bit, and left."

"What did you do then?"

"I waited a few minutes before following my husband out of the library."

"Did you see anyone in the hallway or that floor?"

"No. It was empty."

"Where did you go?"

"I went in search of my husband to tell him I was going home."

"Did you find him?"

"No." She took a deep breath. "After he left the library, I never saw him again. Alive anyway."

A commotion clattered outside the room. "Sounds as though the police have arrived." Unfortunately, I hadn't asked her how she'd come to discover her husband's body with Newcastle by her side. There had been no time. But there was time enough to provide her some advice. "Tell the truth, but do not volunteer any information. With any luck they won't notice your bruises." It would depend on who had been assigned as the investigator. I prayed it would not be Inspector Crawford for he would not miss a thing.

CHAPTER NINE

INSPECTOR CRAWFORD INVESTIGATES

OF COURSE, MY PRAYERS WERE NOT ANSWERED evidenced by Inspector Crawford's entrance into the room. As always, he was perfectly attired in a three-piece bespoke grey suit that perfectly framed his tall, fit physique. "Lady Wakefield. Miss Worthington."

"Inspector Crawford." Should have known he would be assigned to the investigation. After all, he had a stellar record and was noted for his ability to engage with members of the nobility.

"I understand I have you to thank for securing the scene." He addressed the statement to me.

"Seemed the logical thing to do, Inspector."

"But you were the only one to realize its importance." Approbation was clear in his gaze.

Even though I really shouldn't, I couldn't help but be pleased by his praise.

"I need to speak to Lady Wakefield in private. But don't go far. I'll need to talk to you, as well."

Made sense. He would want my take on things. "Of course. Do you need anything Lady Wakefield? Something to eat or drink perhaps?"

"Tea, please."

I nodded. "I'll ask a footman to bring it to you."

As I made my way through the ballroom in search of my family, I couldn't help but notice the guests congregating in small groups, no doubt discussing the murder. Even though ball etiquette required them to remain masked until midnight, many had removed them. But then the purpose of the ball had changed. It had now become a murder investigation, so the usual rules no longer applied. After asking a footman to deliver a pot of tea, cups, and an assortment of the food offerings to the receiving room, I located Margaret and Mother in a secluded alcove, enjoying some of the wonderful repast.

"Might as well enjoy the food and drink. Wouldn't want it to go to waste," Margaret said before biting into a petit four glacé.

My stomach rumbled with hunger. No wonder. Anxious about the ball, I'd eschewed supper, and tea had been hours ago. "Of course." I helped myself to a maid of honour, one of the many pastries that had been brought to them on a tray.

"How long do you think we'll be here?" Margaret asked, polishing off another appetizer.

I scrutinized the ballroom. Although two hundred guests had been invited, those who arrived late had never reached the front of the receiving line. So there were less than that to interview. Still, at least one hundred were present. "With this many guests as well as staff to question? A while."

"I don't see why." My sister shrugged. "I doubt most would have seen anything."

"You don't know that, Margaret. But even if that's true, Inspector Crawford needs to know names, addresses, and their locations at the time of Lord Wakefield's death."

"The police officers seem to be questioning everyone." She nodded toward the throng where half a dozen uniformed officers were going from guest to guest and writing in their notebooks. As I watched, some of the guests were allowed to leave. Either they had been cleared of suspicion or had nothing to offer. Others, however, were held back, probably so Inspector Crawford could interrogate them.

Our turn came half an hour later when an officer approached. But rather than request our information, he asked us to accompany him. Apparently, Inspector Crawford needed our presence. Rather than lead us to the last place I'd seen Inspector Crawford, he took us on a labyrinth route through the ballroom and a rear corridor, up a set of service stairs to the first floor. Eventually, we ended at the family's library where Lady Wakefield and Inspector Crawford were its sole occupants.

While he stood in the center of the room wearing a pensive expression, she was seated on a settee with her eyes downcast. I could only imagine how harrowing the interview must have been.

"Good evening, Mrs. Worthington, Miss Worthington," Inspector Crawford said.

Mother and Margaret responded in kind.

"I'm done discussing matters with Lady Wakefield."

Well, that was one way to refer to an interrogation.

"She needs an escort home, Mrs. Worthington, and I was wondering if you'd be able to offer that kindness to her."

"Of course, Inspector," Mother said. "We would be glad to do so."

"I don't really need—" Lady Wakefield protested.

"My dear," Mother took a seat next to her and held her hand. "You've been through a terrible ordeal. Allow us to assist you in your hour of need." That was Mother all over. Kindness itself.

Lady Wakefield's gaze was filled with contrition. "Thank you, ma'am. Please forgive my rudeness."

"There's nothing to forgive, dear."

"I've taken the liberty of asking your chauffeur to bring your motorcar around to the back of the house, Lady Wakefield. It would be best to leave that way."

"Thank you."

"Can Margaret and Kitty come as well?" Mother asked.

"Miss Worthington may leave, but I'll need Catherine to remain behind."

Mother blinked. It was the first time he'd called me by my first name in front of her. "You'll make sure she gets home safely, Inspector?"

He nodded. "I give you my word, ma'am."

After their outer garments and Margaret's spear were fetched—apparently, the police had confiscated it deeming it a weapon—they made their way out.

Mother, of course, could not leave without a few parting words. "Try not to keep her too late, Inspector."

"I'll do my best, ma'am." He bowed, and they departed, with Mother and Margaret supporting Lady Wakefield on the way out.

"This has to be an ordeal for her."

"So it seems," the inspector responded. "Would you like some tea or other refreshment?" he asked, once we were alone.

"No, thank you. We were well catered to for the last half an hour." I hitched up my chin. "Now what do you wish of me?"

That charming smile of his made an appearance. "Now, there's a question."

Was he flirting with me in the middle of an investigation? After he hadn't called or written? How dare he?

He must have noted my mood because he suddenly became all business. "I want your take on things. What did you see? What did you hear? What conclusions did you reach?"

I explained that I'd barely made my curtsy to the Duchess of Brightwell when the outcry occurred. As soon as I'd realized what had happened, I'd prompted the duke to secure the house, which he did. And then I headed toward where Lord Wakefield lay. After a brief cursory examination in which I noted the blood beneath him, Lady Wakefield made herself known. I'd subsequently accompanied her to the receiving room where I held a brief conversation with her.

"And what did she say?"

I was not falling for that gambit. "She must have told you, Inspector."

"I did not ask her about your conversation with."

"And yet, you do so with me."

He fixed his steely gaze on me. "You will not answer me." A statement, not a question.

"No, I will not. It was private."

"How did she appear?"

"Much as she appeared just now." He could make of that what he willed.

He took to wandering about the room, picking up an object here and there. After close to a minute, he turned back to me. "I understand Newcastle was with her earlier in the evening."

"Was he? How very interesting."

"She didn't share that with you?"

I remained silent. He would easier get blood from a stone than words out of me.

He scraped his jaw while carefully studying me.

I knew what he would see. Chin set to a stubborn angle. Eyes wielding my most cutting glare. Lips flattened into a white line.

"You're upset with me," he finally said.

How very observant of him. "Please don't bring my feelings, whatever they may be, into a murder investigation."

His mouth lifted into a quirk. "So, you think it is murder?"

If he thought he could jolly me out of my mood, he was sorely mistaken. "A slip of the tongue, nothing else."

"I would prefer to think of it as your intuition, Catherine. One that will more than likely prove correct."

Well, that got my attention. "It was murder, then?"

"It certainly appears that way."

Oh, he was a devil to use my weakness—my avid curiosity —against me. But what did my being angry at him get me? Nothing. If I wanted to learn what he knew, I would need to put my hurt pride aside. Very well. Let it be so. "How can you tell?"

"Lord Wakefield suffered blunt force trauma."

"It wasn't a mere fall?"

"No. Somebody hit him over the head. The weapon was not hard to find. It lay at the top of the staircase, bloodied brain matter stuck to it."

My stomach pitched as nausea rose.

In the next instant, a glass of whiskey appeared in front of me. "Drink."

I tossed it back. At the rate I was going, I would end up tipsy, if not downright sloshed, by the time I arrived home.

"More?" He held up a decanter.

I started to shake my head, but then realized that was a mistake.

He took the glass from me and placed it on a table. "Better?"

"Yes," I croaked out. "Any suspects?" I dared to ask.

"Other than the very obvious ones?"

"They didn't do it!"

He arched an inquiring brow. "They?"

When I remained mum, he suggested, "Another slip of the tongue, perhaps? You do know, Miss Worthington—"

Apparently, I was no longer Catherine.

"—withholding evidence can be considered a crime."

"I'm not."

"Then why are you not opening up?"

"They're my friends."

"And there's that *they* again." After a moment, he proceeded, "Shall I tell you what I think?"

"Please do."

"I think Lady Wakefield was abused one too many times by her husband. She wanted to cry off from the ball, but her husband insisted on her attendance. She did her best to cover up the bruise. As fate would have it, Newcastle had already arrived, and he noticed."

"Did she tell you this?"

He fixed me with a superior stare. "You're not the only who can keep silent about a source, Miss Worthington."

Fair enough. "Very well. Go on."

"Being a friend of the duke, he knew about this room. He brought her here so she could repair her maquillage. Somehow, Lord Wakefield found them. A row ensued."

"And then what? Newcastle coshed him over the head and threw him down the stairs? He didn't do that. He left."

"Is that what Lady Wakefield told you?"

There was no sense denying it. Not when I'd blurted it out. "Yes."

"What if they lied about the whole thing?"

"They? Have you talked to Newcastle?"

"Of course, I have," he scoffed. "He's the main suspect."

My blood ran cold. Inspector Crawford was usually more circumspect, more analytical, more methodical. For him to have reached this conclusion so quickly meant the evidence against Newcastle was overwhelming. "How did you determine that?"

"He's in love with Lady Wakefield and has been for an age. Time and again he's seen evidence of Wakefield's abuse of his wife. An honorable man can only stand by for so long and not protect the woman he loves. He reached that limit tonight. Something in him snapped, and he did what he had to do."

"But how could he have done such a thing? He left," I reiterated.

"Obviously, he hid somewhere. Plenty of rooms and alcoves on this floor. When Wakefield exited the study, Newcastle used the nearest object at hand, a porcelain statuette, and bludgeoned him with it. And then he pushed him down the stairs."

"Is this fact or conjecture?"

"Fact. We have a witness. A maid. She'd been asked to deliver a tea service to the drawing room. The servant stairs were unavailable, so she walked around to the ones the family used. As she approached, she discovered Lord Wakefield at the bottom of the stairs. That's when she screamed. She glanced up and spotted Newcastle with the statuette in his hand."

Oh, dear heaven. "She wasn't there when I arrived."

"She was hysterical, so she was taken to the kitchen and

administered a strong cup of tea to calm her down. Once she had, I talked to her."

"He didn't do it. He couldn't have." My voice trembled with emotion.

"Why? Because he's your friend?" He scoffed. "You must do better than that, Miss Worthington. Facts do not lie."

"Maybe. And maybe you're seeing only what you want to see," I snapped out.

"The evidence is overwhelming. I'd be a fool to ignore it."

"Nobody is asking you to. I'm only urging you to look beyond what you've discovered tonight."

Suddenly, he grabbed the arms of my chair and confronted me, his face mere inches away. "Why are you so certain Newcastle is innocent?"

I wasn't. But I was not about to admit it when he'd practically placed a noose around Newcastle's neck. "I just know he wouldn't kill Lord Wakefield."

Straightening to his full height, he jerked a hand through his dark, wavy hair. "Catherine—"

A knock on the door interrupted whatever he was about to say.

"Come!" Inspector Crawford said.

An officer stepped into the room. "My apologies, Inspector, but the Duke of Brightwell is ready to see you in his study."

"Well, at least you won't have to go far," I said in an attempt to dispel his sour mood.

Unfortunately, it didn't work as he shot me a look filled with frustration before addressing the officer, "Constable, Miss Worthington needs an escort home. Can you please arrange it?"

"Of course, sir."

And then Inspector Crawford walked out without once glancing back at me.

CHAPTER TEN

THE INQUEST

$\mathcal{I}$ DIDN'T SEE HIM AGAIN until the day of the inquest. By then, matters had gone from bad to worse.

The newspaper accounts had been full of the murder at the Duchess of Brightwell's masquerade ball. But the actual details that emerged had been few as neither Inspector Crawford nor any of the principals were talking. Lady Wakefield had sequestered herself at Wakefield House. And Lord Newcastle was nowhere to be found. The newspapers wildly speculated that he'd boarded a ship bound for the Americas to avoid arrest. Not that any proof of that had been provided.

Unfortunately, the same could not be said about the motive for the murder. An explosive article had appeared in *The Tell All* in which a maid claimed Wakefield had abused his wife more times than she cared to count, and it was no wonder he'd ended up dead.

As I discovered the day after the ball when I visited

Lady Emma, the maid's sentiments provided tinder to an already brightly burning fire. I'd hoped to spend time discussing a way she could remain in London, but that proved impossible. Her home had been invaded by chattering mavens eager to prattle about Lord Wakefield's death.

"Everyone knows he was abusing her," one of them said. "Hardly a day went by that she didn't venture out with a black eye or a bruise on her arm."

"And Lord Newcastle has been in love with her since her debut," another commented. "Of course, he could no longer countenance the abuse and took matters into his own hands." An echo of Inspector Crawford's sentiments.

Lady Emma attempted to stem the tide. "You don't know that's what happened."

But they roundly ignored her.

"The newspapers reported that a servant from Brightwell Mansion saw a gentleman at the top of the stairs holding a bloodied statue in his hand. They hinted it was Lord Newcastle."

I tried to interject some common sense into the conversation. "How would the maid even know his name?"

I got back a haughty sniff. "I'm only repeating what the newspapers are saying, Miss Worthington."

"Not only that but another servant overheard a row. Apparently, Wakefield and Newcastle engaged in another round of fisticuffs in the Brightwell library."

Unwilling to listen to more innuendoes, half-truths, and downright lies, I decided to take my leave. "How do you countenance this?" I asked Lady Emma, as I stood in the foyer jamming my hands into my gloves.

"I couldn't stop Mama if I tried. She lives for the scandals."

"They all do." Gossip was mother's milk to them. They

positively thrived on it. "We'll find out the truth at the inquest tomorrow."

Worry showed clear in Lady Emma's eyes. "I fear for Newcastle, Kitty. I truly do."

I sighed. "So do I."

* * *

ON THE DAY of the inquest, Ned accompanied me. Newcastle was his friend, and he wanted to show his support. In the past, I'd worn mourning clothes to those proceedings, but that was when I was closely connected to the suspects. Newcastle, while a very dear friend, was no relation to me. So, rather than wear my funereal outfit, I chose a burgundy frock and a matching cloche hat hoping the dress would help me blend with the crowd.

But that proved not to be the case. As soon as we stepped off a taxicab, we were swarmed by reporters who recognized us both. Barely tossing a glance at them, we marched into the Coroner's Court, our heads held high. The gallery was packed, not a surprise given the notoriety of the matter, but we managed to find space at the end of one bench.

The first witness called was the Duke of Brightwell who provided general details about the ball. When asked about Lord and Lady Wakefield's arrival, he answered, "I apologize, but I did not notice the time. My guess would be around nine." He may not have noted it, but the majordomo who received us certainly had. The duke should have anticipated that question would be asked of him and taken the trouble to find out. And yet, he had not. I wrote it in my journal as it was something to consider.

While the duke barely earned a murmur from the crowd, mad whisperings and snickers echoed through the courtroom when Lady Wakefield approached the witness chair.

But the strong reaction did not affect her, as she ignored it all. Although, I had to admit, it was hard to tell as she was dressed in widow's weeds from head to toe. When she was sworn in, she tipped back her veil, revealing the shadows that bruised the skin beneath her eyes. Not only that but her face was an unearthly shade of pale. The courtroom went silent as everyone seemingly was struck by her tragic beauty.

"Lady Wakefield," the coroner addressed her in a gentle voice, "I realize this might be difficult for you, so I'll try to make this as painless as possible."

"Thank you," her husky voice answered.

"What time did you arrive at Brightwell Mansion?"

"Around nine. We were early. My husband had arranged a meeting with someone, a business associate I believe. He wanted to do it before the ballroom filled with guests. As soon as we arrived, he went in search of that person."

"Do you know what he wanted to discuss?"

She glanced down at her hands. "He did not share it with me. My husband preferred to keep business matters to himself."

The coroner noted something in a notebook. "Very well. What did you do?"

"I sought the refreshment table as I was parched and needed something to drink."

"Did you talk to anyone?"

"Lord Newcastle. He approached me." Her lips trembled. She'd grown visibly upset. "He became concerned once he noticed my appearance."

"What was wrong?"

She gazed downward once more. "I was not ready as quickly as my husband wished. He grew angry and . . . struck me."

A ripple of shock ran through the gallery.

"I covered it up with foundation. But it was a warm night,

and it did not prove adequate. Unfortunately, Lord Newcastle saw the bruise."

"How did he react?"

"He knew it would cause comment from the guests, so he suggested I withdraw to the family's personal library where I could repair my maquillage."

"And did you do so?"

"Yes. Lord Newcastle accompanied me. In case someone approached, he could draw them off. And, of course, he could ascertain that the library was empty."

How very clever of her to put his actions in the very best light.

"Where is this family library?"

"The first floor. It can be reached through a private staircase on the side of the ballroom. Having visited Brightwell Mansion on other occasions, he was familiar with it."

"But you were not?"

"No. It's my husband—pardon me—Lord Wakefield was the one who knew the Duke and Duchess of Brightwell."

"What happened then?"

"I'd just finished repairing my makeup when Wakefield walked into the library. I don't know how he found us." She appeared confused.

"How did he react?"

"He was furious. My husband was an extremely jealous man. He couldn't bear to see me in the company of another gentleman."

Clever answer. It put the onus on Wakefield, rather than Newcastle.

"Before I could explain why we were in the room, he swung a fist at Newcastle, who dodged the blow. He grew even more angry and came after me. Newcastle stepped in and struck Wakefield to prevent my being injured. Further injured, I should say." She gazed down at her gloved hands, a perfect study of tragedy. After a moment's stretch, she collected herself. "My husband fell by my feet. I yelled for them to stop for I didn't want to see either hurt. Newcastle bowed to me and left."

The coroner shook his head, seemingly disgusted with what she'd had to endure. "And Lord Wakefield? What did he do?"

"He scrambled to his feet. Without another word, he walked out. That's the last time I saw him until . . ." A handkerchief made an appearance which she used to dab her eyes.

I was in awe of her. You would have thought she'd truly cared for the man.

"Until?"

"I saw him sprawled at the bottom of the stairs no longer breathing." Her breath hitched. "I apologize, your Honor. This has all been too much for me."

If anyone in the courtroom didn't feel sympathy for her, that person owned a cold, stone heart.

"Very well. Thank you, Lady Wakefield. You may step down."

He then called the medical examiner. His exhaustive explanation came down to Lord Wakefield being hit in the back of the head with some object and had either fallen or thrust forward. Death was instantaneous. But the most interesting bit came at the end.

"Lord Wakefield was only five eight. The person who struck him was taller, between five ten and six feet and right-handed as the blow came from that direction."

"A man?"

"Not necessarily. A tall woman could have struck the killing blow."

"What was used to kill Lord Wakefield?"

"A statuette about six inches in height and four inches

across. It was found at the top of the stairs smeared with blood and brain matter."

"Blimey!" somebody said as whispers spread through the courtroom.

The coroner banged down the gavel and demanded silence before calling Inspector Crawford to the stand. He explained how the police secured the scene and took statements from approximately one hundred guests and twenty-five staff members. After providing their names and addresses and a summary of where they'd been and what they'd seen, most were released. The few who had noticed something he interrogated. Unfortunately, remarkably few had, but then the body had been found in a private area of the house.

"How would you describe the manner of Lord Wakefield's death?"

"As the medical examiner stated, Lord Wakefield was struck on the back of the head. It appeared he then fell forward, landing at the bottom," Inspector Crawford explained reading from his notebook.

"What was he struck with?"

"A statuette of a young woman seated, undressed, her hands folded demurely in front of her."

The coroner harrumphed and made a note of it.

"Were you able to ascertain the sequence of events leading to Lord Wakefield's demise?"

"Once he was greeted by the Duke and the Duchess of Brightwell, no one saw Wakefield the rest of the night, except for Lady Wakefield and Lord Newcastle, that is. So, we only have their accounts as to what happened."

"Very well."

"After I arrived, I located Lady Wakefield and escorted her to the family's personal library so we could talk." Inspector Crawford pretty much repeated what Lady Wakefield had said. "I then interviewed Lord Newcastle. His testimony matched that of Lady Wakefield's to a certain extent."

"What extent was that?"

"Well, after the altercation with Lord Wakefield, he did not proceed to the ballroom. Rather, he entered the duke's study. He didn't feel it prudent to wander too far from Lady Wakefield. He feared her husband's intemperate temper might result in her suffering further injury."

"When did he leave the study?"

"He heard a scream and rushed out thinking it was Lady Wakefield, but she was nowhere in sight. He wandered to the top of the stairs, tripping over the statuette which lay on the carpet. He picked it up and found it smeared with blood. Someone was still screaming at the bottom of the stairs. A maid, he thought."

"Can any of this be corroborated?"

"Only the time he was in Lady Wakefield's presence."

"Very well. What about this maid?"

"A Mary Seward. She'd been asked to bring some sandwiches and tea to the family drawing room as the dowager duchess was entertaining there. She'd just made the stairs, when she spotted Lord Wakefield's body, causing her to drop the tea service. At that point, she screamed. That's when she noticed Lord Newcastle at the top of the stairs with the statuette in his hand."

"Is Mary Seward present?" the coroner asked the courtroom.

"Yes, your honor," a timid female voice answered.

"Please come forward."

Inspector Crawford changed places with the maid who turned out to be a slip of a thing. No older than eighteen would be my guess. After she stated her name and was duly sworn in, the coroner asked her about that night.

"Well, sir, a footman came into the kitchen and asked

Cook to have sandwiches and tea delivered to the family drawing room. Apparently, the dowager duchess was entertaining friends. They were meaning to play cards or some such thing. So, I got the tea service together and started toward the servant stairs. But two guests were there doing something untoward." Her face flushed bright pink. "I thought it best not to disturb."

A ripple of laughter rang through the gallery.

The coroner brought down his gavel. "Quiet." Once the hilarity subsided, he asked the maid to proceed.

"Yes, sir. Thank 'ee, sir. So, I decided to go up the family stairs, sir. It's not normally allowed, but I thought it best under the circumstances."

He nodded. "Most assuredly."

"Well, when I reached the family stairs, I saw a gentleman sprawled out at the bottom of them. It took me a second to realize what it was. Dead as a doornail he was. Gave me a fair turn, he did. I screamed, dropped the tea service. Such lovely china, too. Hope the broken crockery won't come out of me wages." Worry was clear in her eyes.

"I'm sure it won't come to that," the coroner assured her.

"Yes, sir. That's when I looked up to the top of the stairs. The landing, that's what the fine folk call it. A young gent stood there, holding something in his hand. It had blood on it. I screamed again. It was awful, sir."

"Would you recognize the gentleman if you saw him again?"

"Oh, yes, sir." She smiled. "He was ever so handsome."

Another round of laughter rippled through the crowd, but the coroner's gavel quieted them down.

"Could you search the courtroom and see if he's here?"

She took her time, but it was a foregone conclusion. "It was him, sir." She was pointing to Newcastle.

"Thank you, Miss Seward. You may step down. Lord Newcastle, would you come forward?"

A murmur of oohs and aahs spread through the courtroom while he approached the stand. No wonder. With his periwinkle eyes and dark hair, he was most handsome indeed. His black suit was all that was proper and so was his demeanor. Clearly, he was taking the proceedings very seriously. As well he should since his neck was on the line.

After he gave his name, he was duly sworn in. The start of his testimony matched Lady Wakefield's.

"So where did you go when you left the library?" the coroner asked.

"I headed toward the duke's private study. It was adjacent to the library. I wanted to remain close in case Lady Wakefield needed my help."

The implication was clear. He expected Lord Wakefield to take out his anger on his wife.

"About a minute later, I heard the library door open and close and a heavy tread walking away. I assumed it to be Lord Wakefield's. I didn't trust him not to return so I remained in the study. The Duke of Brightwell keeps excellent whisky there."

If he intended it as a joke, it fell flat as no one laughed.

"How long were you there?"

"Half an hour, I think. After a couple of whisky tumblers, time got kind of muddled."

The coroner's arched brow signaled his disapproval. "When did you leave?"

"When I heard somebody scream. A woman. Thinking it was Lady Wakefield, I rushed out. I tripped over something in the landing, a white statuette which I picked up. That's when I noticed the blood on it. I glanced toward the bottom of the stairs and saw Wakefield lying still. I've seen enough ruined bodies in the battlefields to know he was dead."

"Did anybody see you in the study? Or emerge from it?"

"No."

"If I may ask, Lord Newcastle, how tall are you?"

Not hard to see why the coroner was asking that question.

"Six feet."

"And are you right-handed or left, sir?"

"Right-handed."

The coroner raised a brow, but all he said was, "Thank you. You may step down."

The verdict was a foregone conclusion—death by unlawful killing. Inspector Crawford arrested Newcastle the next day.

CHAPTER ELEVEN

KITTY IS ASKED TO INVESTIGATE

"*I*'M BEGGING YOU to investigate the murder of my husband," Lady Wakefield said. As soon as Newcastle was arrested, she'd sent me a note begging for an audience. I had no doubt what she would ask of me. And even though I had strong reservations about the case, I'd agreed to the meeting.

"Lady Wakefield, I'm not qualified to do such a thing." It was the same argument I'd used before for it was true. I'd been overruled then, and I expected I would be again.

"You investigated two murders, Miss Worthington," she argued.

Which, of course, I countered with the truth. "I did neither of those alone, Lady Wakefield. My family helped, along with some very dear friends, Lord Newcastle himself included."

"Of course, I know about their involvement. I will ask them to help as well. Beg if I have to. Whatever I need to do.

Newcastle did not murder my husband. And please call me Sybil."

It would not do to call her by her first name, not when I would have to keep her at arm's length if I indeed investigated. "The evidence against him is overwhelming, Lady Wakefield. He had motive, means, and opportunity. And there was a witness to it all." Well, almost. The maid had not actually seen Newcastle cosh Wakefield on the head.

Her breath shorted. "I know it doesn't look favorable, but he doesn't have it in him to kill a man."

I gazed at her with sympathy even as I offered my surest argument. "He was a soldier in the Great War. I imagine he was responsible for a few deaths."

"That was different. Newcastle would not murder an unarmed man."

"Even if that man was hurting the woman he loved?"

Her breath caught. "He's not—"

"He is and has been so for a long time." I didn't add she was also in love with him for she would only deny it. "If I undertake this endeavor, I'll need to delve into your relationship with him, and your husband's . . . mistreatment of you. You will have to be deadly honest with me. Are you prepared for what it all will entail?"

"I will do whatever it takes to save Newcastle from the gallows." For the gallows it most certainly would be.

I capitulated with grace for there really was no other option. "Very well. I will see what I can do. Be forewarned, however. I will not be able to carry out the investigation by myself. My friends and family will need to assist. If they find themselves unwilling or unable to do so, it will be extremely difficult to proceed."

She looked off into the distance before returning her gaze to me. "As I said, I'm more than willing to ask for their help."

"I would recommend you don't as they would find it difficult to deny your request. They need to come to this willingly, with no undue influence from you."

I thought she would argue further, but she didn't.

"I will leave it in your capable hands then. You will contact me, either way?" Her voice trembled toward the end.

"I will. I should have an answer for you by tomorrow." I pressed Lady Wakefield's hands. "Try not to worry too much." Whoever had killed her husband, it hadn't been her, not after she'd taken his abuse for years. But then, what if Lady Emma was right and Wakefield was planning to end her life, and somehow she'd found about it? Would she then plot and plan to kill him before she ended up dead? Something I would need to consider.

As soon as Lady Wakefield departed, I chased down Margaret to ask her opinion. As usual, she was in the library. This time writing a paper on the women suffrage march. She would need to submit it to her tutor once she returned to Oxford.

"How are you progressing?"

"Fine." She stretched her back. "Being hunched over this typewriter tires me out, though."

"You could have written it out longhand."

"Have you seen my handwriting?" A rhetorical question for, of course, I had. Her penmanship resembled a spider crawling across a piece of paper with no rhyme or reason to its path. "Besides, my professor specifically requires all reports be typewritten." She came to her feet. "Just had some tea and crumpets brought in. Join me?"

I nodded.

She took on the task of playing Mother, offering me tea and a lemon scone. Ever since Sebastian had planted lemon and orange trees in the conservatory, we had no lack of citrus fruits. Cook had turned that bounty into lemon bars, drizzled cakes, and, of course, scones.

"How was your meeting with Lady Wakefield?" she asked. I'd told her about it beforehand, of course, for I did not wish to keep it secret from her. "Did she ask you to investigate her husband's murder?"

"She did."

"And what did you say?"

"That I could not do it alone, and I would require some help. Of course, she knows all about our investigations into the other murders."

She bit into a scone. "And you've come to ask for my help."

"Among other things. I hate to do so. I know how busy you are with the women's clinic and your school paper. I wouldn't blame you if you said no."

She tilted her head. "Kitty, how could I do that after Newcastle helped clear Sebastian? Of course, I'll help. I daresay Sebastian will be eager to do so as well."

I released a pent-up breath. "Well, that's a relief. I don't know how successful we will be. The evidence is so clearly against Newcastle."

"The evidence was clearly against Sebastian as well. Remember that. There's no telling what we will find."

"That's true." I came to my feet. "I think I'll telephone everyone, rather than send notes around. It will take less time."

"Excellent idea."

By the end of the day, everyone had agreed to investigate the murder. Lord Marlowe and Lady Emma, Ned, Sebastian, and even dear Lily, all were eager to join in the fray once more. And then there was one surprising addition—Lord Hollingsworth. Somehow, he'd gotten wind of our endeavor, probably from Ned who apparently was handling his finances, and asked if he could join our team. Since it would take time to raise enough capital for his next expedition, he was searching for something to do. This investigation seemed just the ticket to him.

As there was no time to waste, we set our first meeting for the next day. In the meantime, I needed to bathe and dress for I, along with Mother, was to attend supper at Lord Rutledge's tonight. I had no knowledge of his guest list, but there was a strong possibility Inspector Crawford would attend as Lord Rutledge was his mentor. I would need to stay away from him if he were indeed present. After all, I was set to investigate Lord Wakefield's murder, and he was the Scotland Yard inspector in charge of the case. But as it turned out, my good intentions came to naught.

CHAPTER TWELVE

SUPPER PARTY AT LORD RUTLEDGE'S

"*M*AY I JOIN YOU, MISS WORTHINGTON?" Once the ladies retired to the drawing room after supper, I'd sought an obscure corner of the drawing room, hoping to avoid a discussion with him. But much as he'd done in the past, he sought me out.

This time, however, I was in no mood to consent. "I don't know if that's wise, Inspector. I've been asked to investigate Lord Wakefield's murder."

He raised a brow. "Ahhh. I understand. But surely there are other topics we can discuss. The weather, for instance."

That old staple of British society, sometimes used as small talk, other times to avoid uncomfortable subjects. Very well. I would bite. But I would keep it to the barest minimum. "It's a pea soup out there. You can barely see two feet in front of you. There. We've discussed it."

Allowing himself a small smile, he rounded the sofa to sit next to me. Leaning against it, he rested his arm along the back, his fingers mere inches from my bare shoulder. "How about if I tell you about the Yorkshire case?"

Curiosity battled my common sense, and, of course, the former won out. "I did want to know."

For a few seconds, he studied me, probably trying to gauge my mood. After all, at the masked ball we'd parted in less than amicable terms. I kept an interested expression on my face which seemed to satisfy him.

"A three-year old boy was abducted from his bed in the middle of the night. Someone had broken into the house."

"The nursemaid didn't hear it?"

"She'd taken a sleeping powder, or so she said."

"You suspected her?"

"Almost right away. Her answer did not ring true to me."

"And the local police did not suspect her of any wrongdoing?"

"The constable, a friend of her family, took her at her word. When a week elapsed with no progress, the wife's father contacted Scotland Yard. He's not only a baron but holds a rather important position in the government. So, the Yard felt compelled to send someone."

"That's where you came in."

He nodded. "They were desperate. The boy is their only child, and as matters stand, likely to be the only one. The mother apparently suffered complications during childbirth."

"Oh, my. It made it even more important to find the boy, not that it wouldn't be anyway."

"Exactly. It didn't take long to resolve. The nursemaid crumbled when I questioned her. The problem then became finding the child. Her intended hadn't told her where he'd taken him, and he was a much harder nut to crack."

"How did you manage it?"

"He was a hail-fellow-well-met sort, so I put him in isolation in a darkened room. By day three, he was screaming to be let out. On day five, he provided us with the child's location."

"Where was he?"

"With the intended's cousin, if you can believe it. He claimed the tyke was his son, and he needed her to watch over him while he handled a job. The none-too-bright relative didn't suspect a thing. She lives a county away in a rather desolate area, nearest neighbor two miles away. She had no idea of what had occurred. Thankfully, the boy suffered no harm." He took a deep breath, and his tone changed. "The mother, however, was another matter."

"What happened to her?"

"She suffered a mental breakdown. Didn't even acknowledge her son when he was returned to her."

"Oh, dear heaven. How sad."

"Yes." For a second, he glanced away but then shifted his gaze back to me. "So, you're investigating Wakefield's murder."

"Inspector Crawford," I chided. "We shouldn't be talking about this."

He roundly ignored me. "Are you sure you want to do this? The evidence is very clear."

Very well. If he wished to discuss the subject, it would be to his detriment, not mine. He would be the one affected if Scotland Yard found out.

"The evidence was very clear in the previous matter we investigated," I said, "but the interpretation was wrong."

"I wasn't in charge of that case. I wouldn't have made the same mistakes."

"Are you that sure about Newcastle's guilt?"

He shifted in the settee to face me more fully. "I don't trade in matters of guilt or innocence. As an officer of the law, I only search for the truth."

"What if you only know some of the facts?"

"Then I will find the rest."

Well, that gave me hope. "You're still investigating?"

"Of course."

"But at the ball, you said—"

"I said the evidence was clear, which it is."

"But you arrested Newcastle."

"Because the evidence pointed that way. It would have been a dereliction of duty on my part if I hadn't done so."

I breathed a little bit easier. That was something, at least.

"You'll be using Owen Clapham as a resource, I suppose," he said.

I frowned. "Now how did you find out I'd hired him?"

"Word spread at Scotland Yard."

In other words, Chief Detective Inspector Bolton talked. How very inappropriate of him. But it would be highly unfair of me to vent my frustration on Inspector Crawford. "It would be foolish of me not to use his expertise. If he agrees. I want him to advise our group."

His mouth twisted with disapproval. "Beware, Catherine. He left Scotland Yard under a cloud."

"But Inspector Bolton recommended him."

"He would. They're birds of a feather, those too."

"What do you mean?"

"They often employ methods not sanctioned by the law."

He was interfering again. Something he'd done before. But I reminded myself he intended it for my benefit. So I accepted his advice with good grace. "Very well. I'll be on the lookout then."

"Now, about Lord Hollingsworth."

This was the second time he'd raised the issue of the aristocrat. "Yes?"

"You should cut that connection."

That was a surprising thing for him to say. "Why?"

"He courts danger. Unreasonably so at times."

I grinned. "I can very well believe that."

"I don't want you near him when things go awry, Catherine." He'd now stepped over the line as his tone had become quite dictatorial, and one I did not care for at all.

I was no missish young thing to be ordered about. So, I made my position clear. "Inspector, you have no dominion over me. You're neither my father, nor brother, nor anything else. If I choose to associate with Lord Hollingsworth, that's my decision."

"Why would you want to do so?"

Although I did not have to explain myself, I chose to do so. "He's interesting, different. He's done something with his life. He's not satisfied with lying about betting on some idiotic race or gambling all night or consorting with women of the night."

He scoffed.

I couldn't understand why he was acting this way. "Is there something in particular I should know about Lord Hollingsworth?"

"He's a pirate."

I snorted. "A pirate? Really, Inspector. Is that the best you can do?"

"He absconds with objects from other cultures."

"He pays for them!"

His gaze bounced back to me. "Is that what he told you?"

"Yes."

"And you believe him?"

"Of course, I do."

He blew out a breath. "Just beware of him."

"You warn me away but refuse to provide a logical explanation." One would think he was jealous of all the attention Hollingsworth was paying me. Ludicrous, for Hollingsworth was barely an acquaintance.

"I'm doing it as a friend."

I hissed in a breath. "Is that all I am to you, Inspector? A friend?"

I thought he'd explain, but all he said was, "That's all I can give you at the moment."

Three weeks ago, he'd kissed my palm in a terrace, made me feel things I'd never felt before. I thought it was the start of something. Maybe it was the moonlight, or my own naïveté that made me believe he was offering more than mere friendship. Apparently, he was not. Very well. I would accept it and move on.

"Thank you for your honesty, Inspector." I opened my purse and retrieved the handkerchief he'd lent me when I spilled tea on a dress. "I'd meant to return it before now, but with things the way they were, it slipped my mind." It hadn't. I'd kept it because it belonged to him. I'd touched it, felt it, held it in my hand every night wondering who had given it to him. Embroidered with a flourished "R", it was the kind of linen only a woman would own. But before I could give it to him, a discreet cough alerted me to someone else's presence.

Lord Rutledge, our evening's host. He was not only a close friend of our family but Inspector Crawford's mentor. "Are you enjoying your evening?" he asked.

"Yes, thank you," I said in a tight voice. The inspector merely nodded.

His gaze grew wide when he noticed what I held. "May I?" When I placed it in his hand, he asked, "You kept it all these years, Robert?"

"Yes."

"You recognize it?" I was surprised, to say the least.

"I should. It belonged to me once upon a time."

"It was yours?"

"Yes. I used it to stanch Robert's blood the night he was attacked saving me."

"Oh." I flushed with embarrassment. And here I'd thought it belonged to Lady Cookson.

Taking the cloth from Lord Rutledge, the Inspector said, "If you hadn't used it, I would have bled to death. I keep it to remind me of the fragility of life."

I felt like the biggest fool on earth.

* * *

ON THE WAY HOME, I repeated that sentiment to Mother. "I'm an idiot."

"Yes, dear."

I laughed. "You don't have to agree with me."

She gazed at me, warm understanding in her eyes. "I suppose this pertains to Inspector Crawford."

"Yes. I thought. Oh, never mind what I thought. I made a cake of myself."

She patted my clenched hands. "I'm sure that's not true, dear."

I remained silent.

"Did I ever tell you how I met your father?"

"He was Lord Higginbotham's personal secretary, and you were the minister's daughter. You were invited for supper, and he was instantly smitten with you."

"I may have embellished that tale a little."

"Which part?"

"All of it."

I barked out a laugh. "Mother!"

"Some of it, anyway," she said with a small grin. "The truth is slightly different. Would you like to hear it?"

"Need you ask?"

"Very well." She settled against the back seat of the Rolls and began her tale. "After I turned eighteen, I was deemed old enough to be invited to supper at Lord Higginbotham's castle, and one day I was. Excited beyond belief, I dressed carefully in my Sunday best. Father and I were to ride in our gig, but just as we were about to leave, a parishioner arrived. He had an urgent matter he wanted to discuss with Father. So he sent me ahead so I could explain his delay. It'd rained earlier that day so there were puddles on the road. I was taking my time, making sure I evaded them. All of a sudden, your father came riding up, hell for leather on a spirited stallion. I was so astounded I fell backward into a mound of mud."

"Oh, no." I pinched my lips to keep my laughter from making itself known. "What did he do?"

"Nothing. He never even noticed. Fuming, I returned to the rectory and changed into another frock. *Not* my Sunday best. By that time, Father had finished with the parishioner. So, we climbed into the gig and made our way to the castle. When I was introduced to your father, I snubbed him. And when a private moment arose, I told him in no uncertain terms what had happened. He stood there calmly looking at me while I called him rude and ungentlemanly and all manners of names not befitting a minister's daughter."

"Mother!" This time I couldn't keep the laughter from spilling out. "How did he respond?"

"He said nothing that night. But the next morning he arrived at the rectory with a batch of ginger cookies and a bouquet of wildflowers. He'd taken the time, you see, to discover my favorites. And then he explained the reason why he'd been in such a hurry. Lauren, Lord Higginbotham's seven-year-old daughter, suffered from asthma, and she'd had a coughing fit. Her medicine had run out. So, his employer asked him to ride to the chemist in the village and obtain a fresh dose. That was why he was in such a hurry, because of the urgency of the situation."

"Did he make it in time?"

"Yes. Her breathing returned to normal once she was administered her medicine. Needless to say, I felt like a fool. So, you see, dear, you're not alone in thinking yourself less than worthy." She pressed my hands once more. "Now how did you come to feel this way?"

I told her about how I'd spilled tea on my dress one day while visiting Inspector Crawford at Scotland Yard. And he'd offered me his handkerchief to prevent a stain. "The handkerchief was embroidered with a fancy, flourished R. I thought a lady had given it to him. And then I met Lady Cookson, whose first name is Rachel, at Hollingsworth's lecture. Inspector Crawford had escorted her so I thought it'd been she."

"If I had seen it, I could have told you it was Lord Rutledge's. But I sense that's not the only reason you're upset."

"He only wants to be a friend."

"Did he say that?"

Not wishing her to see my tears, I looked out into the night. "He said that's all he can give me at the moment."

"Well, it stands to reason, don't you think?"

I returned my gaze to her. "What do you mean?"

"Kitty, you're involved in the same murder investigation as he, or you soon will be. Of course, all he can give you is friendship for now. It doesn't mean it won't be something different once this matter is settled."

"He warned me against Hollingsworth, you know."

"Did he? What did he say?"

"That Hollingsworth is a pirate."

Mother smiled. "Well, I suppose he is in a way. He travels the high seas, collecting booty."

"I hate that we can't be more than friends. I hate that he always sticks to the rules."

"He is an officer of the law, Kitty." She thought for a moment. "But it may also come from him being an orphan."

"What do you mean?"

"As you know, the Ladies Benevolent Society contributes to the Children's Home orphanage."

"Yes, of course."

"A few lucky ones are adopted, usually the younger ones. We visit the homes, usually three and six months out, to make sure everything's proceeding smoothly. By and large, those children are perfectly behaved. Too perfectly."

"Please explain."

"They feel they must be on their best behavior. That they cannot do anything wrong. Because, if they do, they will be returned to the orphanage. So, they overcompensate by sticking to the rules as closely as they can. Maybe that's why Inspector Crawford acts the way he does."

"But his family loved him, treasured him."

"Which made it even more important for him to be a perfectly behaved child. In fact, he loves rules so much, he became a police officer."

"He doesn't follow them always, though. He approached me tonight even though I warned him against it."

"Obviously, he wanted to be near you. It was a private setting, among friends. Not a public venue, or, heaven forbid, Scotland Yard. He felt safe talking to you there."

That made me feel a bit better, but not much.

"Give it time, dear. Wait until this matter is settled and then you can discuss with Inspector Crawford where you stand. In the meantime, there is Lord Hollingsworth."

A laugh burst out of me. "You never give up, Mother."

"Not when it comes to my children's happiness, I don't."

CHAPTER THIRTEEN

MEETING OF THE INVESTIGATIVE COMMITTEE

"*T*HANK YOU FOR COMING IN A DAY EARLY, Mister Clapham." We'd held several tutoring sessions in the Worthington House Library, where we met twice a week. Yesterday, I'd telephoned and asked if he could attend to me today because there was something I wanted to discuss with him, and he'd readily agreed.

"No trouble at all, Miss Worthington. As it turned out, I was free."

"How very fortunate." I cleared my throat. "I've been asked by Lady Wakefield to investigate the murder of her husband."

He nodded, a pensive expression to his face. "A logical request for her to make given the success of your previous inquiries."

"Thank you." I paused for a second to determine the best way to explain matters to him. "Those were carried out by me, of course, along with a group of family and friends. I telephoned them yesterday. They all agreed to join me in this investigation. We're holding our first meeting this afternoon. At two, to be exact."

"And you want to know how I could help." A statement, not a question, but then Mister Clapham was no fool.

"Yes. Your vast experience will prove invaluable. More than likely, there will be things we haven't thought of. And you might be able to shed light on other matters."

He didn't keep me waiting for his response. "I'll be glad to help in any way I can, Miss Worthington. It will be my pleasure to do so."

"I have to warn you, though. I haven't told the committee members. They might resent your presence and be unwilling to have you join us."

"Perfectly understandable. I suggest you make it more palatable by proposing my participation will be as an advisor, and not a full participant."

A weight eased off my shoulders. The last thing I wished to do was offend him, so I was happy he understood. "Thank you. That's exactly what I intended to do." I glanced at my watch. It was close to noon. "Luncheon will be served in a few minutes. Would you care to join us? No sense you leaving only to return."

His head shake signaled regret. "Oh, no, Miss. It won't do. I'm not quality."

"Nonsense. You are my guest."

"I'd prefer not to do so." He winked. "Still eat me peas with me knife, you see."

"You forget I shared a tea with you, Mister Clapham. You have perfectly lovely table manners."

After a pause of a few seconds, he asked, "May I make a suggestion?"

"Of course."

"Would the kitchen be available? That way I would not have to leave."

"Yes, of course. I'll go alert Cook, shall I?"

"If it's any imposition, I'll be glad to eat my meal elsewhere. There's a perfectly lovely chop house not too far."

"I'm sure it won't be a problem, Mister Clapham." My statement proved to be true. As I'd learned from my maid Betsy, Cook had been curious about the retired inspector. This would provide ample opportunity for a nice friendly chat. In between serving the family's luncheon, of course.

At two, we meandered to the library. Sebastian and Lily had joined us for lunch, so they were already present. Seemingly, the committee members were eager to get started as they arrived early. As we'd done during the previous investigation, Margaret had preassigned seating. Margaret and Sebastian would sit on a sofa on the far side of the room to provide them with as much privacy as could be had. Situated somewhat closer to the center of the room Lily and Lady Emma were perched on a settee. The gentlemen—Ned and Lord Marlowe—had been assigned to single chairs, somewhat distant from one another. Lord Hollingsworth, the last to appear, drew a raised brow from Lord Marlowe which for the moment I chose to ignore.

After everyone was seated, I brought up the subject of Owen Clapham who was waiting outside. I explained that I'd hired him to teach me the art and science of investigation before Lord Wakefield's murder had occurred. I thought he would make a valuable addition to the committee, but it was a decision I could not make by myself. The members would need to vote on whether we would allow him to participate. After a short discussion, we decided he would be a useful resource, but only as an advisor. He would not participate in any decision-making by the group. Once the agreement was reached, Owen Clapham was invited into the room. After I informed him of the terms of his participation, he nodded and took a seat in the far part of the library, probably to make himself as invisible as possible. Since we'd learned during our previous investigation that Margaret was best at keeping track of things, she was once more appointed our scribe.

I opened the meeting by thanking everyone for volunteering to help, and then I welcomed Lord Hollingsworth to the group.

True to form, Marlowe objected to his presence. "I don't see why we need him. He doesn't know Newcastle and has been out of England for an entire year. No offense, dear chap," he finished glancing at Hollingsworth.

"None taken." Hollingsworth returned with a grin.

"In my opinion," I said, "the fact he doesn't know Newcastle is a point in his favor as he will be able to look upon the evidence more objectively."

"Here, here," Sebastian declared.

Placing her hand on his, Margaret smiled. Seemingly, she concurred.

"Are there any more objections to Lord Hollingsworth joining our investigation?"

Silence greeted my question. "Let's carry on, then, shall we? I glanced in Ned's direction. He and Lily had been trading surreptitious glances while whispering back and forth. Their conviviality did not surprise me. Last year, Sebastian had given him permission to call on Lily which he had done. But given the fact she had her debut season to enjoy next year, they deferred any decision until she had done so. If she accepted his suit, they would become engaged. In the meantime, they had an understanding. Of what, I had no idea. "Ned?"

"Yes."

"Could you look into Lord Wakefield's financial situation?"

"Of course," he agreed with a head nod.

I didn't need to add anything. With his vast knowledge of finance, he would know what to do.

"Lord Marlowe."

"Present."

"I know you are present, milord. Could you find out about Lord Wakefield's background—friends, enemies, outside interests?"

"Women, you mean?"

"Yes."

"Shouldn't be a problem."

"Sebastian?"

His head came up from whispering with Margaret. "Yes?"

"You have made inroads in the House of Lords. I need you to listen to the scuttlebutt there. Was Wakefield involved in anything nefarious? Are there are any rumors flying around Westminster about him?"

"Will be glad to do so."

"We also need to obtain information about the new Lord Wakefield. Who is he for starters? Was he eager enough for the title to kill for it?"

Sebastian hitched a breath.

How very careless of me. In my rush to assign tasks to everyone, I'd failed to consider what he'd gone through. "I'm sorry. If that cuts too close to the bone, I can ask someone else."

"No, I'll do it. After all, who here would know better than me?" Margaret pressed his hand which gesture he returned with a smile.

"Thank you, Sebastian."

"Don't mention it."

"What would you like me to do, Kitty?" Lily asked, probably trying to take the focus off her brother.

"Since you're adding to your wardrobe, I want you to listen to the gossip when you visit Angelique's. Women tend to speak freely at places they gather, such as the modiste. You might pick up a nugget of information or two."

"I'll be happy to do so."

"Margaret. Since you're the only one amongst us who has any knowledge of the law, I want you to talk to the solicitor. Find out about Newcastle's state of mind and what his chances are. Hopefully, the solicitor will share such with you."

"I'll send a letter to Newcastle asking for his permission for me to talk to his counsel. Once he has done so, I'll make an appointment."

"Splendid."

"Lady Emma, I want you to take on the most sensitive task of all. One of us needs to talk to the Duchess of Brightwell. I find myself reluctant to do so. At the ball, she seemed ill. She was very pale, and her hands trembled. I don't know if it was a temporary indisposition or something more permanent. Have you heard anything?" Given her mother's penchant for gossip, if the duchess was seriously ill, she would know.

"It was discussed at one of mama's gossip fests. Apparently, it was brought on by something she ate. The night of the ball, the duke urged her to rest, but she felt she needed to be present at the receiving line to welcome guests."

"So she's recuperated from her ordeal?" It had been several days.

"I have no confirmation, but I haven't heard otherwise."

I weighed her answer. We really did need to talk to the duchess, and it couldn't wait. But we needed to be solicitous of her health. "Very well. Tell her what we're doing and ask her if she can see her way to providing you with an audience. If she's not feeling well, it will be her decision to decline your request."

Lady Emma jotted my instructions on a small notebook. "Anything else?"

"We need a list of all the guests who attended, as well as the staff. Once we have that, we can gather information on them. You'll need to get her approval to inspect the premises, specifically the stairway and the first-floor social gathering rooms, not the bedrooms on the second floor. Stress that upon her. Do you feel comfortable taking on this task? I know it's a lot to ask."

"She knows me since I'm out, so I'm not a stranger. I'll make sure she knows I'm not there to pry."

"Wonderful. Now, you cannot possibly inspect that large mansion by yourself. Lord Hollingsworth will accompany you. If he's amenable, of course."

"Be happy to," Lord Hollingsworth said. "But are you assuming only a guest or a member of the staff could have committed the murder?"

"Who else could have?"

"Anyone. With as many windows as Brightwell Mansion has, any person with a mind to it could have broken in with very little effort. Never mind that the day of the ball you would've had any number of individuals delivering food and drink," Hollingsworth explained.

"But wouldn't he have been noticed?" Margaret asked.

"Not necessarily. He could have worn a costume. It was a masked ball, after all. As far as deliveries went, I imagine it was mayhem in the kitchen with all the preparations. Someone dressed as a workman could've snuck into the house to deliver a case of spirits and remained hidden in the wine cellar until it was time for the beverages to be served. More than likely, there were extra servants hired for the occasion, so all he would have needed to do was don the livery of a footman. When the time came, he could have tossed a case over his shoulder and taken it to the kitchen."

The stunned silence that met him gave credence to his words.

"It's possible," Owen Clapham said from his corner of the room.

"Yes, well. Thank you for that, Lord Hollingsworth. Hopefully, the duchess will give you permission to fully inspect the house. When you accompany Lady Emma, you can test your theory."

"Oh, she will," he said with that devil-may-care smile of his. "Not only is she a family friend, but a sponsor of my expeditions."

He could have mentioned that sooner.

"What will you do, Kitty?" Margaret asked.

"Visit Lady Wakefield. We need to learn everything there is to know about her marriage to Wakefield." Whether she told the truth or lied, only time would tell.

CHAPTER FOURTEEN

KITTY VISITS LADY WAKEFIELD

*H*AVING ARRANGED A MORNING MEETING WITH LADY WAKEFIELD, I arrived at Wakefield House early the next day. After showing me to her personal parlor, the butler excused himself to alert her to my presence. While I awaited her presence, I had time to study the room, and what I saw surprised me. Threadbare carpeting, a sofa sorely in need of reupholstering, draperies that had seen better days. I'd expected something up to the mark, for Lord Wakefield had seemed flush enough. But then some individuals were all flash and no substance.

I didn't have long to wait for Lady Wakefield to make an appearance. As in the inquest, she was dressed all in black, but her frock was a much simpler one. And, tellingly enough, she wore no veil. While she paid obeisance to the custom in public, in private it was another matter altogether. I didn't blame her. A veil would signal a grief which I very much doubted she felt.

"I hope I did not keep you waiting long," Lady Wakefield said in that slightly husky tone of hers.

I made my curtsy. "Not at all. Thank you for seeing me."

"Oh, please, Miss Worthington. There's no need." She motioned for me to retake my seat as she eased into one herself. "If anyone is pleased it's me as indebted as I am to you."

After a quick knock on the door, the butler entered carrying a tray with a tea service. The china was fine enough, but the service did not include food. Whether that was due to the time of day or a desire to economize, I had no idea.

I had time to observe her while she busied herself with the tea ritual. Although I couldn't say she was happy, she seemed to be in better spirits since I'd seen her last. But then, no one appeared in their best light at an inquest.

Once we had a chance to refresh ourselves, she asked, "How is the investigation progressing?"

"We're gathering facts. That's why I came to you. To find out more information about Lord Wakefield."

"Of course."

I retrieved my journal from my purse. "I hope you don't mind if I take notes."

"Whatever you need to do, Miss Worthington."

"I'd like to start with your acquaintance with Lord Wakefield. Can you tell me how you first met?"

"It was my first season. I was eighteen at the time. My family had great hopes for me. I needed to marry well, you see. He became interested fairly soon, but I deemed him too old, too unattractive."

"Compared to Lord Newcastle, he would seem so."

"Simon was not an earl then. His uncle held that title, but he was . . ."

I could only imagine how, with his smooth manners and

masculine beauty, he would appear to a young girl fresh from the country. "He dazzled you."

"He did." She permitted herself a small smile. "I fell under his spell. And, wonder of wonders, he became attracted to me, so much so he wanted to marry. But my father turned down his offer. He did not have any prospects, you see. His cousin would inherit the title, not him."

"That must have devastated you."

"It did. So much so, I refused to entertain any other proposals. At the end of the season, we returned to our home with me unattached. My parents, as you can imagine, were beside themselves."

"What happened to change your mind about Wakefield?"

A shadow flitted across her eyes. It happened so fast I would not have caught it if I weren't closely observing her.

"Simon wrote me a letter telling me he was enlisting. The Great War was raging, and the army desperately needed fresh recruits. It broke my heart. Not only had I lost him, but there was a real chance he would not get out of it alive. The thought of him dying alone on some godforsaken battlefield, drove me to the brink of despair. I could not eat. I could not sleep. I became a shadow of myself. Wakefield chose that moment to visit so he could press his suit. I had no fight left in me, no hope of a future."

"So you agreed to marry him."

She sought solace in a sip of tea. "A decision I've deeply regretted."

"How long were you married?"

"Five long, miserable years," she bit out.

Now came the difficult part. "I apologize, but I have to ask. Did he always . . ." I searched for the right word to describe what he'd done to her.

"Discipline me?"

"I'm so sorry."

"Not always, no. He didn't touch me intimately until three months after our wedding. Ill as I was, it took me some time to recuperate." For a few moments, she seemed to get lost in her memories. But then, she gathered herself. "The disciplining began two years later, when I proved unable to bear him a son. At first, it was a slap here, a push there. But the violence escalated, more so in recent months. So much, I feared for my life."

"That's horrible." Of course, I'd suspected it since Lady Emma had mentioned it at Lady Clinton's tea. But to have it confirmed? It boggled my mind. How she'd borne the abuse all these years truly astounded me. But then a thought flashed into my head. Had she told Inspector Crawford about her fear? "You didn't share your misgivings with Inspector Crawford, did you?" I sincerely hoped she hadn't for he would see it as a strong motive.

"No. We only discussed what happened that night."

"But you did share it with someone else."

"I'm not sure what you're getting at, Miss Worthington." She was dodging my statement, but I was not going to allow it.

"At the Wynchcombe House luncheon, you and Lord Newcastle were engaged in a discussion. You spoke so low; I could not hear what you were saying."

"It was nothing of note," she said, shaking her head. Her trembling hands, though, gave her away. And even more telling, she avoided my gaze.

Clearly, she was lying, but I decided against challenging her. In the state she was in, she'd balk at any discussion that included Newcastle. And I needed her as calm as possible to continue our discussion. Those matters would have to wait.

"Very well." I glanced at the list of questions I wanted to ask of her and chose one that hopefully would not involve her emotions. "Do you have knowledge of your husband's finances?"

"No. He refused to discuss those matters with me."

"Forgive me for mentioning it, but your home appears . . ." I searched for a polite word to describe it.

"Rather shabby?" A smile made its way to her lips.

"Yes. And yet, you're always dressed in the height of fashion."

"My husband was mainly concerned with how he and I appeared in public. He never invited anyone to our home. Nor did he allow me to do so. The only outings I was allowed were to the modiste or to accompany him to some event."

"But you attended Lady Lily's luncheon."

"I told him I needed to visit the dressmaker, which I did later that afternoon. I couldn't afford to be caught in a lie. He watched my movements most assiduously."

"But surely, he couldn't do so all the time. He had his duties at Parliament, and there must have been other activities."

"He paid the servants to inform on me, especially my maid and the butler."

Heavens!

"I was a prisoner in my own home, Miss Worthington, but not anymore," she finished with a triumphant smile. If Inspector Crawford were here to witness it, he would think she'd been the one to murder her husband. She had cause enough.

"You are now free to come and go."

Her expression soured. "Not for long, though."

"What do you mean?"

"Wakefield failed to provide for me. He left me with neither a widow's jointure nor a place to call home."

The man had been truly a dastard. "What will you do?"

"Return to my family in Gloucester. They won't be

pleased. They deem me a colossal failure as I failed to provide Wakefield with an heir."

What an unfair blame to place on her. After all, it could just as easily have been her husband's deficiency as well as hers.

"At least it won't happen for a little while. Wakefield's solicitor tells me I have a month's grace before the new Lord Wakefield claims possession of the premises."

"Would he allow you to remain?"

"He did offer. But I would feel uncomfortable remaining here. He should be free to shape his life the way he wishes, without the widow of the previous Lord Wakefield haunting his every step."

"My brother Ned is looking into your husband's finances. Maybe he'll discover something of value."

She tossed her head. "I talked to the manager at Wakefield's bank. There is only the household account, barely enough for one month's wages and food."

"Don't lose heart. If there's something to find, Ned will do so. He's very good at that sort of thing." I glanced at my list once more. Only one left, but it was one she might refuse to respond. "I have a rather delicate question."

"More delicate that what we've already discussed?" A small smile blossomed across her lips. "Whatever you wish to know, Miss Worthington, I will answer."

"Did Lord Wakefield have a mistress?"

"He had many through the years. When he got bored with one, he replaced her. His latest, a Mrs. Gascogne, resides on Willow Street. I almost feel sorry for her as she'll be left destitute unless she finds someone to support her."

"Is that what usually happens?"

"Yes, they spend their youth going from one protector to another. If they're wise, they put money aside for those times when men no longer find them attractive. If they're not, well . . ."

She didn't need to finish her thought. The mistress would find herself on the street where only misery and disease awaited her.

"How do you know so much about them?"

"My husband wasn't shy about telling me. He rather kept throwing it in my face. He objected to my lack of willingness to perform certain acts, you see."

I had no idea what she meant, but I would find out when I talked to Wakefield's mistress.

CHAPTER FIFTEEN

LORD WAKEFIELD'S MISTRESS

"*W*OULD YOU LIKE SOME TEA, Miss Worthington?" Mrs. Gascogne, Lord Wakefield's former mistress asked. Former because he'd died, not because she'd ceased to be his *chére amie* while he was alive.

"If it wouldn't be too much trouble." I'd asked Mister Clapham to discover her address. After he'd done so, I'd contacted Mrs. Gascogne who'd agreed to talk to me. For a fee. She was a businesswoman after all.

"No trouble at all. I have a daily who comes in and does for me. MARY!"

The maid who'd opened the front door ran into the small parlor. "Yes, ma'am."

"We'll have the tea now. Plenty of cream and sugar, mind you. I must keep my figure." She certainly wasn't what I thought she'd be. For one thing, she wasn't young. In her early forties would be my guess. The owner of a full figure, she was attractive in a buxom, blowzy sort of way.

Once the tea had been served, and the maid had been dismissed, she said, "You want to talk about Lord Wakefield?"

"If you wouldn't mind."

"Not at all, dearie. My time is yours, given your generous contribution." She patted her ample bosom where she stashed the envelope I'd given her with the fee inside.

"When I was younger, which was more years ago than I care to count, it was all about what happened between the sheets, if you get my meaning."

"Yes, I think I do."

"But as I grew more experienced, I realized there was a whole world out there that needed to be explored." Leaning closer, she whispered, "Some gentlemen, you see, need something different."

She had me there, as I had no personal knowledge of what happened between or outside the sheets. "Different? How?"

"Well, dearie." She stirred more sugar into her tea. Apparently, four teaspoons were not enough. "Some gentlemen have certain preferences. An itch, you might say, that needs to be scratched."

"And Lord Wakefield was one of them?"

"Exactly. Now you must be firm with these gentlemen. You must tell them how far you're willing to go. Otherwise, they'll ride roughshod over you. Some quite literally, if you get my drift."

For a few seconds, I was confused, but then light dawned. "Horse play?"

She nodded.

Well, that certainly explained Lord Pellegrine's predilection. But I doubted that was Lord Wakefield's 'itch,' if you will. His predilection would more than likely include the sort of 'discipline' he inflected on his wife. "I would imagine some of the preferences include a certain amount of pain."

"Only light spanking, dear. If you set limits, everyone is satisfied."

He'd certainly done more than that to his wife. "Lord Wakefield never breached the agreement?"

"Not with me, dearie. I have hard and fast rules. If you don't follow them, I show you the door, and you're never allowed back. Not only that, but I spread the word among others that ply that particular trade. The gentleman will find himself hard up to find future participants for his games."

"I see." Abhorrent as such a practice was to me, she didn't seem to mind. But then, she was probably well paid for her efforts. "How long was your liaison with him?"

"About five years."

"As long as he was married to Lady Wakefield?"

"Yes. My previous gentleman passed on to his glory, you see." She bowed her head in respect. I did the same. "He was such a sweet old thing, too. But not healthy enough for the game. Unfortunately, it got the better of him one day."

"He died in your bed?"

"Oh no, dearie." She laughed. "Not my bed. His stable. That's what he preferred. You see, it was the pungent aroma of horses that motivated him. Not a very comfortable place, mind you. Hay does get into the tenderest of places."

I bit down on my lip to keep from laughing. "I can imagine."

"His widow allowed me to keep the spurs I was wearing that night. Very decent of her, I thought. They were made of gold, you see."

"Quite."

"Well, once he succumbed," —she bowed her head. I did the same— "I put the word out I was looking for a new gentleman. Based on a recommendation from a friend, I chose Lord Wakefield. He was very generous with me, if I do say so myself."

Apparently more than he'd been with his wife who'd been left penniless and without a roof over her head in a month's time. But Mrs. Gascogne was bound to suffer as well now that her source of income had vanished. Curious about her prospects, I asked, "Where will you go?"

"Go?" she asked, a question on her face.

"Now that your liaison is finished."

"Oh, nowhere, dearie. This is my house. Bought and paid for."

Unbelievable. She had a home of her own while Lady Wakefield didn't. But what could you expect when men such as Lord Wakefield ruled the world? If that was not a strong argument for women to obtain an education and have the right to vote, I didn't know what was. One simply could not depend on a husband to do the appropriate thing.

"As for my next engagement," she continued, "I have a list as long as my arm of gentlemen vying for my services. I'm leaning toward a viscount whose mistress retired. He comes well recommended. A clean gentleman. That's very important to me. And he's very generous with his largesse."

So many ways to interpret that last word. But I chose the polite one. "He sounds . . . lovely."

"Ta."

"If we could return to Lord Wakefield."

"Of course."

"Here's what I don't understand. If he had you to satisfy his needs, why would he abuse Lady Wakefield?"

She put down her cup. "Well, that was a horse of a different color, dearie."

"What do you mean?"

"He desperately wanted a child to carry on his name, and she wouldn't give it to him. Can't count the times he talked about it. I need a son, Tibby. Why won't she give me a son?"

"But the blame could be his as much as hers."

"He was never willing to entertain the notion he was lacking in that respect." She bit down on a biscuit. "Although, I must say, I had my doubts."

"Why?"

"Lady Wakefield was his second wife. His first one did not give him a child, either. So, it did make me wonder."

"Exactly."

"That's why he took out his frustration on her because she wouldn't give him a son. And he knew she could."

I was confused. "How would he know she could bear a child?"

She pinned me with a knowing stare. "Because she had already borne one, of course."

What?!!! Lady Wakefield had given birth to a child? How could this be? "How do you know this?"

"He told me the whole story one night. When she first came to town for her debut, he'd been interested in her. But she was all moony eyed about some good-looking bloke, so he gave up the chase. And then just like that" —she snapped her fingers— "she left town."

A different version of what Lady Wakefield had told me. "Do you know why?"

The family put it about that she'd grown ill. But apparently, she hadn't shown any sign of sickness, so he wondered about it. So much so, he paid an inquiry agent to investigate. Turned out the good-looking bloke had put a babe in her belly. Well, since he desperately wanted a son, he arranged to marry her. After the babe was born, of course. He was not about to claim another man's by-blow as his."

"What happened to the child?"

She shrugged and grabbed another biscuit. "I don't know. He never said."

CHAPTER SIXTEEN

A REVELATION AND A CONFESSION

I RETURNED HOME TO FIND LILY waiting for me. Strange, for we hadn't made an arrangement. Not that it mattered. I was always happy to see her. As both Mother and Margaret were absent, Carlton had simply shown her to the drawing room to await me.

"Kitty, I'm so glad you're home." Her usual ladylike demeanor had gone astray, so much so I grew instantly worried.

"What's wrong? It's not Sebastian, is it?" Margaret would be devastated if anything had happened to him.

"He's fine." Her gaze bounced around the room. "Is there somewhere more private where we can talk?"

I could understand her concern, as anybody could walk in. But what did she have to share that required privacy. "The library?" I suggested.

She shook her head. "No, that won't work. How about your bedroom?"

"Fine." What had her in such a frazzle she required that much secrecy?

We made our way up the stairs. Once I closed the door to my room and we sat on the burgundy silk settee, I turned to her. "What is it, dearest? What has driven you into such a state?"

"You asked me to visit Angelique's to find out what everyone was talking about."

"Yes." Frankly, I hadn't expected much, for it was bound to be idle gossip. More than likely, most of it would have no bearing on the case. But apparently, she'd discovered something of interest.

"Well, I'd gone in for a fitting for a new gown I'd ordered, and, Monique, one of Angelique's assistants, was making some minor adjustments. Apparently, she's been there an age. At least ten years."

"I know her."

"While she was pinning the hem, I remarked how very sad it was about Lady Wakefield's husband, even though nobody really cares about that man being dead."

"No, indeed." I had to agree with her on that issue.

"So, I asked if she'd ever attended to Lady Wakefield." Her eyes lit up. "And, oh, Kitty, she had! When Lady Wakefield was a debutante—well, she wasn't Lady Wakefield then. She was Miss Pearson."

"I understand. Go on."

"Monique worked on her court presentation gown."

That couldn't be the reason Lily was so excited. There had to be something else. "Did something happen then?" I asked.

"Not at that time. But Monique attended to her once more. Apparently, Miss Pearson's mother needed a new gown so her daughter could catch the eye of a special gentleman. So Monique measured and sewed. When it was ready for a final fitting, Miss Pearson returned. That's when Monique discovered she'd gotten the measurements wrong." She ended with a triumphant flourish.

After the revelations from Wakefield's mistress, I knew what to expect. But I held my tongue and allowed Lily to tell the story at her own pace.

"Monique couldn't believe it. She always double checked her ladies' measurements. But somehow, Miss Pearson had grown two inches around her waist. Monique made a joke about it, putting the blame on herself for being careless. And that's when it happened."

"What?"

"Miss Pearson burst into tears."

"Oh, my."

"Monique couldn't have that as it was bad for business. So, she sat her down and fetched her a cup of tea. In between sips and tears, Miss Pearson revealed all." She paused before her dramatic conclusion. "Oh, Kitty, she was *enceinte*."

French for pregnant. While it was horrible, it was good to have it confirmed by a different source. Mrs. Gascogne hadn't lied. "Yes, dear."

Kitty's face fell. "You knew?"

"I found out just this morning. From Lord Wakefield's mistress, of all people." On the way home, I'd deduced what must have happened six years ago. Lord Wakefield found out about Miss Pearson's pregnancy from his inquiry agent. That's why he was so eager to marry her. Because he knew she could give him the son he craved. He would have then traveled to Gloucester and offered for her. Her parents, facing a daughter's disgrace, must have not only agreed but insisted she marry him. After the babe was born, of course. And Miss Pearson, miserable as she'd been, relented. Was there no end to this man's evil? It was no wonder somebody had put paid to his existence.

"Do you know what happened to the babe?" Lily asked. "I can't stop thinking about it."

"No. But I intend to find out." I patted her hand. "Now, dearest, you are not to repeat any of this to anyone, not Sebastian, not even Margaret."

"I won't." She looked off into the distance. "I wonder if Newcastle knows. He must be the father, don't you think?"

"That would be my guess. Leave it to me. I'll get to the bottom of this."

She nodded.

"Now I want you to go home and go about your usual routine. Act like nothing's out of the ordinary. Can you do that?"

"I think so."

I frowned. "You must do better than that, Lily."

She nodded with firm resolution. "I will. I promise."

"Good. I'll talk to Monique, bribe her if I must to keep quiet. This must not get out, especially now."

"Why not now?"

"I doubt Newcastle knew about the babe six years ago. If he had, he would have done something about it. Married Miss Pearson at the very least. Once they met again, she wouldn't have told him as she was already married to Lord Wakefield. And she had to keep quiet for her sisters' sake, lest the scandal tarnished them. But what if Newcastle recently discovered what happened?" He and Lady Wakefield had had that rendezvous at The Majestic. What if she told him not only about her growing fear of getting killed but the child they'd conceived?

"It would provide an even more powerful motive for him to kill Wakefield," Lily answered.

"Exactly."

After thanking Lily for her report, I suggested she return home. She caviled, for she would have preferred to remain and discuss things with me. But I had so much to think about I felt it was best to study what I'd learned by myself. Not that it did any good, as I came up with more questions than answers.

An even bigger problem surfaced the next day. A server at The Majestic had overheard Newcastle and Lady Wakefield discussing her husband. I knew enough about Scotland Yard protocol to suspect Inspector Crawford would bring in Lady Wakefield for interrogation. I would need to question her before he did. With no time to send a polite note, I telephoned her and asked if I could call that afternoon. She must have heard the urgency in my voice, because she readily agreed.

I arrived to find her waiting for me in the shabby drawing room. Since the police could very well be on their way with a summons for her to attend Inspector Crawford at Scotland Yard, I wasted no time on the niceties. "Why did you meet Newcastle at The Majestic?"

Her hand rose to her throat. "I . . ."

"Please, Lady Wakefield. We can't afford a delay. You must answer now."

She firmed up her chin. "I needed his advice."

"Regarding what?"

"A way out of my marriage. As I told you, my husband had grown more violent. I was afraid of what would happen to me. It wouldn't have been the first time he got rid of a troublesome wife. His first wife fell down the stairs to her death." A bitter laugh escaped her. "Ironic, is it not, that Wakefield died the same way?"

"You feared the same thing would happen to you?"

"No. Wakefield was too wily to use the same method. He would have gone about it quite differently. I take a sleeping potion every night. My guess is he would have arranged for an overdose."

I couldn't imagine living with that kind of fear. But I wondered what his motive would have been. "Why would he desire your death?"

"To marry again, of course. He had his eye on one of this season's debutantes who hails from a fertile family. I won't reveal her name. The thought of another young girl under his dominion makes me ill. So, please don't ask."

"I won't." It no longer mattered, anyway. "Now, what did you say, exactly if you please, at The Majestic?"

She became preoccupied with her hands. "At one point I remarked that it would be so much easier if Wakefield were dead." And then she rushed to say, "But at no time did we make actual plans. It was an offhand remark, that is all."

"Unfortunately, it seems the waiter must have overheard you." I sighed. "Inspector Crawford will have no choice but to request your presence at Scotland Yard to question you. When he does, you'll need to make it emphatically clear that you never discussed killing your husband."

Her shoulders drooped. "Do you think he'll listen?" She seemed to have given up.

"He will. He's a fair man. Whatever you do, don't lie to him. He'll know if you do."

"Very well. I shall follow your advice."

"There's another matter I wish to discuss. One a great deal more sensitive."

Her hand went to her throat. And then a resigned look came over her face. "Go on."

She knew what was coming. No sense extending her agony. "You had a child."

"Yes."

"Newcastle's?"

She nodded.

"Tell me about it."

CHAPTER SEVENTEEN

A TRIP TO GLOUCESTER

*T*WO DAYS LATER, LORD HOLLINGSWORTH ARRIVED to escort Betsy and me to Paddington Station where we would board the train for our three-hour journey to Gloucester. After my conversation with Lady Wakefield, I'd telephoned Owen Clapham and asked for his assistance in discovering the address of the person I sought. While he searched for that information, I'd telephoned Lord Hollingsworth and requested his company for the trip. To his credit, he readily agreed, even though I'd provided the barest of details.

"Thank you for escorting us, Lord Hollingsworth," I said as soon as he stepped into the drawing room.

"Your servant, Miss Worthington." He was immaculately dressed in a dark business suit. But his dark hair had grown in length, making him appear the pirate Inspector Crawford claimed him to be. "Anything I can do to help."

Before we could depart Worthington House, of course,

Mother had to have her say, same as she'd done with Inspector Crawford during our previous investigation. "I'm entrusting my daughter's safety into your keeping, Lord Hollingsworth. I'll have your word as a gentleman nothing untoward will happen."

He gazed at me, a question in his eyes.

"We can't leave until you promise," I said.

Losing that devil-may-care smile of his, he said, "You have it, ma'am. Miss Worthington will be safe with me."

Only then were we allowed to leave. It wasn't until we were comfortably settled on the train that he asked, "Why did you ask me to escort you? Why not your brother or Marlowe?" We were alone. Knowing we would need to speak freely I'd situated Betsy in a separate compartment and reserved a private one for us.

"Ned has enough to deal with Father's business and the investigation into Lord Wakefield's finances. And Marlowe, well, if we find what I think we'll find I doubt he'd keep the information to himself. And that would cause more complications."

"But why trust me at all? You barely know me."

"Lord Rutledge vouched for you. That went a long way toward obtaining Mother's approval."

"But that didn't weigh with you." A statement more than a question.

"I would never ignore Lord Rutledge's opinion, but mostly I relied on my own intuition."

"And you found me worthy of escorting you?"

"I believe you're an honorable man, Lord Hollingsworth, and would never hurt me. I also believe that if we were to encounter danger, you'd readily deal with it." I leaned toward him and whispered, "I think there's a little bit of the pirate in you."

"Ho, ho, ho, and a bottle of rum," he joked.

I laughed, as he'd intended.

"So all hilarity aside, why are we traveling to Gloucester?"

I'd told him very little when I'd asked him to escort me, so his question was not unexpected. "We'll be trying to find the whereabouts of a child."

His carefree air disappeared. "A child?" Obviously, I'd surprised him.

I laid out for him the facts as I knew them. Lady Wakefield had given birth to a little girl. Her parents, fearing a scandal, had forced her to give up the babe. She was told that a nice couple, who hadn't been able to have one of their own, would adopt the child. Prior to the birth, she insisted on meeting them. They appeared quite presentable. After they said all the right words, she agreed to the adoption."

His reaction was more than I'd hoped it would be. "The cruelty of forcing Lady Wakefield to relinquish her child. How could any parent do such a thing?"

"They were trying to salvage her reputation. They also had three other daughters to think about. If Lady Wakefield had been tainted with scandal, her sisters would have been tarred with the same brush. I don't know that they had any other choice."

"You would never give up a child." An accurate assessment. It wasn't the first time Lord Hollingsworth had correctly evaluated me.

"No, I wouldn't. But I'm in a different position, milord. I have a small fortune at my disposal. I could set up a separate household from my family's. Not that I'd have to. Mother would never allow a child of mine to be raised in such a way." I smiled thinking what she would do. "She'd probably dream up a distant cousin who perished from some awful disease and left a babe in our care."

"You don't think Lady Wakefield's daughter was in fact adopted?"

"I don't.

"Owen Clapham discovered the couple are performers who work the stage circuit during the season. The rest of the year they offer their services to anyone willing to pay them coin."

"And you think someone hired them to pose as the adoptive parents of her child?"

"It had to have been Lord Wakefield. Her parents couldn't afford their fee."

"To play devil's advocate, the couple very well could have adopted the babe."

"But the thing is, Lord Hollingsworth, they have no children."

"Ah, well." He tossed his head. "There goes that argument. Where are we going exactly?"

"To visit the midwife who assisted with the birth, a Mrs. Merryweather. She would know where the child ended up. Mister Clapham obtained her address." I heaved out a heavy sigh as I recalled what Lady Wakefield told me about her ordeal. "She was barely allowed to hold her child as the babe was taken away minutes after the birth."

"What hell she must have gone through." Kindness glowed in his eyes. He may have resembled a pirate, but he possessed a kind heart.

"It was. The birth was difficult. So much so, she was not able to rise from her bed for several days. To allay suspicion, her family passed it off as an illness. And then miraculously, Lord Wakefield showed up and offered for her hand. Her family insisted she accept him claiming she was a fallen woman, and no other man would have her. So, she did. Little did she know what the future held for her."

The rest of the trip we discussed the investigation and the avenues of inquiry. When we finally arrived in Gloucester, we hired a taxicab to drive us to Mrs. Merryweather's address. She turned out to be a merry soul with a cheerful countenance, a match to her name. As I'd sent a telegram ahead, she was expecting us.

"Come in. Would you like some tea?"

"Please don't put yourself to any trouble."

"'Tis no trouble at all. It's not often I have a Lord and a Lady in my parlor."

Rather than correct her, I simply thanked her.

Once the tea had been enjoyed, I asked, "Do you remember assisting Miss Sybil Pearson with a birth about five years ago?"

She nodded. "I do indeed. Such a lovely young lady. A difficult birth, as I recall, but she stood fast. In the end she delivered a beautiful little girl. Dark-haired and rosy-cheeked. She named her Rose. Well, Lavender Rose. Apparently, lavender was her favorite perfume."

"It still is."

"Poor thing. She cried when I took the babe from her. But it's best not to let the mother get too attached when the child is to be removed. I understand she married an earl, so it ended well for her."

Not so much, I wanted to say. But I kept silent since it wouldn't aid our purpose. "Do you know what happened to the child?"

"Why, I took her to the foundling hospital. That's where the children of unwed mothers are placed." Her manner hinted it was something everyone knew.

"And where is this foundling hospital?"

"On Upper Lower Street. Mind you, don't confuse it with Lower Upper Street."

"No, of course not. Do you know if the child is still there?"

"I don't. But the directress will be able to provide you with that information. They take very good care of the children, you know. Three meals a day, two uniforms, and they're taught their letters and numbers. When old enough, they're taught a trade so they can go into service and such."

Such was the future of the daughter of an earl. "Yes, I'm familiar with the concept. My mother manages the Ladies Benevolent Society in London. One of their charities is an orphanage."

"There, you see. All's well that ends well."

Except that a mother's arms had been left empty, and a little girl had never known her mother.

"Thank you, Mrs. Merryweather, you've been very accommodating. May we contribute to your welfare?"

"Oh, no. Not to me. I'm very well compensated. But I'm sure the foundling hospital would benefit from a donation."

"Very well."

After collecting Betsy from the kitchen, I took a moment to breathe.

"Are you well?" Lord Hollingsworth asked.

"No. The thought of that little girl growing up in a foundling hospital when she had a mother who would have loved and cared for her is too much to bear."

His gaze filled with sympathy and understanding. "How about we enjoy a luncheon? I noticed a pub down the street."

"Thank you, but I couldn't eat. We must first find the child."

"Very well." As we stepped into the street, a taxicab came in sight. After he hailed it, we soon were standing in front of the foundling hospital. When we revealed the purpose of our visit, we were shown to the office of the directress, a Mrs. Hodgkins. Eagle-eyed, dark hair pinned back in a tight bun, she appeared the type to suffer no fools gladly or otherwise.

"Miss Worthington, Lord Hollingsworth. Please sit."

"Thank you for seeing us. We've come all the way from London in search of a child. Mrs. Merryweather informed us she delivered a babe here about five years ago. Her name is Lavender Rose."

"Oh, yes."

"She's here?"

"Of course." She directed that gimlet stare at us. "What is your interest in her?"

I couldn't simply say I meant to bring her to her mother. Mrs. Hodgkins would need proof. "We've been charged by her mother to find her."

"Is there a reason she didn't come herself?"

"Unfortunately, she's not able to do so at the moment. It's a delicate situation. But she very much would like to have her daughter brought to London."

"I can't just hand over the child, you understand."

"Of course."

"And I would need proof she's in fact the mother."

"Such as?"

"A birth certificate."

"And where may we obtain one?"

"At City Hall. The registration office. As a midwife, Mrs. Merryweather would have done her duty and registered the baby's birth." She glanced at the watch she'd pinned to her dress. "They're closed now. You'll have to wait until morning."

Of course, we would. "Any chance we could meet Lavender Rose?"

"No, I'm sorry. It would be unfair to the child."

"What do you mean?"

"When a couple who wishes to adopt visits us, we discuss their preferences. They then select a child who is brought to them. If the meeting is successful, we arrange for subsequent visits. Unfortunately, Lavender Rose has already suffered several disappointments. I would hate to put her through it again. Unless I was assured of success, that is."

"Couples wanted to adopt her?"

"Oh, yes. She's quite beautiful, you see. But once they met her, they changed their mind."

"Why? Is there something wrong with her?" Mrs. Merryweather had not mentioned any defect.

"She's perfect in every way, except for one. She does not speak."

CHAPTER EIGHTEEN

OVERCOMING OBSTACLES

*T*HERE WAS NO HELP FOR IT. We would have to spend the night in Gloucester.

"We'll need rooms at a hotel," I said on our way out of the foundling hospital after we'd met up with Betsy at the reception area.

"Blimey, Miss," she exclaimed, her eyes wide as saucers. "What will Mrs. Worthington say?"

Nothing good, to be sure. While Lord Hollingsworth hailed yet another taxi, I explained the situation to her.

"I didn't pack fresh clothes for you, Miss. What will you wear in the morning?"

"We'll manage, Betsy. Don't you worry."

After obtaining suggestions from the taxicab driver, we chose the New Inn, a hotel which had stood in place for 500 years, since the Tudors reigned. Once we booked our rooms, we inquired about a trunk telephone call and were assured it would be no problem. Since that weighed foremost on my mind, I asked to be shown to the manager's office where apparently the telephone was located. We left Betsy to handle the room arrangements while Hollingsworth and I conducted the call.

"What will you tell your mother?" he asked, biting back a grin. He knew enough about Mother to predict her likely disapproval of our news.

"Nothing. I'll let Ned deal with her." Yes, I was being a coward, but I had more than enough to deal with at the moment. Besides, Ned would be able to provide a more thorough explanation as to the need for our remaining in Gloucester. With his brilliant mind, never mind his contacts, he would be the one to obtain what was required. "I explained matters to him before we left in case we needed an ally. As it turns out, we do."

All I got from Hollingsworth was a raised brow.

It took a few minutes to put the call through to Worthington & Son. As I expected, my brother was still at the office. He almost never left before seven, and it was barely five o'clock. Once I got through to him, I explained the situation and what he would need to bring in order to bring Lavender Rose to London.

"I'll need a Power of Attorney notarized and signed by Lady Wakefield that I can bring the child to her," I said. "Also, the directress needs a surety that the child will be well taken care of. It's apparently a requirement of the law before they release a child into someone's custody. And we'll need to post a bond of 20 pounds to show we can afford to take care of her."

He repeated everything back to me. "Hopefully, I'll be able to arrange all this tonight. If not, I'll call you. Where are you staying?"

"The New Inn in Gloucester."

"If you don't hear from me, you'll know I'm on my way.

Mother will not be pleased, you realize that? A hotel stay with a bachelor with only your maid for company is bound to upset her."

"Betsy will sleep in my room. We've arranged for a trundle bed for her."

"Betsy is not the stoutest of chaperones, as you well know, Sister."

I grinned. "I disagree. She's little, but she be fierce."

Hollingsworth took the telephone stick and mouthpiece from me. "You need not fear anything from me, Mr. Worthington. I have no interest in debauching your sister."

I tossed him a reproving glance. Ned would not appreciate his humor.

After terminating the call, we retired to our rooms for a quick wash before descending to the hotel pub for our supper. Having missed our midday meal, we were all starving. Supper consisted of a surprisingly good bangers and mash which we chased back with a good stout ale.

Hollingsworth proved to be an entertaining supper companion. No surprise there. His tales of the South Seas and his encounter with a rather amorous penguin kept us laughing throughout. But exhaustion after a long day, and the effects of a wonderful meal, had us soon nodding off. So, we said our goodnights and headed off to our respective rooms. I fell asleep as soon as my head landed on a rose-scented pillow. Before I knew it, it was morning.

Betsy had arranged for a brisk brush of our clothes and launder of our undergarments. After a soak in the tub, I felt ready to face whatever came our way. While Hollingsworth enjoyed a full English Breakfast, Betsy and I satisfied ourselves with eggs and toast. Thankfully, the hotel served excellent coffee as well. Fortified after a good night's sleep and a filling breakfast, we set out for City Hall to obtain the birth certificate. Once we obtained the document, we roamed around Gloucester to inspect the sights, including the cathedral, until it was time to head to the train station.

Thankfully, the train was not delayed. But I was surprised to see not only Ned but two more travelers.

"Mother!"

"Hello, Kitty dear." She kissed me on the cheek, before turning to my escort. "How are you, Lord Hollingsworth?"

"Fit as a fiddle, ma'am."

She arched a brow. "Ummm."

Hollingsworth flashed one of his wicked smiles.

"If you don't desist this behavior," I cautioned him, "Mother will have us wed at Gloucester Cathedral by nightfall."

He scoffed. "No wedding can be arranged in so short a time."

I countered with, "You vastly underestimate my mother, sir, and her strong desire to see me wedded to someone with a title. You are a marquis, are you not?"

He visibly blanched under that healthy glow of his. And then, serious as the grave, he took three steps away from me.

Fighting back a grin, Ned introduced the third member of their party, a solicitor who specialized in child adoptions and welfare cases. If we encountered any problems, he would handle them.

"I brought you a change of clothes, in case it's needed," Mother said, pointing to a portmanteau.

"No need, Mother. Betsy has taken excellent care of me."

"Shall we proceed then?" Ned asked. "The directress will be waiting for us."

Same as the day before, we were shown to her office where introductions were made all around. When asked, the solicitor produced the necessary documents and explained that everything was in order. "But, of course," he said, "you will want to examine them."

She took what seemed like forever, before gazing up, seemingly satisfied. But then she folded her hands in front of her and addressed us with that gimlet stare of hers. "I made a trunk telephone call last night to the Children's Home orphanage in London. I was informed that Mrs. Worthington, as chair of the Ladies Benevolent Society, is a generous contributor to the home. So I'm glad to see her present. I will feel better knowing she'll be taking over the care of the child."

"I beg your pardon," Mother said.

She was surprised. No wonder. So was I. Yesterday, the directress had not mentioned such a thing.

"Mrs. Worthington, Lavender Rose is a very special child. She'll need a steady influence over her. I'm not sure her mother is the right person seeing how she's involved in a murder investigation. I read the London papers. Apparently, Lady Wakefield has been summoned to Scotland Yard for questioning."

"Was she?" I asked Mother.

"Yesterday, dear. After you left."

"So, I can't in good conscience allow Lavender Rose to be given to a woman who might soon be in jail for her husband's murder. The only way I will relinquish her is if you, Mrs. Worthington, take responsibility for her care."

"We could appeal your decision," the solicitor said.

Mrs. Hodgkins stiffened up.

"There will be no need, sir," Mother rushed to say. "I will be more than glad to take responsibility for Lavender Rose, Mrs. Hodgkins. I raised five of my own, and we have a large, lovely home in Mayfair. She'll have her own room. We'll find a nanny for her. She'll be well taken care of."

Mrs. Hodgkins nodded while offering a tight smile. "I'm glad we're of like minds, Mrs. Worthington. Now, shall I have the child fetched?"

Fetched. Like a dog. Mother shot me a warning look, and I tamped down my ire. The important thing was to remove Lavender Rose from this place.

"If you would, Mrs. Hodgkins," Mother said, with the pleasantest of smiles.

CHAPTER NINETEEN

LAVENDER ROSE

*N*O DOUBT ABOUT IT, Lavender Rose was a beautiful child. Rosy-cheeked with dark hair that curled about her shoulders, she appeared well fed. She was neither tall, nor short, but of middling height. Her most striking feature were the color of her eyes, periwinkle just like her father's. No denying whose child she was.

She'd been presented to us clean and dressed in the same plain cotton gown all the girl children at the orphanage seemed to be wearing. The shoes, scuffed beyond what was acceptable, appeared a size too large for she kept tripping over her feet. While we finalized the paperwork that would allow us to take custody of her, she sat quietly taking in the world with avid curiosity.

When it came time to say her goodbyes, Mrs. Hodgkins was all business. "Lavender Rose, Mrs. Worthington is taking you home with her."

The child's eyes grew large as saucers. Clearly, she understood language. She just chose not to talk.

"She has a fine house in London where you'll have your own room. You won't have to share any more. Won't that be nice?" And then Mrs. Hodgkins grew misty-eyed. "Be a good girl, sweetheart." After giving Lavender Rose a quick hug, she turned the little girl toward Mother who took her hand with a smile.

I was slightly shaken after that farewell, for it had been more emotional than I'd expected. But Mother, being Mother, focused on practical matters—shoes for Lavender Rose. With an hour to go before the train departed, she decided to shop for a new pair.

As a result, we barely made the train. The poor child was so terrified of the big engine belching dark smoke she howled with fear. We tried to calm her. When that did not work, Lord Hollingsworth picked her up and stepped into the train with her screaming like a banshee. When we walked into the first-class compartment we'd reserved, she struggled out of his arms and landed on the seat, kicking and screaming for all she was worth. Seemingly with one mind, the men looked at each other and, cowards that they were, fled, leaving us to deal with the wild thing.

"Nothing wrong with her lungs or her voice box," I commented.

"No. There doesn't appear to be," Mother said. Having raised five children, she allowed Lavender Rose to vent her fury while continuing her conversation with me. "Where did you stay overnight?"

"The New Inn. Don't worry, Mother. Betsy and I shared a room. I was chaperoned the entire time."

"Ummm. We'll discuss this in more detail once we arrive home."

"Yes, Mother." I was truly in the soup, but, honestly, I don't see how we could have done anything else.

Lavender Rose's cries soon dwindled to the occasional sob and eventually hiccups.

"Would you like something to eat?" I asked her when there was a momentary pause.

She shook her head.

"She needs sustenance," Mother said.

"I'll fetch something from the restaurant car," I volunteered.

"Some tea and biscuits. Oh, and scones if they have them."

I went in search for Ned and found him in the bar car, enjoying a drink with the solicitor and Hollingsworth. Men!

I gave him the tea order. "For four, if you please."

"Of course."

I returned to the compartment to find Lavender Rose had been persuaded to sit next to Betsy who appeared to be making some headway with her. "Would you like to play patty cake?" she asked.

The child nodded.

Pat-a-cake, pat-a-cake, baker's man.
Bake me a cake as fast as you can
Pat it and prick it, and mark it with a B,
Put it in the oven for Lavender Rose and me.

By the time the waiter arrived with the tea service, Lavender Rose was laughing and giggling. Her eyes lit up when she saw the food.

Heaven only knew if she'd ever enjoyed decent fare.

It took no time for the little girl to eat her fill. Soon after, she nodded off, with her head resting on Betsy's lap.

"Seems you've gained a new friend," I said, smiling at Betsy.

"Yes, miss. We were a family of eight. With me right in the middle, I had the care of the little ones."

Mother had a thoughtful look on her face. I had the feeling I was about to lose a maid. "No, Mother. We can find someone else to care for Lavender Rose."

"Surely, she needs Betsy more than you do, at least while we search for a nursery maid."

I would make sure it would be only for a little while. Betsy was invaluable to me.

"Agnes also comes from a large family, Miss," Betsy said. Agnes being one of the downstairs maids. "Between the two of us, we can watch over the young miss until you find someone."

With that I had to be satisfied, for Mother had already made up her mind.

Thankfully, we did not suffer any delays and arrived at Paddington Station around seven. The solicitor quickly parted from us, and Hollingsworth also bid us adieu. I thanked him profusely for his assistance. To my surprise, so did Mother. And then the four of us piled into a taxicab and headed for home. Once he saw us settled, Ned left as he was eager to check on matters at the office.

Mother had sent a telegram to our housekeeper to prepare a room for Lavender Rose. So as soon as we arrived, Mrs. Simpson led the way upstairs with Betsy holding Lavender Rose's hand. Mother and I followed in their wake for we would need to bathe and change before supper. The addition of a child, especially one who did not speak, was bound to change things around the house. How much I had no idea. Only time would tell.

CHAPTER TWENTY

SECOND MEETING OF THE INVESTIGATIVE COMMITTEE

*A*NXIOUS TO MEET HER DAUGHTER, Lady Wakefield arrived bright and early the next day. But before she could do so, Mother and I needed to explain the situation to her. It was bound to be a difficult conversation. Not only would we need to inform her she could not take Lavender Rose home, but we'd have to tell her she did not speak. Mindful of the pain Lady Wakefield was bound to experience, Mother sought to provide comfort in her usual way—by offering tea and scones in the drawing room.

Naturally, Lady Wakefield was heartbroken as she'd looked forward to making a home for her daughter. But she understood why the arrangement had been made. Once matters were settled, Mother assured her, Lavender Rose would be free to join her. Until then, we would take excellent care of her. Her daughter's lack of speech distressed her, of course. But Mother explained the little girl was capable of making noise. She just chose not to talk. With time and patience, she believed Lavender Rose would speak one day.

Having delivered the bad news, Mother asked for Lavender Rose to be brought down so she could meet her mother. Last night, Mother had asked for boxes of our children's clothes and toys to be fetched from the attic so she could find some things for the little girl. After different articles of clothing were chosen, they'd been washed and pressed, and Lavender Rose had been provided a wardrobe any little girl would envy.

As Lavender Rose stepped into the drawing room, tightly holding on to Betsy's hand, we were able to see how well one of the gowns suited her. She was wearing a soft cotton dress that matched her name, as it was lavender blue in color. On her feet were black leather, laced-up shoes I remembered wearing and a pair of white socks. From the box of toys, she'd chosen a bisque doll, which she was now clutching for all she was worth.

"Come closer, dear," Mother said kindly when the little girl paused just inside the door.

When she wouldn't step farther into the room, Lady Wakefield approached and knelt in front of her. "Hello, Lavender Rose. My name is Sybil."

The little girl stood shyly without saying a word.

"I love your dress. Would you like to see the present I brought you?"

Lavender Rose nodded while her eyes grew wide.

Rising, Lady Wakefield held out her hand. After a moment's hesitation, Lavender Rose let go of Betsy and took it. Together they walked back to the sofa with Betsy bringing up the rear.

"You are so beautiful. Is that your doll?"

The little girl nodded.

"Does she have a name?"

The little girl tucked in her chin.

Lady Wakefield glanced toward Mother. "Do you think we could have some time alone?"

But before Mother could answer, the little girl grasped Betsy's hand and shook her head. Clearly, it was going to be an uphill battle for Lady Wakefield to befriend her daughter.

"That's all right. We don't have to if you don't want to. We can just sit here."

"She likes scones." I pushed a plate of the freshly baked pastries across the small table toward her.

"Is that right, Lavender Rose?"

The little girl nodded.

"Would you like to have one?"

Another small nod.

Lady Wakefield placed one on a plate and handed it to her. The little girl put down her doll long enough to take the plate. And then together, she and her mother ate scones.

To give them some privacy, Mother and I left the room. Betsy, by necessity, remained as Lavender Rose was not likely to let her depart.

Mother asked Carlton to show Lady Wakefield to her personal parlor once she emerged from the drawing room. And then we made our way there so we could hold a private discussion. "It'll take some time but eventually she'll come to love her mother," Mother said.

"If Lady Wakefield is not arrested for the murder of her husband."

Mother's brow wrinkled as she weighed my words. "Do you really think she could have done such a thing?"

"The man was a brute, and she was growing fearful for her life. So, she could have been pushed into it. But then it could have been Newcastle. Or anyone else for that matter. So far nothing points to any one person. Except for Newcastle, that is." Frustrated, I let out a heavy breath. "We have a meeting scheduled today. Let's hope things will become clearer then."

About twenty minutes later, Lady Wakefield entered the parlor. A sense of calmness emanated from her that hadn't been there before. "Thank you, dear Kitty, Mrs. Worthington, for finding her and bringing her to me. I will never be able to repay your kindness."

"It was our pleasure, Lady Wakefield," Mother said. "Be assured, we will take good care of her until you can be reunited with your daughter."

"Thank you. I just wish circumstances were . . . different."

Didn't we all?

"How is the investigation progressing?" she asked.

"The committee is meeting this afternoon. With your permission, I would like to tell them about Lavender Rose."

Dismay rolled over face. Only to be expected for the information was scandalous in nature. But I truly felt the investigation would suffer if they were hidden. Something I would need to explain to her. "It will aid our investigation if everyone is aware of all the facts." Never mind that if they saw Lavender Rose, there were bound to be questions. Her resemblance to Newcastle couldn't be denied. "Ned and Hollingsworth already know, of course. I can assure you the rest of the committee will keep the information in the strictest of confidences." Hopefully, the staff would do so as well.

Mother had told our housekeeper that Lavender Rose was an orphan, the daughter of a distant cousin who'd recently perished. Her presence was not to be discussed with anyone outside our home. No staff member would ask questions, but they'd be bound to notice Lady Wakefield's frequent visits. Never mind that many of them—the footmen, and some of the maids, certainly Carlton our butler—had seen Lord Newcastle for he was a friend of Ned's. The striking resemblance between Lavender Rose and Newcastle was bound to be noticed and remarked upon. I just hoped they kept those discussions to our household.

Having taken the time to consider my suggestion, Lady Wakefield capitulated. "Whatever you think is best, Miss Worthington." She turned to Mother. "May I visit again tomorrow, say two o'clock?"

"Of course. Either Kitty or I will be here to greet you."

"Thank you." When she left, she seemed lighter in step, as if a weight had been lifted from her shoulders. Which stood to reason. Not only had she been reunited with the beloved daughter she'd thought lost, but she knew, whatever happened to her and Newcastle, we would take care of the little girl.

Mother and I spent the next hour in the nursery, showing coloring books and primers to Lavender Rose to see what appealed to the little girl. We determined she knew her letters and some numbers. Although she could not yet comprehend the written word, she sat quietly while Betsy read to her. By the time her luncheon arrived, we'd made a list of additional materials we would order. Mother had always been a great believer in educating her daughters as well as her sons. She would do no less for Lavender Rose.

By two o'clock, I was eager for the investigative committee meeting to start. With everything that had been happening, I hadn't preassigned seating. Something I came to regret.

The first order of business was my report about our trip to Gloucester. Everyone was stunned to say the least.

"And Newcastle doesn't know?" Marlowe asked.

"No. And you're not to tell him," I cautioned him.

"How could I? He's only allowed visits from his solicitor or family members. His only relation is a distant cousin, who's next in line for the title, and he lives in Chichester."

"Good. Now if we could get down to business. Ned, why don't you provide us with your report." I knew I could always count on him to be ready, even though he was up to his neck with work.

"I investigated Lord Wakefield's finances and the state of his business affairs. I will divide the discussion into two parts."

Marlowe groaned.

I shot him a pointed look. "Do you have something to contribute, milord?"

"I have an appointment with my barber at four. I'd hoped to wrap this up no later than 3:30."

"Then you should keep silent and allow someone else to have their say," Lady Emma remarked. "No need to interrupt with your antics."

"I was not—"

I clapped. "Children!"

They both hushed. Those two would either murder each other or end up madly in love. Right now, I had no idea in which direction they were headed.

"Go on, Ned."

"Lord Wakefield's personal finances are, to put it succinctly—

"—Too late!" Marlowe exclaimed.

Lady Emma elbowed his ribs.

"Ouch!" Marlowe said, rubbing his side.

I should've insisted they sit in separate chairs instead of the settee they'd chosen. But it was too late now.

"—a disaster," Ned finished, ignoring Marlowe's outburst. "His only source of income is from a very small estate in Devon which has been sadly neglected. Most of those who worked the land have left so his income is practically nil. He gambles, but he's not good at it. So, he loses more than he gains. His business affairs, however, are quite a different matter. Five years ago, a sudden influx of cash appeared on his business account. Unfortunately, I was not able to make further inquiries since I had to attend to the matter at Gloucester."

"You're not giving up?"

"Certainly not," he affirmed. "Now that I'm back in London, I'll follow through on some leads." Ned was like a dog with a bone. He never desisted until he found the answers he sought.

"Splendid. Let us know how it goes. Now, let's see." I glanced at my list. "Sebastian, why don't you have a turn? Did you look into Wakefield's interests at Parliament?"

"I did. He focused on Admiralty matters. Which makes sense. Once upon a time, he was a lieutenant in the Navy. He left the service when he inherited the title."

"His friendship with the Duke of Brightwell must stem from those times. The duke holds an Admiral's rank," I declared. "Did you find out about Wakefield's heir?"

"I have. His name is Archibald Morgan, hails from Devon as well. His place is close to Wakefield Hall. It seems that family did not wander far from each other. He attended Oxford before me. Brainy sort of chap. Got a first in Engineering. He devised a more efficient way to burn coal on steamships. Made him pots of money as a result. So, he wouldn't need to depend on income from the Wakefield estate. Five years ago, when his invention proved profitable, he moved to London. He's taken advantage of business opportunities and engaged with others who have similar interests ever since. His sister, Abigail, keeps house for him. He appears to be something of a parsnip. Only spends what he absolutely must. From all accounts, he does not drink, gamble, or" —he cleared his throat— "visit the ladies."

"Sounds like a deadly dull chap," Marlowe interjected.

"He's an excellent example of what a proper gentleman

should be, unlike some I know." Lady Emma glared pointedly at Marlowe.

"Are you implying that I—"

"If the shoe fits, milord."

These two were bound to draw blood if I wasn't careful. "Marlowe. Lady Emma."

They turned toward me.

"Why don't you provide your report? That way Lord Marlowe can leave for his appointment."

"With pleasure." Lady Emma retrieved a notebook from the satchel she'd brought and began reading from it. "I sent a note around to the Duchess of Brightwell explaining our mission. As you suggested, I inquired after her health. In her response, she assured me she was in fine mettle. More than that, she appeared eager to help. It seems our reputation preceded us as she'd heard of our previous investigations and successes. I arranged the visit for two days ago. Lord Marlowe" —she nodded toward him— "accompanied me."

"And a good time was had by all," Marlowe quipped. Clearly, he was not taking this as seriously as he should.

"Since I needed Lord Hollingsworth to escort me to Gloucester," I explained to the committee members, "I asked Lord Marlowe to step in for him. He graciously agreed."

"Makes sense," Sebastian said.

"After we arrived," Lady Emma continued, "she gave us pretty much carte blanche, allowing us to not only inspect the premises, but to question her staff. I must say, though, she appeared—"

"Oh, for the love of—"

I blew out a frustrated breath. "Marlowe. You may leave now."

His head swiveled toward me. "What? But I haven't provided my report about Lord Wakefield or what I discovered at Brightwell Mansion." He appeared crestfallen.

"I can obtain that from you later. In the meantime, Lady Emma is fully capable of discussing your visit to Brightwell Mansion. I thank you for your time."

"Very well." He came to his feet, straightened his jacket. After one last glance toward Lady Emma, he walked out, head held high.

A few seconds of stunned silence later, Margaret exclaimed, "Brava, sister! That was masterfully done."

Since I did not wish to humiliate Lord Marlowe by reveling in the praise, I simply said, "Thank you, Margaret. Now, Lady Emma, please continue."

"As I was saying, she appeared jittery, anxious. When I once again asked if she was amenable to our inspection, she said yes."

"Maybe she was concerned about what you would find?" I suggested.

"Maybe so." Lady Emma reviewed her notes. "Lord Marlowe and I inspected the staircase, the drawing room, the study. And the hallway, of course. There is a hidden door next to the stairs that leads up to the second floor where the family bedrooms and bathrooms are located."

"So only someone familiar with the house, such as family and staff, would know it was there."

Lady Emma glanced up. "We wondered about that. After our inspection, we questioned the duchess. She revealed that others knew as well, for they held social gatherings on the first floor where the drawing room, library and study are located."

"So we can't rule out anyone intimately connected with them."

"No. That would include Lord Wakefield, of course, as he was a friend of the duke." Lady Emma referred to her journal. "Marlowe was given permission to access the floor where the bedrooms are located. He concluded somebody could've fled that way."

"How so?"

"The murderer could have climbed up to the bedroom floor and gone down the servant stairs on the opposite side. Those lead to the kitchen."

"I doubt that happened. There were too many servants around that day."

"He could have been disguised as a servant. They had to have hired additional staff for that night," Hollingsworth said. "Did either you or Lord Marlowe explore other exits?"

"Such as?" Lady Emma asked.

"The family rooms are located on the second floor, but the house has four floors. The ground floor are the more public rooms, the first, the private social gathering rooms, the second the bedrooms and bathrooms. I'm assuming the top floor would be the staff quarters."

"We didn't visit that floor, but that's a natural assumption. I'll be glad to follow up with her."

"Do the servant stairs run through that entire side of the house?" Hollingsworth asked.

"Yes."

"Then, somebody could have gone up, instead of down and made their escape that way."

"But how would they escape from the top floor?"

"Through the roof. I imagine there's a stairway that leads to it."

"But that would be quite a drop," Lady Emma declared.

"Sailors climb masts which are of similar heights. Whoever did it would have had to secure an anchor to the roof. It would have had to be planned ahead of time, of course. After he committed the murder, he could have easily scampered down the side of the house and made his getaway with no one the wiser. Plenty of bushes about the ground he could hide behind to cover his escape. Someone needs to check the roof and the grounds for evidence."

"Very good, Lord Hollingsworth," Mister Clapham said. "Such a feat is not only possible, but it has already happened. Arthur Edward Young, named the cat burglar by London papers, carried out several acts of burglary in Streatham not too long ago."

Heavens! I would need to talk to Mother about securing the roof. "Since you know what you'd be looking for, Lord Hollingsworth, why don't you accompany Lady Emma at her next visit. Hopefully, the duchess won't object."

"Be happy to."

"Anything else, Lady Emma?"

"We obtained a list of the guests and the staff from the duchess, but I haven't had a chance to study it. I will do so before our next meeting."

"Excellent! You've done stellar work."

She blushed. "Thank you."

"All right. Let's move on." I glanced at my list once more. "Margaret, what did the solicitor have to say?"

"Lord Newcastle is despondent, as is to be expected. The solicitor thinks he can introduce reasonable doubt—a masquerade, plenty of guests there. As long as Newcastle does not do anything foolish, he thinks they have a good chance."

"Very well."

I glanced down at my list. "We're missing Marlowe's report on Lord Wakefield. I'll ask him to submit it." I allowed myself a small smile. "In writing."

"Oh, ho. That should go down well," Hollingsworth said.

"I wouldn't ask that of him," Lady Emma said, pinking up a little.

"Why not?"

"He has atrocious handwriting."

"A good time to practice it then."

"Kitty," she glanced at me in such a direct way I felt she was trying to communicate something important. "Just have him tell you. It really would be for the best."

After a beat, I agreed, "All right. I will do that."

"Thank you."

What did she know about Marlowe the rest of us did not?

"With as many things that need to be researched or followed up on, we'll need to meet again. Say next Tuesday. That's five days from now. It should provide everyone with enough time to do what needs to be done. I'll telephone Marlowe and ask him for his report. His verbal report."

Lady Emma quietly nodded.

"Wait. What about Lily's brief?" Margaret asked.

"She spoke directly to me. She found nothing of note at the modiste. I didn't want to waste valuable time reporting a negative."

Lily did not react but simply kept her sweet smile in place. Before the meeting, I'd taken her aside and explained what I was planning to do about what she'd learned. It would do Monique a disservice to reveal she'd been the one to tell Lily about Lady Wakefield's pregnancy. It was one thing for a dressmaker's assistant to listen to gossip. It was quite another to spread it. To inform the committee that she'd shared that information with Lily might very well put her job in jeopardy. And that was the last thing I wished to do, especially since Monique had assured me she'd told no one else and wouldn't do so in the future.

As we were ending the meeting, Mother arrived clutching *The Tell-All* in her hand. Never a good sign.

Fearing the worst, I asked, "What's wrong?"

Dismay was clear in her eyes. "Newcastle confessed to Lord Wakefield's murder."

CHAPTER TWENTY-ONE

DEALING WITH THE AFTERMATH

*I*NSTEAD OF ADJOURNING, we spent the next half hour discussing the possible strategies to deal with that disaster. None were viable, except for two. The first one being the path we'd already chosen—finding Wakefield's murderer. The second? A discussion with Inspector Crawford to determine where things stood which, of course, would be up to me. Having reached those conclusions, we went our separate ways so we could get on with our tasks.

As soon as the meeting broke up, I sent a note around to Inspector Crawford which he answered quite promptly. A meeting between us would be perceived by Scotland Yard as an attempt to unduly influence an officer of the law. So, he suggested a private room at the Cock and Bull, a pub on St. Martin's Lane in the City of Westminster, for our rendezvous.

Having settled that matter, I went in search of Mother to share what we'd discussed at the meeting, as well as my asking Marlowe to leave. At the very least, I expected an objection about the latter, for Marlowe was a favorite of hers.

But she took a quite different tact. "I've often felt the same at some of the Ladies Benevolent Society meetings. But I haven't dared exclude anyone. You've shown determination and courage. I'm proud of you, Kitty."

To say I was surprised was an understatement. "Thank you, Mother. Your good opinion means the world to me."

"You'll always have it, child," she said somewhat misty-eyed. And then she squared her shoulders, "Now, what are you going to do about Lord Marlowe?"

"I'll invite him to come tomorrow afternoon to provide his report. I should be done with the meeting with Inspector Crawford by then."

"Very well. What else?"

"I hadn't thought beyond that."

"He needs to attend future meetings, does he not?"

"Oh, of course. I never intended to exclude him permanently." I thought about what was necessary. "He'll need to apologize to the group, though."

She patted my cheek. "That's my girl. Glad to see my lessons did not go amiss."

"Yes, Mother." I hadn't always appreciated her wisdom, but the older I grew, the more I did.

The next day, I arrived at the Cock & Bull with Betsy, my ever-present chaperone, in tow. She'd temporarily ceded her child-minding duties to Grace, who was more than happy to watch over Lavender Rose. She was doing so well with the little girl, Mother was considering reassigning her to those duties. Something with which I heartily concurred, as it would free Betsy to attend to me once more, not only as my maid, but as an assistant in my investigations. Something she thoroughly enjoyed, and I highly valued.

After we entered the pub, we discovered Inspector Crawford had arranged for her and Neville to enjoy a luncheon in the public area. While she was accommodated at a spot by the window, I was shown to the private room where Inspector Crawford waited for me.

As soon as I walked in, he stood and bowed. His impeccable manners were one of the qualities that attracted me to him with the others being, well, everything else. It wasn't only that he was handsome, which he was, or that he had a keen mind, which he did. But that he always treated me as his equal. In this day and age, when men so often looked down upon women, thinking us the weaker sex, he never did. Of course, that did not mean we never argued. My point of view often differed from his, as it was bound to today.

"Since time was of the essence," he said, "I ordered simple pub fare for both of us. Shepherd's pie, to be exact. Hope you don't object. We can change it if you do."

"That's fine." I doubted I would have anything to eat as worried as I was about Newcastle. I didn't engage the inspector in conversation until the food was laid out before us, and the server had left the room. And then I blurted out what brought me here, "Newcastle did not kill Lord Wakefield."

His gaze was steady on me. "His fingerprints were on the murder weapon. Do I really need to remind you he confessed?"

"Because you brought in Lady Wakefield for questioning. He's trying to protect her. Can't you see that?"

A doubtful look rolled over his face.

"You think she's guilty as well? Unbelievable."

"They could have planned it together."

"But she was searching for her husband in the ballroom to tell him she was returning home."

"There is no proof of that. No one recalled seeing her."

"Because she was disguised. Unless somebody knew what she was wearing, they wouldn't have recognized her."

"Except for Lord Wakefield. He knew what she was wearing. Once he noticed her, she could have led him back upstairs to lay in wait so she could murder him. The more logical explanation, and the one that appeals to me, is she never actually left the library. She remained there and waited for her husband to return."

"Why would he follow her? Or return for that matter?"

"He was a very jealous man. He would want to make sure she wasn't with Newcastle."

His explanation made sense, but I couldn't, wouldn't believe she'd plotted with Newcastle to kill her husband. But then, maybe I was being naive. She'd told me she feared for her life. Maybe she believed this was the only way out. "I wouldn't blame her if she did kill him. He deserved it, the brute."

"She's not allowed to take the law into her hands, Catherine, even if Wakefield deserved punishment for his treatment of her."

"What protection did she have against an abusive husband?" I snapped out. "He had all the rights, and she had none."

His gaze softened. "I agree. The law needs to change. Too many husbands commit atrocities knowing they will not be held accountable."

At least he agreed with me on that point. But that didn't help Lady Wakefield. "You're not really going to arrest her?"

"We're considering our options."

An evasive answer which did not reassure me. "You can't, Inspector. Someone needs her."

"Yes, I know."

Alarm bells rang through me. Could he have learned about Lavender Rose? Owen Clapham had approached someone at Scotland Yard for information about the midwife in Gloucester. Could Inspector Crawford have heard about that inquiry and deduced the implications? "What are you referring to?"

"Her family, of course. The last thing they'd want is for their three unmarried daughters to be tainted by a scandal. So, of course, they would not want Lady Wakefield charged with murder."

I scoffed. "Yes, they would want to preserve a daughter's reputation, no matter the cost."

His brow furrowed. "Are you implying anything in particular?"

"No. Just a general observation. Surely, there are other avenues of investigation."

"We're aware and are looking into them." He pointed to my plate. "Now eat your food. It's getting cold."

Ignoring his suggestion, I said, "It could have been an old sin coming back to haunt Lord Wakefield. Rumors abounded when his first wife died after she fell down the stairs."

"That was seven, eight years ago. Why would somebody wait this long to exact revenge?"

"Maybe that someone was out of the country and did not return until recently. Maybe he was not aware of what occurred until now."

He shrugged off my suggestion. "Doesn't ring true."

I took another tack. "Lord Wakefield appeared to be quite flush." At least in public. In private, it was quite another matter. "The money could not have come from his estate as it's sadly neglected. Maybe he's involved in some nefarious scheme."

Well, that got all his attention. "And you know this how?"

"We've been looking into things." I couldn't say more than that. I did not know what methods Ned had used to discover what he had. He wouldn't do something illegal, but he might have pulled a questionable string here and there.

His eyes flashed with emotion. "Catherine, you must not pursue this facet of your investigation. If Wakefield was in fact involved in sordid dealings, there are dangerous people out there who'd do anything to stop you."

Oh, ho! I'd struck a chord. Maybe we were a lot closer to the truth than we thought. Owen Clapham, with his Scotland Yard background and connections, might know something, or, if he didn't know, who did. Sordid dealings meant dangerous places and people. If he needed to talk to someone, and more than likely he would, I'd insist on going with him. Maybe Hollingsworth as well, for he certainly could handle himself in a fight. Yes, this was the right line to follow.

He gazed at me with dismay. "You are not going to listen to me, are you?"

I'd waited too long to placate him. Very well. It was what it was. "You have your investigation to conduct, Inspector. And so do I."

By the time we said our goodbyes, he was visibly frustrated with me. But at least we parted somewhat amicably.

I arrived home to find Marlowe waiting for me.

"Miss Worthington." Much as Inspector Crawford, he stood and bowed as soon as I stepped into the room.

"Lord Marlowe." I curtsied.

"If you'll excuse me," Mother said. "I have matters to attend to. It was a pleasure talking to you, Lord Marlowe."

"Ma'am." He nodded to her.

Such was the sign of her trust in him she didn't ask for Betsy to join us. Not that there was a need. Marlowe was always on his best behavior, at least with me.

I took the seat on the sofa Mother had just vacated. "Thank you for coming."

He accommodated himself back on his chair. "My pleasure. Before we get started—"

"Yes." I gazed expectantly at him.

"I would like to offer my most sincere apologies. My behavior at the meeting was unacceptable. I was a total, unmitigated ass."

"Yes, you were."

A laugh escaped him.

I arched a brow. "Was I supposed to disagree with you?"

"No. I just expected—"

"A polite reply."

"Something of that nature."

"If I may ask, why did you behave in such a manner?"

"I . . . really don't know. I normally don't act that way."

"I can attest to that. You've always been a perfect gentleman with me."

"It's Lady Emma. She—"

I cut him off. "It's not Lady Emma. It's you. You're attracted to her and don't know what to do about it."

He jumped to his feet. "Attracted to that, that . . ."

He collapsed on his seat. It took him a minute to come to terms with his feelings. "It's true, isn't it?"

I fought back a smile. It would not do for him to see me grinning. "I do believe so."

"What am I going to do?"

"What any rational person does. You make yourself agreeable to her. Engage her in pleasant conversation. Ask her to the theatre as you did with me."

"But I can't."

"Why not?"

"She's not . . . she finds me repulsive."

"Oh, heavens." I laughed. "She does not. If you would stop acting like an idiot for two seconds, maybe you'd realize she likes you as well." When had I become a matchmaker?

"She does?" There was a note of hope in his voice.

"I believe so. Now we should get down to the matter of the investigation. Should I ring for tea?"

"Your mother most graciously offered it to me."

"How about whisky?" He looked like he could use a good stiff drink, even though it was barely two.

"Oh, yes, please."

I rang for Carlton to bring me tea and whiskey for Marlowe.

Once he held a glass of the amber liquid in his hand, I said, "Now tell me about Lord Wakefield."

"I think you can guess most of what I have to report. He was in his fifties, married once before. His first wife died when she fell down the stairs. Although rumors of murder abounded, nothing was ever proven. It was declared a tragic accident. He married Lady Wakefield five years ago. Been trying to sire an heir since. He wasn't any more successful with her than he'd been with his first wife."

"Everything we already know."

"Just explaining it to get you up to the present. His estate is quite small and rather ramshackle. Hardly earns enough money for its upkeep much less the house in London. He made do but was well on his way to having to rusticate in the country to preserve economy. His so-called friends had drifted off."

"Ned discovered the same thing."

"But then about five years ago, he was suddenly flush with money and was soon invited to all kinds of events— card parties, horse races, and such. He also rejoined his club. Apparently, his account, which had been in arrears, was paid off. Only then was he allowed back. Having said all that, he's not well liked at all. Not only for the way he's treated his wife, but some thought he cheated at cards. Again, nothing has ever been proven."

"So, in other words, we know nothing more than what Ned reported, and what we already knew." How very disappointing. I'd been hoping for much more.

"There is one thing I discovered that we were not aware of."

I impatiently waited for him to continue.

"A servant. A young woman, girl really. She was no more than sixteen. She worked at Wakefield Hall during the period between his marriages. Her name was Eleanor Tibbett." His face flushed red. "Apparently, he was quite besotted with her. So much so, he brought her to London with him."

I gasped. "A sixteen-year-old girl? A member of his own staff?"

"It happens, Miss Worthington. More often than you'd think, I'm sad to say."

"Did he . . ." I couldn't bring myself to say the words.

"Take advantage of her?" He finished my thought.

I nodded.

"He tried, but she managed to evade him most of the time. The cook apparently hid her when he was on the hunt."

I didn't have enough words to condemn Lord Wakefield's actions. "How did you discover this?"

"From one of the Wakefield House servants. I obtained Lady Wakefield's permission to talk to them, of course. They proved quite recalcitrant to discuss Lord Wakefield. Until I flashed some cash, that is. And then one of the maids was more than willing to talk. She's worked there for ages. Since the flood, according to her."

"You said most of the time. Did he ever catch up to her?" For her sake, I hoped not.

"Unfortunately, one night he did. In the scullery of all places. She stabbed him to save herself. A flesh wound, as it turned out. But next day, she was gone. She seemed to have simply vanished."

"I could see why that would be. She would have been charged with a crime for assaulting an aristocrat. Thrown in jail at the very least." But maybe she'd sought refuge back home. "She didn't return to Devon?"

"No. I checked."

I whooshed out a breath. "People don't simply disappear. She must have gone somewhere. We'll need to look further into this matter. It might be important. Someone close to her could have murdered Wakefield for revenge." If Eleanor Tibbett had fled into the mean streets of London, no telling what happened to her. Nothing good, that was for certain.

"That's what I believe as well. But the thing of it is, though, why wait more than five years to exact retribution?"

Same question that Inspector Crawford had asked about the death of Wakefield's first wife. "I don't know but we'll need to find out if she has any living relatives."

"I'll take care of that."

"That may be too much of a reach for you. Let's have Owen Clapham check into it. He found our midwife in Gloucester, after all."

"I'll share with him what I know, then."

"Do that. Miss Morgan may know something as well," I said more to myself than him.

"Miss Morgan?"

"Her brother is the new Lord Wakefield. They lived in that area before moving to London. She may know something."

"Stands to reason. Country folk love to talk."

"Our next meeting will be next Tuesday. I would like you to attend."

His complexion flushed with more than likely chagrin. "I'll be there."

"You'll need to apologize to everyone, especially Lady Emma."

He nodded. "I'll talk to her in private, if you don't mind."

"Of course not."

He stood. "Thank you for your honesty and kindness."

"You are most welcome, Lord Marlowe. Don't muck it up."

He laughed. "I'll try not to."

CHAPTER TWENTY-TWO

A DANGEROUS DECISION

*T*HE NEXT DAY I encountered Lady Wakefield as she emerged from the drawing room. She arrived promptly at ten every day to spend time with her daughter. Going by the giggling that could be heard, the visits were doing her and Lavender Rose a world of good. No wonder she appeared happier than ever before.

"How are you and Lavender Rose faring?" I asked.

"As well as can be expected," she said smiling. "She laughs when I make a joke. Turns out she loves pretty dresses, so I make a point of bringing a new one every day."

Thank heaven the little girl could make noises. She just chose not to talk. With infinite patience, I prayed one day she would. "Along with a new pair of shoes and a bonnet I'm willing to guess."

"After so many years of being deprived of her company, I can't help but shower gifts on her." She held up her left hand. "Compliments of my wedding ring. I sold it to buy clothes for her." Her mouth twisted. "I will never forgive my parents for taking her away from me."

"But you have each other now."

Resolution blazed in her eyes. "And I will keep her. No one will separate us ever again."

She'd lived the last five years in the shadow of her cruel husband, browbeaten and abused by him. But now her true personality was emerging, one that was fiercely protective of her daughter. Whatever it took, she would move heaven and earth to care for Lavender Rose. But more than likely she would pay a hefty price. Once her daughter's existence came to light, high society snobs would deem her a fallen woman and shun her. I doubted she would care much. Neither would Newcastle. Once he learned he had a daughter, he would make provision for them both. I prayed that someday the three of them would be able to live in perfect harmony. Once that happened, I imagine they would count the world well lost.

"Any progress on the investigation?" she asked, anxiety clear on her face.

"Some. Have you been in contact with Newcastle?"

"Only in writing. I'm not allowed to visit since I'm not family. I told him what an idiot he'd been to confess."

I grinned in response. She was right. He had been an idiot, even if his intentions were good. "Inspector Crawford hasn't stopped his investigation, regardless of that admission."

"He hasn't?" She asked, a bit of cheer in her voice.

"He's eager to discover the truth, whether it leads to Newcastle or someone else."

"Simon did not kill my husband, Miss Worthington. He couldn't have."

"What do you mean?"

"He can't raise his arm above his head, an injury from the Great War."

Well, that was a surprise. "That's tremendous news. Did you inform Inspector Crawford?"

She nodded. "He didn't seem to think much of it. Probably thought I was lying to protect Simon."

That was not the only reason. Newcastle could have knocked down Wakefield before hitting him with the statue. In such a scenario, he wouldn't have needed to raise his arm. But at least it was something to be used. "Can the injury be proven?"

"Oh, yes. He consulted physicians as he'd like to have it repaired. They advised against it, however, arguing he might lose mobility of his arm altogether."

"But he punched Lord Wakefield in the study." And one other time at a ball in full view of many witnesses, a row that has no chance of being forgotten. Or that a prosecutor would fail to bring up at trial.

"Simon struck out." She demonstrated with a straightforward motion. "He didn't raise his arm. There is a difference."

"That's certainly a point in Newcastle's favor. Unfortunately, his confession would be used to disprove that."

The spark she'd been showing seemed to evaporate. "If only he hadn't."

I pressed her hand. "Keep the faith. The truth will prevail."

Once she departed, I went in search of Owen Clapham who was waiting in the library to conduct our lesson. Unfortunately, after I shared what I'd learned from Lady Wakefield, he didn't hold out much hope.

"People will say anything to save a loved one from the rope."

"But couldn't it be used to inject reasonable doubt into the case against Newcastle?"

"Yes, of course. The information will need to be verified, but not by us, by his solicitor. If proven true, Lord Newcastle's barrister can use it at trial."

It wasn't much, but it was something. "Inspector Crawford mentioned something yesterday."

A slow-moving smile rolled across his face. "Did he now?"

Of course, he knew about my consultations with Inspector Crawford during prior investigations. On one previous occasion, my visit had been discovered by an enterprising journalist and splashed all over the news, thus forcing my clandestine meeting with the good inspector.

"He warned me against investigating Wakefield's financial situation, claiming he might have been involved in sordid dealings."

"Funny he said that." He cleared his throat. "I've been doing my own inquiries and heard some things."

"Such as?"

"Rumblings in St. Giles."

The worst part of town. During my last murder investigation, I'd gone there in search of information. It hadn't gone well. "What kinds of rumblings?"

"The kind that get people killed. I arranged to meet someone there tonight to find out more. I should have something to report at the next meeting."

Maybe this related to what Inspector Crawford warned me about. "I'd like to come."

"No, Miss Worthington. It's too dangerous. And you'd stand out like a sore thumb."

"I've gone to St. Giles before to obtain information. Disguised. No one suspected my identity."

He arced a doubting brow. "This information you sought. Did it involve payment?"

"Yes, of course."

"They knew you came from money. Nobody offers to pay

in St. Giles unless he's flush or a copper. And you're the wrong gender for the police."

I took offense at that. "There are no policewomen on the force?"

"A few. Not enough to make a difference. And they're certainly not dispatched on perilous missions."

"Well, that needs to change. Women can add a lot of value to police work."

He leaned back against his seat. "I'm not arguing that point. Just saying that's the way it is."

"They didn't suspect who I was before," I offered in my defense.

"Oh, sure they did, Miss. They just wanted the money."

"We can offer your contact that then."

He refused the suggestion. "That won't work. The man I'm seeing tonight isn't sharing information for the money. He wants to right a wrong. But he's scared. If whoever he's afraid of found out he'd talked to me, he would not live to see another day. That's why I chose a meeting spot no criminal is likely to visit."

"What place is that?"

"A place the riffraff avoid."

Ahhh. He'd given it away. "When are we leaving?"

"*We* are not going anywhere."

I shrugged. "Fine. I'll go by myself then."

A cocky smile popped up on his lips. "You wouldn't know where to go."

He thought he had me; he was that sure of himself. But he was wrong. "You are going to a church, and there's only one in that area. St. Giles in the Fields. That's how that part of London got its name."

The smile vanished as he cursed softly under his breath. "You're too intelligent for words." He rubbed a hand across his jaw as he weighed my suggestion. "You'll have to stay quiet. The moment you open your mouth, the jig will be up. Your elegant speech will give you away."

"Fine. What time?"

"Midnight. I'll wait for you in the mews."

"I'll be there." I took a deep breath, let it out before I continued, "There is one other matter that has come up. Lord Marlowe reported it yesterday to me. It pertains to a young woman who worked at Wakefield Hall in Devon."

A stillness came over him, one I barely noticed eager as I was to relay the information I'd learned.

"What about her?" His tone had turned gruff. How very odd.

"She caught Wakefield's eye, so much so he brought her to London with him."

"Did he hurt her?" Anger blazed out of his eyes. Well, no wonder. Any decent man would feel the same way about a young woman trapped in such a perilous situation.

"Not for lack of trying. Apparently, she managed to evade him most of the time. When he finally caught her, she stabbed him. Next day she vanished. The Wakefield House servant Marlowe talked to does not know what happened to her."

He gazed off into the distance, probably considering what I'd said. Having reached a conclusion, he turned back to me. "I feel for the lass. But what connection would she have to the investigation?"

"Maybe nothing, but something tells me it does. I think we should try to find her."

"After all these years, the trail would have gone cold." He was trying to dissuade me from my course of action, probably because he thought it'd be a waste of time.

But no matter his mood, I was resolute. This was a path that needed to be followed. "We'll never know unless we try. We should start with the Wakefield Hall staff. The housekeeper should be able to tell us something. We'll need to travel to Devon, of course."

"We?"

"As soon as it can be arranged, but no later than Saturday."

"Do you think me a magician, Miss Worthington? That's only two days from now."

"No, I think you a former Scotland Yard Inspector. Whatever police station is near Wakefield Hall should have a telephone. Have them contact the housekeeper and set up a time for us to talk to her."

"With everything that's going on here in London, I think you best leave it to me."

"I think not. You yourself said it when we first met. Women feel more comfortable talking to other women. The housekeeper might not find it easy to discuss unsavory matters with you."

He sighed heavily. "Very well. I'll do my best."

"I'll also be talking to the Morgans tomorrow. They lived close to Wakefield Hall. They might know something as well."

Since the telephone call to Devon took priority, we never did get around to my lesson. But I did not mind. I was too excited about going adventuring once more.

CHAPTER TWENTY-THREE

A MIDNIGHT ADVENTURE

*P*ROMPTLY AT MIDNIGHT, suitably attired in a dress, shawl, and hat Betsy acquired from the rag shop, I sneaked out to meet Owen Clapham. Thankfully, my clothes didn't reek of gin and onions as the previous ones had.

"You're punctual. I give you that." He was attired in workman's pants, a heavy cotton shirt, a weathered brown jacket and a gray cap that had seen better days. "Any trouble getting away?"

"No. As I've said, I've done this before."

He led the way through the mews to the street that bordered Grosvenor Square. Only there would we find transportation.

The moonless night was foggy and damp. So much so, we could barely see two feet in front of us. Not only that, but it was downright chilly. As the cold seeped into my very bones,

I wrapped the thin shawl about my shoulders. It didn't help, and soon I was trembling.

"Told you, you shouldn't have come."

"I'm not complaining."

He scoffed. "Let's hope you won't have to."

A taxicab seemingly appeared out of nowhere, almost running into us. But noticing it just in time, we hailed it.

"Where ya goin, mate?" the cabbie asked after we'd climbed into the taxi.

"St. Giles," Mister Clapham answered in a ruff voice, "and make it quick."

"Oi don't go there, especially this late at night. Best oi can do is Covent Garden."

"Take us there, then."

The driver let us off at Bow Street, once the home of the famous Bow Street Runners, the precursors of Scotland Yard.

Once we alighted, Mister Clapham cautioned, "Eyes on the back of your head, mind you."

"I brought a weapon." I thought it only fair to let him know.

He glanced at me askance. "What sort of weapon?"

"Nunchucks." I retrieved them from the deep pocket of my skirt and showed them to him. The black chainsticks had dragon symbols painted on them.

"What the devil are those things?"

"They originated in Japan. They're used in martial arts training."

"Do you even know how to use them?"

"I learned self-defense at finishing school." Eager to demonstrate, I widened my legs, spun the nunchucks forward and back parallel to my body before catching one of the sticks.

"Blimey. Never seen anything like that. Those things are dangerous."

"That's the point," I said triumphantly.

As we traveled from Covent Garden into the St. Giles district, the streets became filthier. The air stunk of rotten cabbage, refuse, and some ungodly stench. Having been here before, I'd known what to expect, so I'd brought a perfumed handkerchief to ward off the stink.

Mister Clapham stopped in his tracks and turned to me. "What is that smell?"

I shrugged. "Haven't the foggiest. Dead rats would be my guess."

"Not that. Your handkerchief."

"Oh, that's attar of roses." I wafted the handkerchief in his direction.

He grabbed my wrist. "You want to get us killed? Put that away. They'll know you for a gentry mort if you keep that up."

"Sorry." I buried the handkerchief deep in my pocket.

After another twenty minutes, we reached St. Giles in the Fields. The Palladian style structure had been built in the 12th century, but ravaged by time, it had been rebuilt twice. Within, everything lay silent as a tomb, not even the skittering of creatures could be heard.

Pointing to a pew situated in the dark shadows of the nave, Mister Clapham signaled me to stay quiet. I did as I was told while he sought a more visible seat closer to the altar and next to the aisle, probably so he could easily be seen.

While the minutes ticked by, we waited for his contact to appear. And then finally somebody did. A man, not that I was expecting a woman. As dark as it was inside the church, I couldn't discern his features. The only thing I noted was that he was tall and nervous. Twitching and glancing over his shoulder, he dropped into the pew behind Mister Clapham and leaned over to engage in a whispered back and forth. Having apparently reached some sort of agreement, they came to their feet and left.

Time dragged on for what seemed like an eternity. Without any worthwhile thoughts to occupy my mind, my imagination came alive with phantasms who shifted and faded in the dark. The frigid temperature inside the nave did not help and soon my teeth were chattering, and my body trembled. Clearly, I couldn't remain where I was. I needed to move before the cold or fear claimed me as a victim. I had just decided to stand when someone crept up behind me and clamped a hand over my mouth.

Heart thumping wildly in my chest, I scratched at the hand that held me captive.

And then a voice breathed into my ear, "Stop struggling. It's me."

Inspector Crawford. Relief flooded through me as I turned around. Unlike every other time I'd seen him when he'd been dressed in the height of fashion, he was now wearing the threadbare clothes of a common man, torn and dirtied by time and use.

"How did you know I was here?"

"I caught a whiff of your perfume three streets away and followed the scent. What the blazes are you doing here?" Clearly, he did not approve.

I hitched up my chin. I would not allow him to browbeat me. "Owen Clapham and I are gathering information."

"Didn't I warn you against getting involved?" he bit out.

"You did."

"Yet, you ignored my warning."

I tossed my head in defiance. "As I explained earlier, you do not direct my moves, Inspector."

In the quiet of the place, I heard his growl.

"What is Clapham investigating?" he asked.

"He's trying to find out what Wakefield was up to." A shiver ran through me, one I could not hide.

"You're freezing."

"It is rather cold, inspector," I said, through my chattering teeth.

He heaved out a heavy sigh, before peeling off his coat and draping it over me. "Here."

I sank into the warmth, fragrant with his scent. "Th-thank you."

"You should have let Clapham handle it, Catherine. This is no place for a lady. You need to go home."

"I've done this before, Inspector," I reminded him.

"And look where that landed you."

Caught up in a street fight, where I came very close to getting seriously hurt. I had to admit he did have a point.

A man suddenly rushed into the church, seemingly in search of Inspector Crawford. "Sir. You need to come. We found something."

Curious as to what was so urgent, I came to my feet.

With a frown, Inspector Crawford clamped his hands on my shoulders."Where do you think you're going?"

"With you?" I asked hopefully.

He shook his head. "This is a Scotland Yard operation. No civilians allowed, never mind that you're a woman."

Not that again. "Do you think women are incapable of investigating police matters?"

"Inspector Crawford? Now, sir," the man urged.

He glanced at the man. "Officer, I want you to watch over this woman. She is not to leave. Do you understand?"

"Yes, sir." The man's shoulders drooped. No wonder. He'd been ordered to guard a female rather than participate in whatever urgent matter had just arisen.

The inspector turned to me. "You will stay here. You will

not move away from this place. I'll return to escort you home."

When I didn't respond, he said, "If you don't do as I say, I will tell your mother what you've been up to." He slipped away before I could call him a snitch.

No sooner did he leave than Owen Clapham returned. "Was that Inspector Crawford?" He must have seen him leaving the church.

"Yes."

"Right. We better go."

"I can't. He told me to stay put. And he asked that officer to guard me." I nodded toward the man who was standing in the shadows.

Mister Clapham approached the officer. After a brief conversation during which Mister Clapham flashed a paper of some kind, the man nodded.

Returning to my side, Mister Clapham said, "You can leave now."

"But what about him?" I nodded toward the officer. "I don't want him to get into trouble."

"He won't. I'll square things with Inspector Crawford in the morning. Come on." And without another word, he grabbed my elbow and rushed me out of the church.

"What did you discover?" I asked, as we reached the street.

He searched the surroundings as he answered, "Enough. I'll tell you when we're in safer surroundings."

With a hand on a revolver, he carried by his side, he remained vigilant as we quickly moved through the streets. It wasn't until we were clear of St. Giles that he breathed easy. We kept a lookout for a taxicab, but as late as it was, none was to be found. We were left with no choice but to walk. The night had not improved. It was still foggy and damp and chillier than before, but at least I had Inspector Crawford's coat to keep me warm.

When I started to ask questions, Mister Clapham signaled silence as it was best to make as little noise as possible. You never knew who was walking the streets. The slog was long and tiring. By the time we reached Worthington House, I was more than ready for my bed.

"Better go in, before you're caught," he said.

"In a minute." I was not about to let him leave without finding out what he'd discovered. "What did you learn?"

He blew out a breath. "Wakefield was involved in the illegal importation of cocaine."

"What?" I exclaimed.

"Keep your voice down, Miss," he cautioned. "Someone might hear you."

"Sorry," I whispered.

"Wakefield was the middleman. Somebody brings it aboard ships. He arranged for its delivery to a warehouse. Apparently, he employed a different one every time. Someone else arranged the distribution. All this I already knew."

"You did? How?"

"Scotland Yard. But this is what's new. At the masked ball, Wakefield was supposed to inform his contact about the location of the latest shipment. But somebody killed him before he could do so."

"How do we know he didn't pass on the information?"

"Because the goods are still there. They were never picked up."

"How does your friend know all this?"

"He knows some of the people involved, and they have loose tongues. They're complaining they haven't been paid because no one knows where the warehouse is located. My friend's life won't be worth much if they find out he talked to me."

"Why did he risk it?"

"His sister became an addict. She died last month. This is his way of getting justice for her."

"So, Scotland Yard knows about the drug smuggling and Wakefield's part in it."

He nodded. "They've been trying to nab Wakefield for the last two years. They knew he was involved, but they couldn't trace it back to the bastard—I beg your pardon, Miss."

"No need to apologize, Mister Clapham. Go on."

"He was never caught making the payments or passing on the information. He was a wily old beggar if I do say so myself. And now somebody's gone and killed him. And they still don't know who's in charge of the whole thing."

"Are they sure it wasn't him?"

"Scotland Yard doesn't think he has the brains to pull off such a complex scheme. He was used as an errand boy, nothing more. The big fish still has to be caught."

"Why didn't you mention this at the meetings?"

Even in the dark, I caught his wary stare. "Well, Miss, seeing how one of the committee members has a ship that sails the seven seas."

"Hollingsworth? I can't believe he would be involved in such a dastardly thing."

"His ship cuts across the Panama Canal from one ocean to another."

"And Panama is next to Colombia, a country infamous for its cocaine crops."

"Exactly so. Easy enough to arrange for the transportation."

"You think someone aboard his ship has engaged in this nefarious trade?"

"I do."

"I don't see how. A captain as savvy as Lord

Hollingsworth would certainly be aware of what's happening right under his nose."

"I don't think you're seeing matters clearly, Miss."

"What do you mean?"

"He could be the one responsible. Those expeditions of his are very expensive. What's there to say he isn't engaging in drug trafficking to get the funds he needs?"

"He wouldn't! He couldn't!" I protested. Hollingsworth was an honorable man. I would bet my life on it.

"Time will tell, Miss. Now you better get inside before somebody sets off an alarm."

"Very well. Goodnight and thank you." I kissed his stubbly cheek and slipped inside before he could protest.

Mister Clapham had certainly given me plenty to think about what he said. And so had Inspector Crawford, for what he didn't say. What was he doing in St. Giles? Was he also investigating the drug trafficking? Or something else? Needless to say, I got little sleep that night.

CHAPTER TWENTY-FOUR

A VISIT WITH THE MORGANS

*T*HE FOLLOWING DAY I made my way to the Morgans' house, sans Betsy. Lavender Rose, who had a case of the sniffles, had refused to relinquish her. Mother, of course, objected and offered to cancel her plans and accompany me. But I convinced her the visit would not last long, and there would be no need for either a chaperone or for Neville to drive me for she needed him more than I did. She reluctantly gave in.

The drive did not take long, but it did take me from the rarefied air of Mayfair to a more humble Lambeth address. The Morgans' house was in a district that barely clung to the fringes of gentility. Situated across the Thames from Westminster, the area was comprised of a hodgepodge of buildings, some industrial and commercial, others residential, with the Waterloo Station railway lines separating them. Not the best locale, but they'd be in Mayfair soon enough. Not for another month, though. Even though Archibald Morgan had inherited the Lord Wakefield title, he couldn't very well ask a widow who was presumably in mourning to vacate the premises.

After I pulled the doorbell, a tall gentleman answered the door. To my surprise, it was someone I recognized. "Mister Brougham? How pleasant to see you again." I was somewhat taken aback to see him employed as the Morgans' butler. It seemed a step down from his last position at an earl's house. At that time, he'd provided vital information to a previous investigation.

"Likewise, Miss Worthington," he responded with a smile while taking my coat and umbrella.

"Brougham, is that our guest?" A shrill female voice called out from deep within.

The butler scrunched his mouth. Probably thought how bad mannered it was to yell. I didn't blame him, as I felt the same way.

The rude summons didn't affect his demeanor, however. He retained the decorum all proper butlers have, and he certainly was that. "If you'll come this way, Miss."

"Of course."

Mister Brougham showed me into a small drawing room where the Morgans were perched on a stodgy couch that held delusions of grandeur. Overstuffed and upholstered with a garish cloth, elegant was the last thing I'd called it.

As I walked in, they rose in unison. Miss Morgan curtsied while her brother bowed.

I curtsied in return. "Thank you for seeing me, Miss Morgan, Lord Wakefield." Rather odd to call him that. But it was what it was.

"Our pleasure, Miss Worthington," Miss Morgan said, all her teeth in display.

Clearly, Miss Morgan wanted to make herself as agreeable as possible, whether it was in my guise as Miss

Catherine Worthington investigating the former Lord Wakefield's murder or the sister of a soon-to-be-duchess remained to be seen. Regardless of the reason, she appeared eager to be accepted by the higher echelons of society. And at least somewhat, she'd succeeded, as she'd obtained invitations to Lady Clinton's afternoon tea and the Duchess of Brightwell's Midsummer Masquerade Ball. What did she, or her brother for that matter, have to offer that would have gained her such prominence? I didn't know, but I intended to find out.

Without first knocking, a servant plodded into the room carrying the tea service. The poor dear didn't appear to be properly trained as everything was rattling on the tray. The offerings were meager. Other than the teapot and china, only a few dry biscuits lay on a plate. It would have been the height of bad manners to visibly react or comment, so I plastered on a pleasant expression and thanked my hostess.

Once Miss Morgan had poured and served, she provided the opening, "What can we do for you, Miss Worthington?"

"Lady Wakefield has asked me to look into the matter of her husband's unfortunate demise." Politeness had to be observed even though no one in acquaintance of the previous Lord Wakefield would mourn his death.

"Yes, of course. Anything we can do to help, although I don't know what we can contribute. We never socialized with them. He roundly ignored us, don't you know? Probably because we reminded him of his mortality."

I suspected she was right. It would have rankled the former Lord Wakefield to associate with his presumptive heir when it had proven impossible to sire a son of his own.

Her brother, Archibald, or I should say, Lord Wakefield, commented, "We know she's not satisfied with Lord Newcastle's arrest."

His sister patted his hand. "Well, brother. It stands to reason. She doesn't think he did it."

"He confessed, Abigail." He looked down at her from his great height. Well, greater than hers, for she was quite tall herself.

"Forgive my brother, Miss Worthington. He's a man of reason. Can't distinguish between the gray areas of life."

"Whereas you do?" I asked trying to get the measure of her.

"I keep an open mind. One never knows."

"Just so. If I may, Miss Morgan. One of the things I'm looking into is the matter of a maid in the former Lord Wakefield's employ. An Eleanor Tibbett. I'm wondering if you were familiar with her."

"I was." For a moment, she cast her gaze downward before raising it again. "Such a sad story. She was barely fifteen when her mother passed, and she was left an orphan. She came to us in search of a job. But at the time we were not in a position to take on more staff. Dear Archie was still working on his invention, you see. I knew there was an opening at Wakefield Hall, so I recommended her. That must have been about, let's see, six years ago." She glanced toward her brother for confirmation.

"If you say so." His absentminded expression told me the subject was of no interest to him.

"Oh, there he goes again. Daydreaming. He does that all the time. Probably thinking about another invention."

Archie could go hang for all I cared. She'd probably dragged him in to make a good impression on me. If that was her aim, she'd failed. As far as I could see, he lacked conversational skills. His countenance was downright unassuming. Unlike his sister, who at least could claim different colored eyes, his were a dull brown. And his physique? Well, let's just say tall and gangly did not appeal to me. "About the maid?" I asked to remind her of my question.

"Oh, yes. Well, about six months later we heard she'd died."

"Died?" That did not agree with the Wakefield House's maid report.

"Yes, indeed," she said putting a dry biscuit on her plate. "The rumors were ugly, very ugly. I knew better than to pay attention to them, country folk being what they are. But then one day I encountered the Wakefield Hall cook and she told me in confidence what had happened."

"Which was?"

"He abused that girl dreadfully. I was horrified, of course, and saddened I had put that poor, innocent child in the path of that fiend."

The words spoken so matter-of-factly sickened me. But I couldn't let them affect me for I had more questions for her. Faking a smile, I said, "Your kind heart does you credit."

She flushed with pleasure. "Thank you, Miss Worthington. It's nice to be appreciated." She glanced askance at her brother, who seemed oblivious to her pointed comment. As she was unwed and appeared to be in her mid-thirties, officially she could be branded a spinster. Her future was bound to be dreary as her brother would soon find a wife. And then, all she would have was endless gossip and trading on the misfortune of others. I almost felt sorry for her.

"Do you know how the unfortunate girl met her demise?" I could barely get the words out.

"Why, she hanged herself," she offered with a smile.

Dear heaven! Could this be true? I swallowed the bile that rose in my throat. For a moment, it was touch and go, but somehow I fought back the nausea.

"Lord Wakefield hushed it up, of course," she went on as if she was talking about the weather. "But he couldn't silence the rumors. No indeed, he could not. At least he gave her a proper burial."

"A burial? Where?"

"Back in Devon, of course. Right next to her mother."

Unwilling to hear any more, I made my excuses and hurried out into the relatively fresh air of Lambeth. Taking big gulps, I sought to settle my stomach. Last thing I wanted was to sicken all over the street. I walked mindlessly through the streets for what seemed like miles, ignoring a taxicab when one stopped next to me.

"Catherine!" Inspector Crawford. I'd recognize his voice anywhere.

Before I had a chance to acknowledge his presence, he'd bundled me into the vehicle right next to him.

"Here. You're soaked." As he'd done in the church, he removed his jacket and draped it over me. "What are you doing out in this rain?"

Glancing out the window, I realized he was right. A soft drizzle was falling. "Th-thank you. I didn't realize." The horrible image of that poor girl dangling from the end of a rope wouldn't release its hold on me. Was it even true?

He placed his arm around my shoulders and drew me to him, sharing his warmth, his scent. "Why are you wandering in Lambeth by yourself?" The rumble of his voice reverberating in his chest offered safety and strength.

For one mad moment, I wished I had the right to his comfort. But I didn't. So, I freed myself from his hold. "I was talking to the Morgans. Abigail and Archibald. He's the new Lord Wakefield."

"Why?"

"We're pursuing a line of inquiry, and they had answers."

That charming smile of his made an appearance. "Line of inquiry. Is that you or Owen Clapham talking?"

"Both. I learned it from him, of course."

"Have you had your tea?"

I'd had a weak imitation, nothing to provide reasonable sustenance, so I answered, "No."

"Would you like to join me, then? There's a pub close by that serves decent fare."

Mother would fret if I went missing too long. But the meeting with the Morgans had rattled me, and I needed to regain my bearings before returning home. Tea with Inspector Crawford would give me the time and space to do that. "Thank you. I'd like that."

The pub was not fancy, by any means. It was crowded with working-class people who quieted when we walked through the door.

"Bobbie Crawford! As I live and breathe." The publican, a roly-poly of a man whose girth seemed to equal his height, greeted Inspector Crawford like a long, lost friend. "Come to visit your old haunts?"

"I am. Do you still have that quiet table in the back? We'd like a bit of privacy." He nodded toward me.

The publican elbowed Inspector Crawford and spoke in a loud whisper. "Got yourself a sweetheart, do you?"

Inspector Crawford grinned. "Something like that."

The publican gave me the once over. "Don't blame you. She's a looker, all right." He swung an arm over his head. "Follow me. I'll set you up." He kept an entire conversation going while he showed us to a room in the back that smelled of fish and chips. The lone table didn't appear too clean, and the chairs had seen better days, but the room offered privacy. "What will you have?"

"Tea and scones?" I suggested.

The publican frowned. "How about fish and chips and a mug of my best dark ale?"

I grinned. "Fabulous."

He winked at Inspector Crawford. "She'll do."

CHAPTER TWENTY-FIVE

A CONSULTATION WITH INSPECTOR CRAWFORD

*T*HE FISH AND CHIPS, AS ADVERTISED, WERE DELICIOUS. I hadn't realized how ravenous I was until the plate was in front of me, and I quickly consumed the food.

"Hungry, were we?" A hint of a smile touched Inspector Crawford's lips.

I flushed with embarrassment. "I'm sorry. That was rather indelicate." The *Young Ladies' Guide to Etiquette and Deportment* would not have approved.

His eyes gaze twinkled with humor. "No need to observe the social niceties with me. I enjoy watching you eat."

He wasn't being polite. He really meant it.

"I don't know why I was so hungry. It isn't like I haven't eaten. I had tea at the Morgans and toast for breakfast."

He frowned. "That's not nearly enough. You need to eat to keep up your strength." When I made a face, he laughed to himself. "My apologies. Lecture's over."

"Did you work in this area? The publican knows you."

"It was the first district I patrolled as a recruit. I wasn't assigned to St. Giles until I gained some experience. That being a more dangerous part of London, the Metropolitan Police only places seasoned officers there."

Made sense since St. Giles was one of the seedier sides of town. "How long did you work in Lambeth?"

He rested back into his seat. "About two years. Got to know the publican well."

"He called you Bobbie. You must have become friends."

"*Bobbie* as a policeman, not as a diminutive of my name."

My face heated up. "Oh, of course." Police officers were often called bobbies after Robert Peel, Queen Victoria's Home Secretary who inaugurated the Metropolitan Police department. "My mistake."

"No need to apologize. Anyone would have thought the same."

"Is there a ladies'?" After drinking a full tankard of ale, nature was demanding a visit.

"Out the door, to your left."

The bathroom was surprisingly clean. It even held a lit candle to ward off noxious fumes.

By the time I returned, our plates and tankards had been cleared, and a pot of tea and two mugs had been brought.

While I poured for us both, he asked the question which must have been uppermost in his mind. "What did you discover at the Morgans that distressed you?"

Of course, he'd want to know. "Lord Marlowe discovered a rather alarming matter about a young maid who'd been employed at Wakefield Hall. Apparently, the former Lord Wakefield had been besotted with her. So much so that when he came to London to attend Parliament, he brought her with him."

A muscle worked in his jaw. "Did he . . . abuse her?"

I took a sip of the tea before answering. "Not for his lack of trying. Apparently, she managed to evade him. The cook was very good at hiding her. But he finally caught her one night. In the scullery, of all places. She . . . stabbed him to defend herself. It was only a flesh wound," I rushed to say. "No lasting harm was done."

His jaw worked some more. "Unfortunately, that wouldn't have mattered to the law. Regardless of her motive, she would have been arrested for attacking an aristocrat."

"She wasn't, though, because she vanished. According to the servant, she was there one day and gone the next. More than likely, she ran away to avoid such an outcome."

"She would have landed in jail had she stayed. But where could she have gone? Did she seek refuge back home?"

"Apparently, not. The Wakefield House maid told Marlowe nobody knew where she went." I swallowed hard. "The thing of it is that Abigail Morgan told me a different story. She said the young maid hanged herself after suffering Lord Wakefield's abuse."

"And that's what caused your upset." His eyes showed nothing but kindness.

I swallowed hard. "Yes." I prayed Miss Morgan was wrong. No young woman deserved to suffer such a fate.

"Sometimes people hear different tales about the same set of events. Maybe that's what happened in this case."

"Miss Morgan supposedly heard her version from the Wakefield Hall cook in Devon, whereas Marlowe learned it from the Wakefield House maid in London. So, the sources are different. Wherever the truth lies, it will need to be verified which means I'll be traveling to Devon."

"Take Owen Clapham with you."

He'd warned me off the retired inspector before. What had made him change his mind? "You trust him now?"

"I trust him to watch over you. He came to my office this

morning and explained how you'd come to accompany him to St. Giles. Faced with the choice of either agreeing to your demand or you putting yourself in harm's way with no one to guard you, he chose the lesser of the two evils."

I jutted out my jaw. "I came prepared, Inspector."

"The nunchucks?" When I startled, he went on to say, "Those are only effective in hand-to-hand combat, and they won't protect you against a bullet. They're illegal by the way, so you'll be handing them over."

Hell would freeze over before I would do that. They were a gift from my finishing school self-defense class instructor when I performed brilliantly. "I don't have them on me at the moment."

"I'll call to collect them."

He hadn't telephoned or written to tell me about his Yorkshire case or pay a social visit, but he would come by to confiscate the weapon. Sheer anger drove me to say, "I think I'll ask Lord Hollingsworth to escort me to Devon. Since he doesn't know you, he won't snitch on me." I wouldn't, as he would be busy inspecting Brightwell Mansion. But Inspector Crawford did not know that.

His head jerked toward me. "I told you to stay away from him."

"What objection do you have to him, other than you think him a pirate? That's a ludicrous charge, by the way. Mother agrees with me as he's a favorite of hers." A sudden thought intruded into my mind. Maybe his objection to Hollingsworth was much more serious and had to do with the illegal trade. "Wait. Is he connected with the drug trafficking matter? Is he transporting cocaine in his ship?"

"How would you even know . . .?" He breathed out a frustrated breath. "Owen Clapham, of course."

"I think it's connected to Lord Wakefield's murder."

"How did you make that leap of logic?"

"It stands to reason, doesn't it?" I asked in a rush. "He was involved in the importation of cocaine. Somebody killed him for it."

"Who would have done it and for what reason?" he asked.

"I don't know. But I intend to find out."

"Catherine. Please be careful. These people will stop at nothing. The people involved in the drug trade will hurt anyone who gets in their way." Anguish dimmed his gaze.

"I will." The least I could do was ease his distress. "As far as the trip to Devon is concerned, I've already asked Mister Clapham. So, no need to worry about that."

He rubbed a hand across his brow before accepting the inevitable. He couldn't stop me from doing what I wanted to do, how I needed to do it. "Very well. He'll know who you should talk to. His last assignment before he left Scotland Yard was in Devon."

"Mister Clapham didn't share that information. How very odd."

"It didn't end well for him. More than likely, that's why he failed to mention it."

"What happened?"

I got nothing but a blank stare. Should have known he wouldn't discuss it.

"The important thing is he'll keep you out of harm's way."

Of course, he wouldn't let it go. Having no desire to have him ring a peal over me, I decided to jolly him out of it. "I didn't get arrested this time." I grinned.

He pursed his lips. "I could have. I should have."

"What for? I did nothing wrong."

"Loitering." By the way his mouth moved, I could tell he was biting back a smile.

He was teasing, of course. "I was doing no such thing. I was praying in a church."

A brow arched with mock derision. "Miles away from your home? Dressed in rags?"

"I could ask the same of you, Inspector. What were you doing in St. Giles that late at night?"

He lost that hint of a smile. "Police business."

"Such as?"

"Nothing I can share."

"Did you discover anything?"

He remained silent.

Very well. I would take another tack. "What's happening with Lord Newcastle's case?"

All his levity vanished. "It's out of my hands, Catherine."

"What do you mean?"

"They've started proceedings against him. Two, three weeks at the most for the trial. And then . . ."

He didn't have to say it. But I knew. If found guilty, Newcastle would be led to the gallows and hanged.

CHAPTER TWENTY-SIX

A TRIP TO DEVON

*T*HE NEXT MORNING, Owen Clapham and I took the train from Paddington Station to Devon. We were to interview Mrs. Saunders, Wakefield Hall's former housekeeper. Apparently, she'd retired several years ago and was now keeping house for her son, a widower.

The train ride was not long, a little over two hours. Sufficient time to share what I'd discovered at the Morgans. But something held me back. Mainly because I wanted to hear what Mrs. Saunders had to say first. After all, she had been at Wakefield Hall. Abigail Morgan had not.

And then there was the fact that Owen Clapham's last case had been in this part of the world. Something he'd failed to share with me. Inspector Crawford had hinted that it hadn't gone well, so that could very well be the reason for his reticence. But I had a strange feeling something else was holding him back. When I'd mentioned the maid from Wakefield Hall, he'd gone suddenly silent. Why? Maybe it had something to do with his investigation. But that had been only a year back while Eleanor Tibbett had worked at Wakefield Hall six years ago. So, I didn't see the connection. I hoped the discussion with Mrs. Saunders would clarify matters.

After our arrival at Devon, we proceeded to the house Mrs. Saunders kept for her son. She appeared to be in her fifties, still comely with a head full of chestnut hair streaked with silvery strands. Her ready smile welcomed us to the parlor where refreshments waited for us. While the china may not have been of the best quality, her pastries certainly were. She waited only until the rules of etiquette had been observed before coming right to the point.

"You're here to discuss Eleanor Tibbett."

"Yes."

She shook her head. "Such a sad tale that was. She was young, barely fifteen when her mam died. She came to work for us shortly afterward. Miss Morgan recommended her." Her mouth pursed with disapproval.

Clearly, Abigail Morgan was not a favorite of hers. I would need to delve into the cause. "When was she taken on?"

"The spring after Lady Wakefield passed. About six years ago."

"She had no other family?" I asked.

"A wastrel of a father. The moment her mam died he threw her out the house. He couldn't afford to feed her, he said." Her eyes flashed with emotion. "But he had more than enough blunt for drink and loose women."

"That's horrible." How could a father toss his child out on the streets, and a young girl at that?

"It was. Her mam used to work for Miss Morgan before she got sick. So young Eleanor sought help from her. Not that it did her any good. She told Eleanor she didn't have a position for her. I'll have you know that was a bald-faced lie."

"Was it?"

"Oh, yes. Eleanor's mam had been the washerwoman, and she hadn't been replaced. She could have taken up her mam's duties."

"Why do you think that was?"

"Well, if you ask me" —she leaned forward to whisper— "I think she was afraid her brother might have been attracted to the girl. She only hired older women, you see, and unattractive ones at that."

"So, Eleanor was pretty?"

A smile rolled across her lips. "Oh, yes. She looked like an angel with her dark hair and rosy cheeks. And always a smile on her face."

"Her mother was not attractive?"

She lost the beatific expression. "She was until that wastrel of a husband wore her down with his demands."

"What happened after Miss Morgan sent her to you?"

"We had no need for more staff, but I couldn't send her away, not after everything she'd experienced."

"So, you hired her."

She nodded. "As the scullery maid. Cook could always use more help in the kitchen. I never once regretted my decision. Eleanor was a very eager lass. And hardworking too. Her and cook got on like a house on fire."

"How long did she work at Wakefield Hall?"

"She came to us in the spring. We were a happy household. Only a few servants. Lord Wakefield, you see, was in London attending Parliament. And then he came home that August and the troubles started."

"What happened?"

"The devil got a hold of Lord Wakefield, that's what happened. Not that he was a saint to begin with. But he was obsessed with her. And here she was, a sweet young thing, an innocent with no knowledge of the world. It didn't stop him from chasing after her, though."

"Did he catch her?" I hated to ask, but it had to be done.

"Not while at Wakefield Hall. Cook and I devised a plan to hide her in the scullery. The master didn't visit the kitchen, you see. Every time he asked about her, I'd say she'd gone into town on an errand or to visit her mam's grave. He never caught on." But when spring came, well, then, I couldn't make no more excuses. When he returned to London, he took her with him."

"Oh, my."

"Cook promised to carry on with our plans to keep her away from that devil. I suffered. Oh, how I suffered not knowing what had happened to Eleanor. And then several months later, I heard she'd vanished."

"She didn't die?"

"No. What gave you that idea?"

"Miss Morgan. She said she heard it from the Wakefield Hall cook."

"I don't see how she could have done so."

"How did you find out she disappeared?"

"From Cook. She traveled to town with Lord Wakefield, you see, and so did the rest of the staff. Well, except for me and Mr. Struthers, the butler. The London duties would have been too much for him, old as he was. He's gone on to his glory, he has." She bowed her head. So, did I.

"Why didn't you accompany Lord Wakefield to London?"

"Me son's wife was feeling poorly. She's passed on since, poor thing." More head bowing. "So, I came here to make do for me son and grandchildren. Three lovely boys. They're the light of my life."

"They must love you as much as you do them."

"They do, if I say so myself."

"Now about Cook. When did you talk to her?"

"Why, she came back to say her goodbyes. She was leaving England, you see. A family bound for the West Indies needed a good English cook. When she heard about it, she applied for the position. Was hired on the spot."

"And she told you Miss Tibbett had disappeared?"

"She did. Apparently, Lord Wakefield finally caught up with her in the scullery. The lass defended herself by wielding a knife and cutting the devil. His doctor patched him up. Turned out to be nothing but a flesh wound. But Eleanor was afraid of what would happen to her. Next morning when she didn't show up at the kitchen, Cook went looking for her. She was gone, her clothes with her. No one knew where. Apparently, Lord Wakefield was beside himself. He swore to visit all kinds of punishments on her once he found her. But he never did."

"What an ordeal she suffered," I said. "She never came home to Devon?"

"No, Miss. We never saw hide nor hair of her after that devil took her away."

"To have to make her way all alone in the streets of London. It's a thought not to be borne."

Mrs. Saunders bared her teeth. "I tell you what, Miss, whoever killed Lord Wakefield did the world a favor. Not only did he attempt to seduce that poor lass, but he was a brute to his first wife. And that I saw firsthand. Poor Lady Wakefield ended up at the bottom of the stairs with her neck broken. Suspicious that's what I called it. I still do. But Lord Wakefield was friends with the magistrate. Between the two of them they hushed up the whole thing. And from what I hear, the second Lady Wakefield experienced the same sort of abuse. It was a good thing someone ended his life, for, mark my words, she would have gone the way of the first."

I couldn't help but feel the same way. Inspector Crawford, though, would have a different view.

After thanking Mrs. Saunders, we went on our way on the taxicab we'd hired for the day.

"The train back to London is not due until two hours from now," I said. "That will give us enough time to enjoy a luncheon."

"Yes," Mister Clapham said, almost absentmindedly. "Would you mind if we visited St. Bartholomew's?"

A church? What business would he have there? Regardless, I couldn't deny his request. "No, of course not."

On the way, we stopped to purchase flowers from a nearby florist, a bouquet of sweet peas, delphiniums, and phlox. When we arrived at the church, I thought to remain in the taxicab to allow him his privacy, but he insisted I come with him. To my surprise, he didn't enter the church but walked steadfastly through the graveyard toward a marker below which a lady had been laid to rest. The stone was a humble one with only her name and the years of birth and death. Ophelia Tibbett, 1880-1917.

I remained quiet while he laid the flowers on the grave.

"She loved sweet peas."

The statement touched a chord within me, something I could no longer ignore. "Who is this lady to you, Mister Clapham?"

He gazed at me with tears in his eyes. "Me daughter."

If Ophelia Tibbett was his daughter, it stood to reason that Eleanor Tibbett was his granddaughter, which would give him a prime motive for killing Wakefield. But rather than address that now, I walked back to the road to allow him time to grieve.

In time, Mister Clapham rejoined me and offered a simple greeting, "I know a pub that serves decent grub."

As my stomach had been making demands for the last

half hour, I went along with his suggestion. "Lead on, Mister Clapham."

We both requested bangers and mash. Mister Clapham opted for a tankard of ale which I eschewed, ordering tea instead. His assertion proved to be correct. The pub indeed served tasty fare. While we ate, I asked no questions, trusting he would reveal the tale in his own good time.

It was only after we were ensconced in a first-class train compartment that he finally opened up. "Me daughter, Ophelia we named her, she was a good lass, smart, hard-working. She was the light of my, and her mam's, eyes. Shortly after she turned sixteen, she met someone." His face burned with a hate I'd rarely seen on anyone else. "He was no good. I tried to warn her off him, but she wouldn't listen. And then, he took her away. Her mam was mad with worry. I searched high and low, but he kept her well hidden from me. One year passed and then another." Sadness rolled over his face. "Her mam, she died from grief."

"I'm so sorry, Mister Clapham."

He went on as if he hadn't heard me. "Wanting to leave the sore amount of grief behind, I moved to London. Became a sergeant with the Metropolitan Police. Even as I rose through the ranks and was made Inspector, I never stopped looking for her. Never. And then one day, a request came across my desk. They needed someone in Devon to investigate a murder. They sent me here thinking I was the best man for the job. The victim was the bastard who'd stolen my girl. Killed in a dark alley. I didn't spend much time on it. Instead, I went in search of me daughter only to find her in that cold, dark grave. Wanting to know more about her life, I asked more questions and was told she had a daughter. Eager to acquaint myself with her, I headed to Wakefield Hall, only to find out she'd vanished without a trace."

Everything he said rang true. "Why didn't you tell me?"

"Because I'm teaching you the ways of investigation. You had a hunch, and you followed your lead. That's the way you become a good investigator."

I could no longer hide my misgivings. It had to be said. "Mister Clapham, you know what this makes you, don't you?"

"Yes, I do, lass. It makes me the main suspect in Lord Wakefield's death. For what it's worth, I didn't kill him. He was the only hope I had of finding my granddaughter. I needed him alive."

I believed him, but would anybody else?

CHAPTER TWENTY-SEVEN

A THIRD COMMITTEE MEETING

*A*S SOON AS I RETURNED HOME, I telephoned everyone and moved up our meeting to Monday, explaining I had urgent news. All agreed to reconvene, including Ned who was busier than anyone else. Not only was he involved with the investigation, but he had his own responsibilities at Worthington & Son.

After the meeting started, Lord Marlowe stepped up to the front of the room and offered his sincere apologies for his behavior. And then he provided his report. When they heard about Lord Wakefield's treatment of the young girl, they were just as sickened as I'd been.

Taking over from him I reported on my trip to Devon, ending with "Mister Clapham will no longer be joining us."

"I should hope not," Lord Hollingsworth remarked. "He's now our main suspect."

"He's a suspect as he definitely has a motive, but we haven't discovered the opportunity. And that is something we must do." Sad that I was using the lessons he'd taught me to determine whether he'd committed the murder.

"Shouldn't we inform the police?" Marlowe asked.

A fair question. But it would be premature to do so. "Not until we have something more concrete. Until then, we keep this information to ourselves."

"I don't think he murdered Wakefield," Lady Emma said. "He had this information a year ago, why would he wait this long to kill him?"

"He was probably waiting for the perfect opportunity," Lord Hollingsworth explained. "The masked ball provided that. He could be masked, and nobody would know who he was."

"That's a logical argument." And one that seriously concerned me. "However, until we have definite information pointing his way, I don't think we should go to the police."

"Can we vote on it?" Marlowe asked.

"Of course."

The vote turned out to be in Inspector Clapham's favor, but by a margin of only one vote. The men—Marlowe, Sebastian, Ned, and Hollingsworth, all wanted to inform the police, the women—Margaret, Lily, Lady Emma, and I voted to wait. According to our rules, in case of a tie, the chair made the final decision. That was me. I cast my vote in favor of keeping things to ourselves for the time being. With proceedings moving forward against Newcastle, it was a risk. But if we grew no closer to the truth in a week's time, I would inform Inspector Crawford as well as Newcastle's solicitor. At the very least, Owen Clapham would create reasonable doubt.

"Now, Ned, have you managed to obtain more information about Lord Wakefield's business?"

"His income seems to have come from the Calypso Shipping Consortium of which he was the head. At least on paper."

He confirmed what I' d learned during my midnight adventure with Inspector Clapham. I allowed him to proceed since it was best for that information to come from him rather than reveal to the committee members I'd gone to St. Giles.

"The consortium owns a fleet of steamships. They bring back goods from South America right up to the London docks. But the thing of it is, the numbers don't match up."

"Please explain," I said.

Each ship carries up to 4,000 tons of cargo. Even if they carried the most profitable goods, it would not add up to the amount of money the consortium has earned for the last three years which amounts to over half a million pounds."

Heavens! "What is being imported?"

He fetched a list from the briefcase he'd brought with him. "Sugar, bananas, cocoa, coffee, tobacco, corn, and wheat, according to the ship manifestos."

"I know the area from my travels," Lord Hollingsworth said. "I've watched them loading foodstuffs onto ships. That's about right."

"It takes two weeks to travel each way to and from South America with a one week break in between. Barring some breakdowns or complications, each ship makes ten trips a year. Let's say, to be generous, each brings in 40,000 tons. Even if they were the most profitable crops, it wouldn't add up to the total credited to its bank account. Only a tenth of that amount would be my guess."

"What else could they be importing?" Lily asked.

"Cocaine. They'd be bringing in cocaine," Lord Hollingsworth said.

Someone in the room gasped. As that was what I'd learned, I simply nodded.

"That's awful," Lily said.

"But cocaine comes from coca leaves," Sebastian opined. "That many would take up a great deal of volume. Much more than could be carried by a few trips."

"They're processed where they're grown and refined into powder. Much easier to transport," Lord Hollingsworth explained.

"Who's in this consortium? Who's funding this operation?" Margaret asked.

"That's just it. No one knows," Ned responded. "Lord Wakefield was the front man. But he couldn't possibly have arranged this high a level of business. As far as I can see, he didn't have the brains for it. For his name, and his name only, he was paid ten thousand pounds a year."

"I can't imagine Scotland Yard not knowing about such an intricate operation," Sebastian said.

They did. But I couldn't reveal that, since it wasn't public knowledge.

"What if they knew about the shipments and Lord Wakefield's involvement but were lying in wait to see what Lord Wakefield would do," my clever sister suggested. "He told Lady Wakefield he was meeting someone at the ball. Maybe he was passing on some information about a shipment."

"And then somebody went and killed him, cutting off that flow of information," Sebastian said.

"Scotland Yard would have to rethink their investigation."

"Not necessarily," Lord Hollingsworth said. "They have an alternate source."

"Who?"

"Me."

We all turned to stare at Hollingsworth. Most were dumbfounded by his statement. I wasn't. I'd always suspected there was more to his interest in our investigation that simple boredom. "Could you please explain, Lord Hollingsworth?"

Leaning forward, he propped his elbows on his knees. "In order to understand the current situation, a bit of history is necessary. So please forgive me if I'm a tad longwinded."

"No apology needed," I said. "We understand. Please go on."

"It wasn't until 1920 that cocaine was declared an illegal substance. The Dangerous Drugs Act to be exact. That, of course, provided impetus to the illegal importation of the drug. Gangs who'd previously imported all sorts of dangerous substances, now got into smuggling. The legitimate shipping companies refused to do so as they didn't want to get into trouble with the law. So, they needed someone who didn't mind a little illegal trafficking, especially after the cost of the drug shot up tenfold. With riches to be made, that left an opening for an enterprising sort to establish a thriving import drug trade."

Ned flipped through his papers. "The Calypso Shipping Consortium was created in 1918, right after the end of the Great War."

"They must have seen the handwriting on the wall and sought to establish themselves before the law was passed." Hollingsworth said. "This consortium has been clever enough to disguise the importation of cocaine by hiding it among the shipments of wheat, sugar, or what have you. For the last two years, they've been under investigation, but they have yet to be caught. Custom inspectors have examined their goods time and again and come up empty."

"Could somebody be tipping them off?" I asked.

"That's Scotland Yard's guess. The night of the masked ball they were tracking a suspect, but, unfortunately, he gave them the slip."

"They know it's a he?"

"That's what I was told."

It stood to reason a man would head such an operation, at least legally, for a woman did not have the power to sign documents. At least not as the current law stood. But why was Hollingsworth recruited to aid with the investigation? "How did you get involved in all this?"

"I was approached by Scotland Yard. They know I travel through that part of the world and asked me to keep my eyes and ears open." He turned to me. "During our first meeting, you asked why my return trip took so long."

"You told me you stopped in Tahiti to recuperate and make repairs to the ship."

"In reality, it was Panama City, the Pacific entrance to the Panama Canal. Using the excuse we were making repairs, we spent an entire month observing the ships traveling in and out of the harbor, especially noting the ones that took on cargo. We telegraphed daily reports to the British government so they could be on the lookout for them."

"But they could have been carrying lawful goods."

"If they were, they would have nothing to fear. But if they were hiding cocaine, they would lose a great deal. As it turned out, a few on my list were indeed transporting illegal drugs. Not only were their ships confiscated, but they lost the license to dock at any English harbor ever again. That includes all our colonies and territories, by the way."

"That's very impressive, Hollingsworth," Lord Marlowe said.

"Thank you, but we still have to catch the leader of the consortium." He took a deep breath. "You've done well all of you, very well. But now it's time to step up the game."

"What do you mean?"

"I'm not privy to everything Scotland Yard knows. Far from it. But they are impressed with your progress in this murder investigation. They believe you can make inroads into the shipping consortium business. You, collectively, have an in with society that Scotland Yard can't replicate. It's their firm belief somebody high up in society is directing all this. They want you to find the person responsible. Once you do, they'll take care of the rest."

I stated the obvious. "But that's not the purpose of our group, Lord Hollingsworth. We're here to discover who killed Lord Wakefield."

"You need not worry about that."

"Why not?"

"Because Robert won't rest until he finds the murderer."

What?!!! "Robert? As in Inspector Crawford? You know him?"

He flashed that cheeky grin of his. "Since our days at Oxford."

Unbelievable. "But he warned me off you!"

"He knew if he opposed me, you would look more favorably upon me. It worked. When I volunteered to help with your investigation, you didn't think twice about it."

I gritted my teeth. Next time I saw Inspector Crawford, somehow, some way, I would make him pay.

CHAPTER TWENTY-EIGHT

THE COMMITTEE SPLITS UP

*W*E SPENT THE NEXT TWO HOURS passionately debating our mission. Half the group felt we should remain focused on the murder investigation, while the other half argued we should investigate the shipping consortium. With suppertime quickly approaching, Mother gently inquired whether she should arrange supper for all. A legitimate concern, for she would have to alert Cook.

As everyone was exhausted, we decided a break would be best. In the morning, after a night's rest, we would reconvene. That night, I slept poorly, all the while wishing I could consult with Inspector Crawford. After I throttled him, of course.

But somehow morning brought clarity. There was no help for it; we would need to bifurcate our efforts. One group, under Hollingsworth's leadership, would investigate the shipping consortium. The other would remain focused on Wakefield's murder. Now the problem became who would be assigned to which group.

When I brought up my idea, silence momentarily reigned. But then Margaret piped up with, "It could work. But how are we going to split things up?"

"Well, here's my thinking," I said. "Obviously, Hollingsworth will head up the shipping consortium endeavor, and I will remain on the Wakefield murder investigation."

"Makes sense," Ned replied.

"You, Ned, belong with Hollingsworth's group since you have the best handle on business and financial matters."

He nodded. "I'd be amenable to that."

"Lady Emma should stay on the Wakefield inquiry. She has a keen knowledge of high society, and we still need to evaluate the guest and staff list for possible suspects." I took a breath before I continued. Given the current state of affairs between Lady Emma and Marlowe, I was wary of asking them to team up again, but there was no help for it. For all their acrimony, they worked well together. "That's a huge task, but you, Lord Marlowe, have an excellent grasp of society. Would you be amenable to working on that endeavor as well?"

For a second, Lord Marlowe startled, but then he answered, "Of course. Whatever you think is best."

Lady Emma did not object. I suspected, in her heart of hearts, she was pleased.

"Splendid. That leaves Sebastian, Margaret, and Lily."

"I don't have any special knowledge or skills. I feel so useless," Lily exclaimed.

"Don't. I'll need to revisit the Morgans." At the very least, I would need an explanation of Abigail Morgan's statement because she had most assuredly lied to me. The question became why. "I have a hunch I missed something. Maybe you'll pick up on what it is."

Margaret and Sebastian had been whispering madly to each other while I was assigning people to tasks. Curious, I called them into the conversation.

"Margaret and Sebastian, do you have something to contribute?" An honest question for they most surely were not breathing sweet nothings into each other's ears, at least not in public. It simply wasn't their style.

"We were talking," Margaret offered.

"About?"

"There are several doping scenes in Soho where cocaine is used for recreational purposes. Sad to say, but we were both invited to join."

I'd learned about those from newspaper articles, most notably one in *The Sunday Post*. I never could fathom why anyone would risk such harm to themselves. "When did this happen?"

"At Oxford. We turned down the offers, of course. But we can contact those individuals and say we're now interested."

"You're not actually going to—" I couldn't finish the question.

"Of course not. We'll tell them we changed our minds when it comes to participating."

"If Mother ever found out—" I shuddered to think what she would do. As it was, Mother barely tolerated wine being served at our suppers.

"She won't. We'll make sure of that."

"All right. That's everything. Is everyone clear about their responsibilities?"

A lot of head bobs.

"Let's adjourn for a short while." People needed to visit the W.C., at the very least. "We'll resume in fifteen minutes. Hollingsworth's group will remain in the library. The Wakefield contingent will gather in the drawing room. We can reconvene the whole committee in an hour. Will that work?"

More head bobs.

An hour later we'd made solid progress. Ned would continue to investigate the shipping consortium's structure and finances to see if he could discover any critical information. Margaret and Sebastian would reach out to those who'd issued invitations to their drug parties. Hollingsworth would alert Scotland Yard as to the new direction of the group and see if they had any new information he could share.

Our group would be responsible for studying the guest list and questioning the staff for possible suspects. Lily and I would visit the Morgans.

"Can I make one point about the guest list, Kitty?" Lady Emma asked.

"Of course."

"The Morgans were on it. Rather a surprise, don't you think?"

"Yes, indeed." Only notable personages and those with titles were invited to the Brightwell Midsummer Masked Ball. At the time of the ball, the Morgans were not members of the aristocracy. So, it begged the question. What attributes did they possess that had gotten them an invitation to the most coveted event of the season? "Had they gained entrance to the ballroom before Lord Wakefield's body was discovered?"

"They had."

"Well, that's something we'll need to look into." And one I would probe the next time I saw the Morgans. "Thank you, Lady Emma."

With that being the last report, we adjourned, but not before agreeing to meet again in three days' time.

I had a premonition something would break before then. As it turned out, something did.

CHAPTER TWENTY-NINE

MAGDALEN HOUSE

"*W*HAT'S THE MATTER, DEAR?" Mother asked after supper that night. "You appear a bit peaked."

Tonight was one of those rare evenings during which we neither had guests nor a social event to attend. Father had retired to his study to handle a financial matter, and Margaret, Sebastian, and Lily were quietly discussing something on the other side of the drawing room. Mother and I were by ourselves on the couch. As usual, she was putting the time to good use by quietly embroidering a seat cushion. I, on the other hand, had been staring rather glumly at the wall, which, of course, she'd noticed.

"I don't know how people do the things they do," I replied.

"Anyone in particular?"

"Lord Wakefield. He was a rotter through and through.

Not only did he abuse his wife, but made life miserable for a young girl in his employ. How could he do such things, Mother?"

"Some men, and women too, believe they have the power to do as they wish, regardless of who they hurt. Wakefield was one of those. He'd lost his soul."

My shoulders drooped. "Or maybe he never had one to begin with."

"Everyone is born with a soul, Kitty. What you do with it is up to you." She put her embroidery aside and reached out to press my hands. "Come with me tomorrow."

"I can't. I have so much to do."

"Kitty, you're carrying the weight of the world on your shoulders. A temporary reprieve will do you good. It will take only an hour or so."

It would take longer than that, but she was right. I needed a respite from the constant worry. I forced a smile to my lips. "Very well. Where are we going?"

"Magdalen House."

The residence for fallen women that the Ladies Benevolent Society sponsored. I was aware of its existence, of course, and that they took in women who'd led unfortunate lives. But I knew little more than that. Before I left for finishing school I'd been deemed too young to discover all that Magdalen House entailed. But now that I was a year older, Mother seemingly believed I was old enough to find out.

After we rose bright and early the next day, Mother and I were on our way. Magdalen House was in Shepherd's Bush, an area located just past Hyde Park, so the journey shouldn't have taken long. But traffic clogged the streets which gave us time to talk.

"Where do the ladies come from?" I asked Mother. She

never referred to the residents as 'fallen women', a term she abhorred. But those who'd created the refuge had named it such, and there was no changing it.

"Jails, as well as the streets of London. That's where those who've fallen on hard times are usually found. Sometimes, a kind-hearted police officer or a man of the cloth brings a lost soul to us. A few wander in, looking to save themselves. We teach them reading, writing, and mathematics, skills they can use to help them successfully reintegrate into society. And for those who seem suited for domestic work, we teach them that trade."

"How many women reside within?"

"Ummm. About twenty or so at a time, sometimes less, sometimes more."

"I imagine for some it must be a difficult transition. Is it difficult for them to stay the course?"

"Some find it easier than others. Those who work hard at their instructions are deemed reformed. But others can't resist the lure of their past lives and return to their former existence. Drink and drugs are powerful temptations. Neither is allowed at Magdalen House."

"What happens to the ones who succeed?"

"We find positions for them. Mostly in commercial establishments—shops, factories, and such. One young lady, an excellent seamstress, obtained employment with a modiste."

I had to ask. "Angelique's?"

"The very same." She gazed out the window and frowned. "This traffic is simply atrocious. Why are horse-drawn carriages still allowed on the streets of the London? They should be banned."

"Maybe not everyone can afford a motorcar."

"That's true." She turned to me. "I apologize, my dear. Seems this trip will take more than an hour of your time."

"No regrets are necessary, Mother. I'm looking forward to the visit."

"Thank you for understanding," she offered with a soft smile. "Now, I do want to caution you about conversing with the residents. We don't inquire as to their past histories. They are just that. In the past. By the time we arrive, they will have finished their daily devotions. We hold those after they break their fast, and then they're released to the classrooms where they spend the next 3 hours."

"What do they do in the afternoons?"

"Well, idle hands being the devil's tools, they're each assigned a task. It could be mopping and cleaning, laundry, helping with the kitchen, tending to the garden or the library."

"They have a library?"

The corners of her lips lifted. "That's my contribution. You see, many have never left London, much less England. It helps them see what other worlds are out there."

Traffic finally eased, and in no time at all we arrived at Magdalen House where we were welcomed by a young woman about my age. Very pretty with dark hair and brown eyes. Going by her wide smile, she was a merry soul.

"This is Mrs. Pennyworth," Mother trilled. "She's one of our successes."

She appeared to be with child and far along at that, something I didn't anticipate. "I . . . see."

Mrs. Pennyworth bit back a smile. "Your expression, Miss Worthington. It's priceless."

Goodness! Had I been that transparent?

"Mrs. Pennyworth is married, dear," Mother explained, "to the pastor who tends to our flock."

The young woman placed a hand on her bulging stomach. "Henry is his name, and he's the dearest man that ever lived."

Clearly, she adored her husband.

A gentleman cleared the doorway and came out to greet us. Of middling height, chestnut haired, not very prepossessing at all, but his eyes brimmed over with love as they lit on Mrs. Pennyworth. Had to be the pastor.

"Henry, Mrs. Worthington has come to visit us, and she brought her daughter with her. Isn't that wonderful?"

"It is, my dear. Mrs. Worthington, Miss Worthington." He bowed his head. "A pleasure to welcome you to Magdalen House."

"I brought Kitty so she could see the splendid job you're doing."

"I can only take a small piece of the credit. The Magdalen House staff does most of the work." He turned to his wife. "Sorry, dear, but I must leave. A couple is seeking counseling before marriage. Ladies," he acknowledged us once more and, after a quick kiss to his wife's cheek, he was gone.

"I must absent myself as well, Mrs. Pennyworth," Mother said, "as there's something I need to discuss with Matron. Do you mind if I leave Kitty in your capable hands?"

"Of course not."

Mother glanced a caution at me. "Remember what I said, dear."

"I will."

And off she disappeared into the bowels of the house.

"So, I gather you've come for the grand tour, Miss Worthington?" Mrs. Pennyworth asked with a grin.

"Yes, please."

"We'll start with the parlor, shall we?"

"Whatever you think is best," I readily agreed.

The parlor was small, but it was magnificently furnished with pieces from the Georgian period which I'd seen before.

"The Duke of Wynchcombe and his sister donated these. Apparently, they are refurbishing their home."

No wonder they looked familiar.

"It's lovely."

"This is where we first meet the ladies who come to us."

Ladies. She did not refer to them as fallen women either. Mother had once explained they were referred to as such to remind them of the status they could achieve. A simple thing, but it made a world of difference to the residents.

Mrs. Pennyworth's hand went to the small of her back. "I apologize, but do you think we could sit for a moment? I easily tire these days."

"Of course. Whatever you need."

After we'd taken repose on two sumptuous sofas, I asked, "Is there a welcome process for the ladies?"

"There is. Before they are admitted, they are examined by a physician. It may seem harsh, but we must maintain high health standards. We cannot allow anyone who's suffering from an illness to join our community."

"Yes, of course. What happens if they're sick?"

"If the illness is one that can be treated, we refer them to the Sisters of Mercy. Once they're given a clean bill of health, we admit them. If the illness cannot be remedied, we find a place where they can live out their lives." A shadow passed over her eyes. "The streets can be really cruel, Miss Worthington."

Is that where she'd come from? She was so young, it seemed impossible. And yet, I knew girls as young as twelve years of age roamed the streets of the city, earning whatever coin they could, whichever way they could.

"What happens once the ladies are admitted to Magdalen House?"

"We assess their level of education and determine if they've received any training."

"Such as?"

"Households, factories, farms—"

"Farms?"

She nodded. "Many young ladies come to London hoping for a better life only to find themselves caught in horrible situations." She smiled to lighten the moment. "Farm ladies make excellent cooks. No one knows how to snap a chicken's neck like a farm girl. And need I say they're a dab hand at growing vegetables? We eat very well in this house because of them, Miss Worthington."

"I can imagine, Mrs. Pennyworth."

"Please call me Bumble. Mrs. Pennyworth is such a mouthful."

"Only if you call me Kitty."

"Be glad to, Kitty."

"Bumble. I bet there's a story to that."

"It's what my mam used to call me. I was always buzzing about like a bumble bee." She tilted her head as she considered me. "Families love to give nicknames to children. We may have that in common as I suspect Kitty is not your proper name."

"You're right. It's Catherine."

"Kitty suits you. But I suspect you'll grow into Catherine someday. Oomph." Her mouth formed an "O" as her hand flew to her belly.

"Anything wrong?"

"The baby kicked. That's all." She rubbed her stomach. "I hope it's a girl, so I can name her after my mam." Her eyes grew misty-eyed. "I wish she were here."

"What was her name?"

"Ophelia. A troupe of traveling players came to her mam's village one summer and put on a play. *Hamlet*, I believe. She fell in love with the name."

As soon as she said the name, everything clicked into place. "I know I'm not supposed to ask about your particulars, but do you mayhap come from Devon?"

Her gaze turned wary. "How did you know?"

"I didn't until now. Is your first name Eleanor?"

Panic raced across her face. "He sent you to find me, didn't he? I won't go back. I'll never go back." She jumped up and, clutching her belly, made an unwieldy run for the door.

I stopped her before she could leave. Heaven only knew where she would go. "No one sent me."

She speared me with a glance. "Vow on everything that's holy that you have nothing to do with him."

"Lord Wakefield is dead, Bumble. Somebody killed him. It was in all the papers."

Her eyes grew wide. "Truly?"

"Truly. Now come and sit down again. It won't do your baby any good for you to be upset." Taking her arm, I helped her back to her seat.

"How do you know my name?"

"From your grandfather. He's been looking for you."

She grew angry again. "I don't want to see him. He abandoned my mother. Kicked her out in the street when she found herself pregnant with me."

"Who told you that?"

"My father."

"What did your mam say?"

"Nothing. She was too scared of him to say much. After she died, he ordered me to leave. He couldn't take care of me anymore."

"He lied to you, Bumble. Your grandfather is a good and caring man. It will be his greatest joy to know you are alive."

"Really?" A light of hope glowed in her eyes.

"Absolutely." That's when I noticed she was shaking. Well, it was no wonder with everything that had transpired. The surge of emotion couldn't possibly be good for her or the baby. I joined her on the sofa and put my arm around her. It took her a few minutes to stop trembling.

"Better?" I asked.

"Yes, thank you."

"Where did you go after your father asked you to leave?"

"My mam had worked for the Morgans, so I thought it best to go to them. But they didn't have anything available. Miss Morgan sent me to Wakefield Hall as they needed help." Her expression turned stormy. "If I knew what would happen, I never would have gone there."

I covered her hands with my own to lend her comfort. "No need to think about that anymore. You're safe, and you're loved."

"Yes, my Henry loves me, that he does. He's a good man."

"I saw that he was." We exchanged smiles. "If you don't mind my asking, where did you go after you left Wakefield House in London?"

"I walked the streets looking for a place to sleep, food to eat. After a week, the little money I'd saved ran out. I was so hungry I stole a loaf of bread." A small grin blossomed across her lips. "That's where my Henry found me. He paid for the food, brought me to Magdalen House. Been here ever since."

"Your grandfather has been looking for you over a year. I wonder why he never found you. I imagine this would have been one of the places he would have looked."

"I didn't give them my true name. I was afraid that devil would come looking for me. I told them I went by Bumble Bee." She grew serious. "I'd like to meet my grandfather, Miss, before the babe is born."

"Once he finds out you're here, wild horses couldn't keep him away. Would you like to hear more about him?"

"If you don't mind."

"His name is Owen Clapham, and he was an inspector at Scotland Yard." I told her all about her grandfather. By the end of my recitation, she'd achieved a measure of peace.

"Miss Worthington."

"Kitty, remember."

"There's something I need to tell you."

"If it's about your past, there's no need, Bumble."

She shook her head. "It's not about me. It's about Lord Wakefield and what he was up to."

"I'm listening."

CHAPTER THIRTY

REVELATIONS

*N*O SOONER DID WE ARRIVE HOME than I telephoned Owen Clapham. When he did not answer, I sent a footman with a note asking him to call on me as I had an urgent matter to discuss. I then notified Miss Morgan that something had come up, and I would need to postpone my visit until the next day. Last but not least, I contacted Inspector Crawford and told him what Bumble had said.

"And she has proof of this?"

"She overheard them planning the entire scheme. At first, she couldn't make heads or tails of what it was all about. But when cocaine was mentioned, it became clear she needed to contact the authorities. Apparently, a friend from Devon had died from taking too much of the drug. She grabbed the signed documents from his desk and hid in the scullery as she often did. Unfortunately, this time he found her. After she stabbed him in the arm, she fled."

"Why didn't she go to the police?"

"She was afraid she'd be thrown in jail. After all, she'd just injured an earl."

"Does she still have the documents?"

"Yes. She kept them as protection in case he ever came after her."

"We have to obtain them."

I gave him her directions. "I told her to expect you tonight. Once word gets out, she will be in danger. She'll need to be taken to a secure place."

"Don't worry. I'll handle it."

"Please let me know once that's taken care of. I won't rest easy until she's safe."

"I'll call in person. And Catherine? You've done well."

Pleasure blossomed within me from his praise. "Thank you, Inspector."

It wasn't until late in the afternoon that Owen Clapham arrived.

"Miss Worthington, I apologize for the delay. I came as soon as I read your note. Did you discover something to aid the investigation?"

"In a roundabout way. Are you familiar with Magdalen House?"

"Yes. They rehabilitate women who've fallen down on their luck."

An excellent way to describe them.

"It's one of the charities the Ladies Benevolent Society sponsors."

"Bless them for doing so."

"Yes, indeed. This morning Mother asked me to accompany her there. She wanted me to see the work they're doing."

He nodded.

"I met the pastor's wife there. Mrs. Pennyworth, a lovely

young lady. She's expecting her first child. She hopes it's a girl so she can name her after her mother."

He must have sensed something because he suddenly grew alert. "And what is her mother's name?"

"Ophelia. She's your granddaughter, Mister Clapham."

His face lost all color as he rushed to his feet. "I have to see her."

"You most certainly will. But not tonight. She needs time to explain it to her husband. You see, she never told him who she was."

"She's me granddaughter, that's who she is. My Ophelia's girl," he said out of breath.

"There is an additional complication, Mister Clapham."

"What sort of complication?"

"She's a witness."

"To what?"

"Lord Wakefield's involvement with the shipping consortium."

"If they find out, she will be in danger."

"That's why I called Inspector Crawford. He's taking her somewhere safe. He'll have someone guarding her until this matter is resolved."

"That won't do her any good." He threaded a jerky hand through his salt and pepper hair. "There's a leak at the Yard."

"I'm sure it will be someone he trusts."

There was a knock on the drawing room door followed by Carlton's entrance. "My apologies for interrupting, Miss Worthington, but supper's served." He nodded to the retired inspector. "Mrs. Worthington has extended an invitation to Mister Clapham if he'd care to join the family."

"Thank you, Carlton." I tossed him a look which he correctly interpreted as his clue to leave.

Mister Clapham shook his head. "I should go."

"Directly to Magdalen House?" I asked Mister Clapham.

He had the grace to look chagrined.

"That's a horrible notion. They have no idea about Bumble's past. It's bound to cause an uproar. Besides, she's not there or at her home. Inspector Crawford would have already taken her to a sanctuary." When he still appeared unsure, I said, "He will call later tonight. Wouldn't you like to hear the news firsthand?"

"Yes," he choked out.

I came to my feet. "Then why don't you escort me to supper?"

Finally giving in, he took my extended elbow, and together we made our way to the dining room.

Of course, I'd told Mother about Bumble, and I'm sure she'd shared it with Father. But there were footmen around and Carlton, of course, so we couldn't discuss what was uppermost in our minds. We'd barely finished our puddings when Inspector Crawford was announced. He'd been shown into the drawing room.

Mother, as always, was ever mindful of the proprieties. "Would you like tea, Inspector? Or maybe something to eat?"

"No, thank you, ma'am. I have but a few minutes before I must return to my duties."

"I shall leave you to it, then."

She walked out, leaving only Mister Clapham and me in the room with Inspector Crawford.

"Well, man, what happened?" Mister Clapham asked.

"I talked to Mrs. Pennyworth. She indeed has information about the shipping consortium which she learned during her employment at Wakefield House. Apparently, certain people kept calling on Wakefield. A strange occurrence for he rarely entertained at home."

"Lady Wakefield remarked on that as well," I said.

"At first Mrs. Pennyworth—Miss Tibbett, I should say, for she wasn't married then—did not think much of it. But then she heard raised voices. A proper shouting match, she said. Curious, she hid in a small side room attached to the study where she could listen without being seen. The meetings continued two and three times a week during which she learned every detail about their operation and the importation of cocaine. She was horrified about what they meant to do. A friend of hers from Devon had died from overuse of the drug. That's when she vowed to stop them any way she could. Given she was barely sixteen, it is quite amazing she possessed such a strong moral fiber."

"Me daughter would have taught her well." Tears shimmered in the retired inspector's eyes.

"She most certainly did, Mister Clapham."

"Go on, Inspector Crawford," I urged.

"The ones who devised the plan for the shipping consortium needed someone to lend legitimacy to their business. That's where Wakefield came in. But he wasn't willing to do it without appropriate compensation. They did not want to pay him what he thought he was worth. After much back and forth, an agreement was reached. Papers were drawn up and properly signed. Knowing she would need proof to present to the authorities, Miss Tibbett took them first chance she got. But after Wakefield caught up to her in the scullery and she stabbed him, she knew she couldn't follow through with her plan. More than likely, she would have been tossed in jail for attacking an aristocrat. So, she fled to keep that from happening. All these years, she kept the papers. If he ever tracked her down, she would use them as leverage."

"Where is she?" Mister Clapham asked, his gaze firmly fixed on Inspector Crawford.

"In a safe place."

"Where?"

"I'm sorry, but I can't reveal her location. Not until this matter's settled."

"You think I would hurt a hair on her head? If a lady weren't present, I'd give you what for, Inspector or not."

"I'm sure that's not what he meant, Mister Clapham," I said in an attempt to calm him down.

"It wasn't," Inspector Crawford assured him. "There are people who know of your association with the Newcastle investigation. If I were to tell you where she is, you would lead them right to her."

"How do you know you weren't followed to her home?" Mister Clapham asked.

"I disguised myself before meeting up with someone I trust. Together, we visited her. No one but him and me, the three of us here, Miss Worthington's parents, and, of course, Pastor Pennyworth know who she really is." He breathed out a sigh. "After the true head of the consortium and his associates are apprehended, you'll be able to see her. It should only take a day or two."

"You know who the head of the consortium is?" I asked. Bumble had refused to tell me, insisting she would only provide that information to the proper authorities.

"I do. But it's not enough. The Yard is setting a trap. If things go the way we hope, we'll have him."

"It is a him then?"

"Most assuredly."

"I want in on it, the trap," Mister Clapham barked out.

"I'm sorry, Mister Clapham. I wish I could allow it, but it's beyond my power to grant that to you." After a pause, he said, "Why don't you go home? I promise to bring you news as soon as I can."

The retired inspector let out a long-suffering sigh. "It goes against the grain to do nothing."

"Your daughter would like her to be safe, wouldn't she?" I asked.

He nodded.

"Then do it for her."

"You're the devil, you are," he retorted.

"Clapham! That's no way to talk to a lady."

Mister Clapham's face flushed bright red. "Begging your pardon, Miss."

I pressed his hands. "I understand. If it were a loved one of mine, I would feel the same. But there's nothing you can do. Go home, sir, and try to get some sleep. It will be over soon."

I thought he'd offer further argument, but with one last nod, he walked out, his shoulders heavy with worry.

Once he'd gone, I voiced the question that was uppermost in my mind, "Is she truly in a safe place?"

"She is." He fixed a steady gaze on me. "I want you to remain safe as well."

I wrinkled my brow, confused as to what he meant. "I am."

"What about tomorrow? And the day after that?"

I gazed away from him.

But he captured my chin and turned me back. "You are very dear to me, Catherine. I would hate to see you hurt. Would you consider remaining at home until things are settled?"

"You know I can't, not when Newcastle's trial date is growing near. We need to discover the truth."

He slowly let go of me. "You will be careful?"

"I'm always careful."

He laughed. "We must have different understandings of that word." When the clock on the mantle suddenly chimed the hour, all his levity fled. "I must go. There's much to do."

"Thank you for coming to tell us."

He cradled my face in his hand, brushed a thumb across my cheek. "You are most welcome, dear Catherine." And then with one last look, he was gone.

Trembling from his touch, from everything that had just transpired, I collapsed on the couch. It took a minute, maybe longer, to regain control of my senses and think through what he'd said. I wanted to feel comfortable with the conclusion he'd reached about the head of the consortium. But something in my bones told me he was wrong.

CHAPTER THIRTY-ONE

VISIT WITH ABIGAIL MORGAN

"*I*'M SORRY ARCHIE COULDN'T BE HERE TO MEET YOU," Miss Morgan said. "He's presenting a paper before the Institution of Mechanical Engineers about an improvement to that invention of his."

"Sounds fascinating."

A smirk shaped her lips. "You don't need to be polite, Miss Worthington. It's deadly boring."

Although I agreed with her, any response would be inappropriate, so I chose to ignore her remark. "May I introduce Lady Lily Dalrymple, the Duke of Wynchcombe's sister." I'd intended to visit Abigail Morgan on my own for I did not know what the outcome of our discussion would be. But Lily had arrived at Worthington House eager to accompany me, and I hadn't had the heart to deny her.

"It's such a pleasure to meet you, Lady Lily," Miss Morgan said, her toadying grimace in full display. "I've been wanting to do so for ages."

"The pleasure is all mine, I assure you," Lily responded with a smile.

I marveled how she'd emerged from her lonely childhood with such a sunny disposition. You would have thought she would have grown bitter with life. But that was Lily all over, politeness combined with grace.

"What a divine dress you're wearing. Please tell me the name of your modiste. I simply must have one like it."

Heavens! Miss Morgan was a sycophant of the worst sort.

"Angelique's," Lily graciously responded.

As busy as Angelique was, I doubted she'd be able to accommodate Miss Morgan, but she was certainly welcome to try.

A foghorn sounded in the distance.

Lily glanced toward the sound, a surprised look on her face. "What is that?"

"A tugboat, I imagine. Situated as close as you are to the Thames, Miss Morgan, that must be a normal occurrence."

"Oh, la, Miss Worthington. I'm much too busy to notice." A cackling laughter burst out of her, intended no doubt to disguise her true feelings. But her narrowed gaze revealed she resented my bringing it up.

I doubted she was speaking the truth. As her home was situated in the northern part of Lambeth which bordered the Thames, I didn't see how she could miss them.

"Please have some tea. I managed to obtain some Darjeeling. From India, don't you know?" she said, preening.

The devil in me decided to test her. "You must have easy access to it, seeing how the ships dock nearby." She could deny it as much as she wished, but the evidence was in full display. All one needed to do was look out one of the upper windows to see cargo boats, barges, and what have you sailing on the river.

A tight smile shaped her lips. "The stores do that. They inform me when a new shipment arrives."

"And one did?"

"Just yesterday. We also have coffee if you prefer. From Colombia. They grow the best beans."

That was not the only thing they grew. "That would be lovely if it would not be too much trouble." I was not just saying that. When given a choice, I opted for coffee over tea.

"You'll excuse me then while I ask the kitchen wench to brew some."

Wench? A rather impolite word for a maid.

It took but a few minutes for Miss Morgan to return. "It shouldn't take long. In the meantime, what can I do for you, Miss Worthington?"

She wanted our visit to be done with as quickly as possible. I did not have to search for the reason. My comments had grated her nerves.

"After our last conversation, I visited Devon."

Her gaze widened. "Did you, really?" Clearly, I'd surprised her.

"Yes, I talked to Mrs. Saunders, the former housekeeper at Wakefield Hall. When I asked her about Eleanor Tibbett, she said the young woman had disappeared. She believed she'd simply walked out. But you told me, she'd hanged herself."

"Oh, no," Lily cried in dismay.

I reached out and covered her clenched hands. "It's fine, dear."

"But—"

"Trust me." I couldn't say more than that without Abigail Morgan sensing I knew more than I was letting on.

Lily bit down on her lip and nodded, seemingly accepting my advice.

Refocusing on our hostess, I asked, "How do you explain the discrepancy?"

Miss Morgan tossed her head in dismissal. "Easily. Mrs. Saunders resides in Devon. She would not know what happened in London."

"Except that the Wakefield Hall cook returned to Devon. Apparently, she'd obtained a position with a family who was leaving for the West Indies and wanted to say goodbye to her old friends. She did not mention anything about Miss Tibbett dying. So, I wonder how your account came to be." Much as I wanted to do so, I couldn't come right out and call her a liar.

Before she could answer, there was a knock on the drawing room door, followed by the maid carrying a tray, a pot, cups, and saucers. With a clatter, she set everything on the table and left.

Ignoring the maid's lack of ability, Miss Morgan presented me with a cup filled with the brew. When she offered cream and sugar, I turned them down as I preferred my coffee black.

"Ooh, that is so fragrant," Lily said.

"Coffee has a rather enticing aroma, doesn't it, Lady Lily?" Miss Morgan said. "Strong enough to disguise other scents."

What an odd comment.

"May I have some, please?" Lily asked. "I admit I've been curious."

"Of course." Miss Morgan started to pour her a cup but only succeeded in spilling the liquid all over the tray. "Oh, I'm so sorry. How very clumsy of me. And now there's no more. I'll ask the wench to brew another pot. If you will excuse me."

"You didn't get it on you, did you, Lily?" I asked as soon as Miss Morgan stepped out of the room. "I would hate to have your lovely frock ruined."

"Thankfully, it missed me," she said with that bright

expression of hers.

"Here, have mine." I held out the cup to her. "I haven't sipped from it. I can wait."

She accepted it with reluctance. "Are you certain?"

"Of course, dear. Go on. Drink it before it gets cold."

She took a sip and scrunched her face. "It's bitter."

"Add milk and sugar."

She did and took another sip. "Much better. I can see why you like it so."

Miss Morgan returned, a repentant look on her face. "I do apologize, but we seem to be out of coffee beans. Archie loves it, you see. I'll need to order some more."

"No need to apologize, Miss Morgan. It's perfectly understandable. Could we return to my inquiry?"

"Of course."

"How did you come to believe Eleanor Tibbett had died?"

"I must have gotten my story wrong, somehow." She wasn't in the least bit sorry. Just the opposite. Triumph was written all over her face. She was expecting something to happen. Something which would give her the upper hand.

And then, heaven help me, something did.

"Kitty," Lily said in a trembling voice. "I don't feel well."

My gaze jerked to her. Her face had grown deathly pale, her pupils had become enlarged. Not only that, but she was shivering. "Dearest, what's wrong?"

"I'm going to be sick." And then she was, all over the carpet. Gazing at me with dismay, she said, "I shouldn't have drunk the coffee."

"*She* drank it?" Miss Morgan spit out, teeth bared. "It should have been you." Her eyes blazed with hate.

Too late I realized what a dangerous creature she was. "What was in it? What did you put in the coffee?" But she didn't have to say. I knew.

Cocaine. She'd laced the brew with cocaine.

CHAPTER THIRTY-TWO

CONSEQUENCES AND REGRETS

J YELLED FOR THE ONLY PERSON I could trust —the butler. "Mister Brougham. Come quick. I need your help."

He rushed into the room and took one look at the scene.

By this point, Lily was shivering, babbling, not making any sense.

He wasted no time in asking, "What do you wish me to do, Miss Worthington?"

"Help Lady Lily to the motorcar outside." Thank heaven I'd asked Neville to drive us today.

When he tried to take Lily's arm, she fought him off. "Don't touch me, you wicked man."

"Pay no attention to her, Mister Brougham. Do what you must."

Somehow, he managed to subdue her long enough to pick her up. I turned to follow them, but before I left, I grabbed the coffee cup Lily had used. We'd need it for evidence.

"You can't do that," Miss Morgan screeched.

With no time to argue, I swung a right hook to her jaw. She didn't so much as twitch when she landed on the floor.

I followed Brougham out of the house and found him trying to put an arms-flailing, legs-kicking Lily in the Rolls. But as I approached, the fight seemed to leach out of her, and she collapsed long enough for him to lay her on the back seat.

"Poor lass." He turned back to me. "What else can I do? You have only to ask."

"I punched Miss Morgan, not enough to kill her. But I did knock her unconscious. She laced the coffee with cocaine."

"Merciful heaven," Mister Brougham said, a look of horror on his face.

"You need to tie her up. Do you understand?"

He snapped into a soldier's stance. "Yes, Miss Worthington. Don't worry. I'll do her right."

"After you do, telephone Scotland Yard and ask for Inspector Robert Crawford. If he's not there, request his superior. Tell him you have the head of the Calypso Shipping Consortium in custody. He'll know what you're talking about. And then wait for them. When they arrive, ask them to analyze the contents of this cup."

Taking it from me, he said, "Yes, Miss Worthington."

"Don't leave her unsupervised. And whatever you do, don't drink or eat anything in that house."

"I'll follow your instructions to the letter."

"Thank you, Mister Brougham. I'll see that you're properly rewarded."

"No need, Miss. It's my duty."

Having done as much as I could about Abigail Morgan and the evidence, I climbed into the back of the Rolls and cradled Lily's head on my lap.

Neville gazed at me out of worried eyes. "Was Lady Lily really dosed with cocaine?"

"Afraid so, Neville. Please drive us to Doctor Crawley. He'll know what to do."

He shook his head. "I've seen this before, Miss. She needs a hospital. St. Thomas is the closest one, only a few streets away."

"I second that, Miss," the butler said.

"Take us there then. Oh, and Mister Brougham. Please let Inspector Crawford know where we're headed."

I caught his nod as we drove away.

After taking one look at Lily and hearing my explanation, the accident and emergency care staff at St. Thomas wasted no time. They placed Lily on a trolley, rolled her into a private care area, and swiftly started administering to her. I requested and was granted permission to call Doctor Crawley, our family physician. Upon hearing what had occurred, he said he was on his way. I telephoned home next. Thankfully, Mother was there along with Margaret and Sebastian. I'd barely gotten the words out, before they were rushing out the door.

Half an hour later, Doctor Crawley arrived. After checking on Lily, he said I'd done the right thing by bringing her to the hospital. "She would have never made it to my surgery."

Dear heaven. We could have lost Lily. I closed my eyes and exhaled. But I had to give credit where credit was due. "We have Neville to thank. It was his suggestion to bring her here."

He nodded. "She's not out of the woods yet. But the staff is doing as much as they can. It's in God's hands now."

"Thank you, doctor."

Mother, Margaret, and Sebastian reached the hospital not

long after him. By the time Inspector Crawford showed up two hours later, Lily was resting comfortably in a private room, with all of us gathered around her, including Ned, who'd rushed to the hospital as soon as he heard. Grief-stricken, he was by her bed gently holding her hand as if he could infuse her with his strength.

"How is she faring?" Inspector Crawford asked, concern clear on his face.

"She pulled through," I said in a quivering voice.

The tension in his body eased. "That's very good news. Is there somewhere private where we can talk?"

"The chamber next door. It's unoccupied." I'd noticed it when I'd stepped into the hallway to discuss the symptoms of cocaine addiction and subsequent withdrawals with Doctor Crawley.

As we entered the room, he closed the door behind us. "How are you doing?"

I thought to lie. Stiff upper lip and all that. But I couldn't stop the tears from rolling down my face.

In a voice filled with compassion, he whispered, "Catherine," as he gathered me into his arms. For a little while, I allowed myself the comfort of his warm embrace. But then from somewhere, I found the strength to step away. "Time and again, you warned me about the danger. But I did not heed it. This is all my fault."

His wrinkled brow disagreed. "How do you figure that? You were not the one who laced her coffee with a dangerous substance."

I glanced up at him. "Was it cocaine?"

"Our lab confirmed it. From what I hear, the drug was intended for you. You would have been the one lying on that hospital bed. If you hadn't perished first, of course."

"You're right. But that doesn't excuse my actions. I knew

Abigail Morgan was involved with the shipping consortium. I should have expected she would do such a thing. But I thought I could get her to admit it when I confronted her with her lies. Instead" —I choked back a tear— "poor Lily paid the price for my arrogance."

"We all make mistakes, Catherine. Look at me. I believed her brother was the head of the shipping consortium, simply because it was his signature on the documents."

"It wasn't him, though. It was her."

Ever so gently, he brushed away the moisture from my cheeks. "How did you know?"

"He seems only interested in his engineering endeavors. She, however, is eager to move among the higher echelons of society. As she has neither class nor a title, she needs money to do so. I suspect his invention may have earned some funds, but not as much as she needed."

"You're right. It was enough to lead a comfortable life, but no more. But that's all about to change. His latest creation promises to burn coal more efficiently, thus reducing a steamship's travel time."

"Which will bring goods to markets faster," I said. "And increase the number of trips, thus earning a higher profit."

"Precisely," Inspector Crawford said.

"But that's all in the future, and her ambition to gain entrance into society was borne several years ago."

"Apparently so," he said. "That's when she devised the scheme to import agricultural goods from South America. To do that, she needed to form a consortium to raise funds."

"But, as a woman, she was not allowed to sign legal documents," I said.

"No, she was not. So, she convinced her brother to become the titular owner by promising him riches to develop his inventions. Like a fool, he signed every paper she put in front of him."

"Then it was a matter of finding some avaricious lord high up in society to become the consortium's public face. That's where Lord Wakefield came in. Once he was brought onboard, he persuaded others to invest." At least that was my guess, for I had no actual knowledge of what had occurred.

But Inspector Crawford did. "Exactly. When the importation of cocaine was made illegal, the consortium switched from food products to mostly cocaine. That's when the serious money started to pour in."

"According to Ned, there weren't sufficient goods to justify the amount they were earning," I said. "You'd think they would have lied about that."

"They could tamper with the numbers in the company's books but couldn't do so in a bank account. The one mistake she made was a failure to account for a bank manager who couldn't be bribed. He was the one who alerted Scotland Yard to what was happening. That was two years ago. We've been keeping track ever since."

"But how did they distribute the money? Ned hasn't been able to find out."

"After the funds were deposited in the consortium's bank account, they were disbursed to several shadow companies they'd created. The structure was so convoluted it took forever to determine the labyrinth path. Somewhere along the way, the investors were paid. They never questioned the largesse. As long as they received a lucrative rate of return, they didn't care about the origin of their ill-gotten gains. The bulk of the money, however, ended up in Archibald Morgan's account. But he didn't manage it, his sister did. And she made sure he never knew exactly how much money was there."

"Unbelievable. How did you learn all this?"

"We apprehended Archibald Morgan at the Institution of Mechanical Engineers, where he was presenting a lecture about his latest invention. When we explained what had been going on, he was dumb stricken. He had no idea what his sister had been doing. Of course, that won't help him. He's the one on the hook."

"Wait. Are you saying he'll be held responsible for the drug trafficking?"

"Unless she confesses which, frankly, I don't see her doing. And, of course, we'll have to find proof they're importing cocaine. Without evidence, we can't charge him or anyone else."

"But what about all the money they earned? Isn't that proof?"

"Circumstantial evidence at best."

"But she'll be charged with poisoning Lily, won't she?"

"She claims she knows nothing about it and blamed the kitchen maid. Well, what little I could understand when she spoke." He bit back a grin. "You practically dislocated her jaw."

"Really? I didn't hit her *that* hard."

"People often underestimate their own strength in a fight." He gently cradled my right hand, its bruised knuckles clearly visible. "Have you had that seen to?"

I hitched up my chin. "There were more pressing matters to attend to, Inspector."

"I'll take you down to emergency care. They'll make sure you didn't break any bones."

"If I had, I wouldn't be standing here." But that was the extent of my protestations. In truth, my hand was aching.

Emergency care determined the damage was minor in nature, although my hand was bound to hurt until it healed. To prevent aggravating the injury, they advised I have it bandaged. I sorely protested the suggestion for I needed my right hand.

But I caved in when the inspector threatened to alert Mother. "You don't play fair, sir."

"Not when it comes to your well-being, I don't. Now let's return you to Lady Lily's room so you can rejoin your family and practice being a good girl."

I gritted my teeth. "Like a dog?"

"Like a young lady who deserves a respite."

But as we stepped out of the examining room, a very young police officer with barely any fuzz to his face rushed up to Inspector Crawford. "Sir, she's escaped."

Inspector Crawford came to a screeching halt. "Miss Morgan?"

"Yes, sir."

Anger poured out of the inspector. "How could you allow such a thing to happen?"

The police officer's face flushed bright red with embarrassment. "She asked me to fetch her a glass of water. When I came back, she was gone."

Inspector Crawford cursed softly under his breath.

Minutes later, we discovered how Abigail Morgan managed to escape. A nurse with lacerations to her arms who was being tended in another examining area explained, "When I arrived with her medication, she attacked me with a scalpel."

"So, you weren't able to administer it?"

"No, sir. She's going to be suffering mightily if she doesn't get it."

Well, that was rather stupid of Miss Morgan to attack her nurse before she'd been given the pain remedy. But then she probably thought the young police officer would soon return and she'd have no other opportunity to escape.

"We'll need to organize a search team," Inspector Crawford said. "And find her before she hurts anyone else."

"I'm coming with you," I said.

Grabbing my shoulders, he turned me to him. "No. You're not. You're staying right here. I'm serious, Catherine."

He thought he had the upper hand, but he didn't. I had an ace up my sleeve. "I know where she's going, Inspector. If you don't allow me to accompany you, I'll travel there myself."

CHAPTER THIRTY-THREE

KITTY AND INSPECTOR CRAWFORD INVESTIGATE

"*H*OW DID YOU KNOW where she was going?" Inspector Crawford asked on the way to the most likely place Miss Morgan would go.

"I read the shipping notices in the *Morning Post*, Inspector. This morning's edition reported one of the Calypso shipping consortium's ships, *The Sea Nymph*, was docked at Billingsgate."

"And how did you learn the names of the ships?"

"Ned. He was very thorough in his research. According to the newspaper, *The Sea Nymph* docked yesterday carrying cargo from South America. Colombia to be exact." Scotland Yard already knew that, of course.

His arched brow spoke volumes, but he remained silent the rest of our trip.

We arrived at Billingsgate to find a contingent of policemen already there. Not a surprise. Before we left the hospital, the inspector telephoned Scotland Yard and requested a search team join us at this location. They were standing in a group, probably awaiting further orders.

Inspector Crawford approached one wearing a uniform with a sergeant's insignia. "Sergeant Fellow, is it not?"

"At your service, sir."

"Have you had time to assess the situation?"

"The ship's captain will not allow us to board *The Sea Nymph*."

"I suppose he's demanding a warrant."

"Yes, sir."

"Where is he?"

"His worship's over there." Sergeant Fellow nodded toward a disreputable looking man with long, dark unkempt hair standing firm at the end of the gangplank. While an earring dangled from his right ear, a big flashy smile revealed a gold tooth. He resembled a pirate more than anything else. All he was missing was a cutlass between his teeth.

"What's his name?" the inspector asked.

"Captain Antone Jeffries."

"You can't just go aboard?" I asked.

"Not without a warrant, reasonable belief that a crime's being conducted, or in pursuit of a criminal."

I huffed in frustration "But she's there. I know she is."

The inspector veered back to the police officer. "Has anyone boarded the ship since you arrived?"

"No, sir. No one has disembarked, either. I alerted the Thames Division, sir." He pointed to the river. "As you can see, they're patrolling the waterway. No one will get anywhere near that ship if they have anything to say about it."

"Where's the chief customs inspector?"

"Right here." An official looking gentleman with mutton chop whiskers and salt and pepper hair stepped forward. "Sheldon Whitehouse at your service."

"Detective Inspector Robert Crawford." They shook hands. "Has the cargo been offloaded?

"This morning."

"What was it?"

"Wheat, sugar, and coffee."

A misty recollection rose from the depths of my mind. Miss Morgan had remarked how the aroma of coffee disguised other scents. At the time, it'd seemed a rather odd thing for her to say. With everything that had happened, I'd forgotten about it. Until now.

"Inspector Crawford," I said recapturing his attention. "While we were at Miss Morgan's house, she mentioned that coffee is fragrant enough to camouflage other odors. At the time, I took it to mean other food items. But I think she meant something quite different."

Lines furrowed his brow. "Such as?"

"What if they're hiding the cocaine in the sacks of coffee beans?"

Inspector Crawford grew suddenly alert. "Well, there's a thought. Did you inspect the bags of coffee, Mister Whitehouse?"

"Yes, sir. Not every bag, of course. We don't have enough men for that. But enough. The cargo passed inspection. We were in the process of releasing it when your men showed up."

"Don't release it."

The customs officer went ramrod straight. "I'll need a good reason to do that, Inspector."

"You heard Miss Worthington. They could be hiding cocaine among the coffee beans."

Mister Whitehouse sniffed at the suggestion. "Never heard of such a thing,"

Ignoring him, Inspector Crawford said, "We'll need to inspect every burlap sack."

Alarm rode over Mister Whitehouse's face. "That will take quite some time, sir. There are at least a thousand of them. And we have another ship docking in the morrow. It simply can't be done."

"Then you better notify other inspectors that they're needed."

"With due respect, Inspector, you have no authority here without a warrant."

"May I make a suggestion?" I asked.

"Will it stop you if I say no?" Inspector Crawford replied with a grin.

Which I returned. "Of course not. I'd like to bring in Sir Winston."

Inspector Crawford frowned. "Sir Winston? Your dog?"

"He has the true nose of a hound. If we provide a small amount of cocaine for him to smell, we can ask him to go fetch. If there's cocaine in those burlap sacks, he'll find it."

"Of all the ludicrous notions!" A red-faced Mister White-house was growing apoplectic.

"How do you know he'll detect the odor of cocaine?" Inspector Crawford asked.

"I don't. But he can smell sausages and bacon a mile away. Cook must well and truly hide them from him."

"I suppose it can't hurt," Inspector Crawford said. "I'll need to get official approval, though."

"While you handle that matter, I'll go get him. Can you ask a police officer to chauffeur me?"

"Of course."

Once I arrived home and made my needs known, Betsy insisted on accompanying me. Not only was it growing dark, and I needed a chaperone, she argued, but she was better suited to handling Sir Winston. And, of course, my hand was bandaged. If Sir Winston took it into his head to run away, I couldn't have stopped him. I had no choice but to agree. Sporting a broad smile, she handed off child minding duties to Agnes and climbed aboard the police car with Sir Winston and me. I really should have remembered how much she adored watching the police at work. At Scotland Yard, she regularly chatted up the police sergeant stationed at the front desk. This would seem like a dream come true for her.

Upon our arrival at Billingsgate, Sir Winston was given a small amount of cocaine to sniff, securely wrapped so he wouldn't accidentally inhale it. Once he'd done so, Betsy led him on his leash to the mountains of burlap sacks filled with coffee beans and told him to "Go fetch." Dawdling all the way, he wandered through the customs warehouse, stopping here and there for a sniff. Half an hour into it, I thought my suggestion a failure when he suddenly stopped, planted his bum on the ground, and howled for all he was worth.

When the customs officer slashed through the burlap sack, a slew of coffee beans spilled over the ground. But tucked among them was another smaller sack. When opened, little packets filled with white powder streamed out.

"Well, I'll be," Mister Whitehouse said, scratching his head. "That dog deserves a medal."

Scotland Yard had set up a makeshift lab to check the substance if one was to be found. It took no time to determine the white powder was indeed cocaine.

Now that he had definite proof, Mister Whitehouse turned to the dozen or so customs inspectors that had been summoned and ordered, "Search every sack. Be careful, though. Best wrap a scarf around your mouth and nose. That stuff can be deadly."

Inspector Crawford's triumphant gaze found me. "Now we have probable cause to board the ship." The judge who'd been standing by provided his approval, and soon the police were swarming the ship.

A wide-eyed Betsy couldn't contain her excitement as she was bouncing on her feet. "Oh, miss, did you ever?"

"Woof!" A tail-wagging Sir Winston seemed to agree.

"Such a good boy you are," I said.

"Woof! Woof!"

"This is all due to you," Inspector Crawford said with a wide grin. "How can you be so intelligent?"

"Mother and Father. Mostly Mother, though. She notices everything."

A cry went up from the ship.

"Excuse me. I must attend to that."

"Of course."

With the mad circus atmosphere around us, I didn't hear Father until he was practically upon Betsy and me.

"Kitty!"

"Father!"

"Thank heaven I found you. Your mother is worried sick about you. What on earth is going on, and what is Sir Winston doing here?"

I filled him in on everything we'd accomplished, concluding with "Sir Winston is a hero, Father. He found the drugs."

In a tone filled with wonder, he said, "I always knew he had it in him. Extra sausages for you tonight, my boy."

Sir Winston barked with joy.

"He's already a chunk, Father." Never mind what they did to his digestive system. He could positively clear a room when he emitted malodorous airs.

But Father brushed aside my objection. "A hero deserves a reward. Nothing like extra sausages. Right, boy?"

Sir Winston woofed madly again.

"The customs official mentioned a medal for him."

"Did he really?" Father's chest puffed out with pride. You'd think he'd sired Sir Winston himself. "Well, I suppose only time will tell. In the meantime, we should head home before your mother sends out the cavalry."

"They're already here, Father." I pointed to the new squad of policemen who'd just arrived. They were needed as a crowd had begun to gather around the docks. As word spread about the drugs that had been discovered, even more people were bound to arrive. The police would not only manage the crowd but safeguard the evidence. I could only imagine what the cocaine contained in those burlap sacks were worth.

I would have loved to remain to find out if Miss Morgan was aboard the ship. But Mother's worry took precedence over my curiosity. Besides, whatever the result of the search, Inspector Crawford would report to Worthington House to inform us. I left word with one of the police officers that Father was escorting me home. He promised to relay the message to the inspector.

We arrived at Worthington House to find Mother and Margaret waiting anxiously for our return. "Oh, Edward, you found her!"

"Yes, my dear." He kissed her on the cheek.

"How did you leave Lily?" I asked.

"The doctors expect a full recovery," Mother explained, a tinge of worry on her face. She wouldn't be satisfied until Lily was home safe and sound.

"Thank heaven," I said, breathing a sigh of relief. If Neville hadn't gotten us to the hospital as quickly as he had, we could have lost her. "Where are Sebastian and Ned?" I asked. They were nowhere to be seen.

"They remained at the hospital. Sebastian commandeered the room next to hers so one of them can watch over Lily while the other one gets some rest."

"Hospital staff found it hard to say no to a duke," Margaret explained.

"I can imagine."

"Did you locate Miss Morgan?" she asked.

I shook my head. "They were still searching the ship when I left. But we discovered the cocaine."

"Where?" Margaret asked.

"Hidden among the coffee beans."

"Well, I'll be," Mother said, a look of wonder on her face.

"How did they find it?" Margaret asked.

Sir Winston barked.

Mother frowned with displeasure. "Does that dog have to be here, Edward?"

Father bit back a smile. "Shall I tell her, Kitty?"

"Please do."

"Sir Winston is a hero, Mildred."

"A hero? Whatever could you mean?"

I told them the shortened version of what had occurred, ending with, "The customs official mentioned a medal."

"For a dog?" Mother said, her tone incredulous.

"I always knew he had it in him," Father said. "I'm off to the kitchen, Mildred, to get him something to eat. He's starving after all that gallivanting." And off he and Sir Winston went.

Once they'd cleared the room, Mother sighed. "I'll never hear the end of this, will I?"

"No, Mother," I said with a grin. "I don't believe you will."

CHAPTER THIRTY-FOUR

INSPECTOR CRAWFORD REPORTS

*W*E'D BARELY FINISHED SUPPER when Carlton announced Inspector Crawford. As we all were anxious to hear what he had to say, everyone proceeded to the drawing room.

"Did you find her? Was Miss Morgan aboard *The Sea Nymph?*" I asked as soon as I stepped into the space.

"Kitty! Give Inspector Crawford a chance to breathe," Mother admonished before addressing him, "Would you like something to eat or drink, Inspector? Some sandwiches perhaps."

"That's very gracious of you to offer, Mrs. Worthington. I did miss my supper."

While Mother gave Carlton the order, Father handed the inspector a tumbler that held an amber liquid. "Whisky, am I correct?"

"Yes, sir. Thank you." He drained it in one gulp. "How is Lady Lily?"

Mother provided him with the details.

"Glad she won't suffer lasting consequences."

"Let's all sit, shall we," Mother said with a smile, no doubt to give the inspector a chance to rest. It had been more than a full day for him. Although he was, as always, immaculately dressed, shadows marred the skin beneath his eyes.

Impatient to hear his response, I once again asked, "Was she aboard the ship, Inspector?"

"I'm sorry to say she wasn't, Miss Worthington."

My shoulders drooped. "Well, that is disappointing. I was so sure."

"If it's any consolation, so was I. I think that must have been her original plan. After she drugged you, she would have needed a quick escape. Living as close as she does to the docks, it would have been a few minutes' journey to *The Sea Nymph*. The cargo had already been offloaded. So, all the captain would have needed to do was pull away and maneuver the ship back up the Thames to the open sea. From there, she would have had the whole world available to her."

"She would have left her brother to take the blame for the illegal importation of cocaine?" Margaret asked.

"I don't think she counted on it being found," Inspector Crawford said. "If it weren't for your hound, we wouldn't have. And without that proof, we wouldn't have been able to accuse her brother."

"But now you do, Inspector?" Mother asked.

"Yes. There's sufficient evidence to hold him responsible."

"That's so unfair to him," Margaret said.

"His name and signature are on all the documents, as well as the bank account," Inspector Crawford responded.

"She must be found and made to confess," I said.

"Oh, we'll find her. She has nowhere to go. The ports and train stations have been alerted. If she tries to flee, she will be arrested and charged with the attempted murder of Lady Lily."

"I think she's guilty of more than that."

His brow furrowed. "What do you mean?"

"I think she killed Lord Wakefield."

Someone in the room gasped, probably Mother.

"How do you figure that?" The inspector asked.

"She was at the ball. Her name, as well as her brother's, were on the guest list."

"There's a long way between being present and committing murder."

"Did you talk to the Duchess of Wakefield at the ball, Inspector?" I asked.

"No. Only the duke."

"At the receiving line, her face wore a deadly pallor and her voice trembled. To my eyes, she appeared ill. And when she heard the news of Lord Wakefield's death, she collapsed into her husband's arms."

"I noticed the same, Inspector," Mother said.

"When Lady Emma subsequently visited Brightwell Mansion, the duchess was jittery, restless, almost manic in her movements. She seemed a totally different person." I paused for a few moments to allow my words to sink in. "At the hospital, I consulted Doctor Crawley, our family physician, about the symptoms a person addicted to cocaine would exhibit. He described almost every symptom the duchess presented."

"Good heavens!" Father said. "You think the Duchess of Brightwell is addicted to cocaine?"

"I do. And I think Lord Wakefield was supplying her with the drug." I turned back to Inspector Crawford. "You'll need to visit her and see for yourself. It wouldn't surprise me if she refused to see you. Now that her source has been cut off, she might be suffering withdrawals."

"I will." For a few seconds, he pondered what I said. "You believe Miss Morgan killed Lord Wakefield because he was supplying cocaine to the duchess?"

"I do. And that put the whole operation in peril. Because once the duchess suffered a tragic collapse, as she was bound to sooner or later, her cocaine habit would be discovered. It would only take a cursory investigation to find out who provided it to her. And once Lord Wakefield was identified as her supplier, he would have been arrested. I have no doubt in my mind he would have given up Abigail Morgan to save himself. So, he had to be killed."

A quick knock on the drawing room door interrupted followed by Carlton's entrance. "My apologies. Inspector Crawford, there's a telephone call for you from Scotland Yard."

"I left word that I would be here," Inspector Crawford said coming to his feet. He then excused himself to take the call.

"Good heavens, Kitty," Mother said after he cleared the room. "You are a wonder."

"Thank you, Mother. But as you know, I didn't do it all by myself. Margaret, Ned, Sebastian, Lily" —I choked on her name— "Lord Marlowe and Lady Emma. Owen Clapham. They all helped."

"Maybe so," Margaret said. "But it was you who put it all together. I was at the ball and didn't have a clue."

"You have other matters that concern you—Sebastian, the women's clinic, your studies. You can't do it all, Margaret. Leave something for me," I teased.

"Well, I have to say I'm impressed, Kitty," Father said. "You have a rare talent for investigation. Maybe you should nurture it."

"Edward! Don't encourage her," Mother said. "She's already thinking about becoming a lady detective."

"Is she, by Jove?" He gazed at me with the same pride he'd shown toward Sir Winston. I was indeed coming up in the world.

A rattle at the door and Inspector Crawford entered. "My apologies. I must leave. A . . . situation has arisen."

What situation, I wanted to ask, but I didn't. He wouldn't have explained.

"But you haven't eaten!" Mother said.

A rueful lift to the inspector's lips evidenced his disappointment. "I regret it, but there's no time."

"Nonsense, Inspector." She addressed our butler who'd followed the inspector into the room. "Carlton, if you could please have the food boxed up."

"I've already done so, Mrs. Worthington." He presented a corded box to the inspector. "I anticipated that duty was calling the inspector back to Scotland Yard."

"Thank you, Mister Carlton."

"You are most welcome, sir." Carlton bowed and retired.

Inspector Crawford said his goodbyes. But before he could leave, I said, "I'll walk you to the door, Inspector."

When we reached the foyer, I asked, "You didn't come in a taxi, did you?"

"No. A police car."

"You will take care?" I couldn't keep the anxiety from my voice. As I'd learned, the criminals involved with drug trafficking wouldn't think twice about hurting him.

The corner of his lips lifted. "I will."

"And return to let us know?"

A grin this time. "And there it is, your real reason for escorting me out."

"Not the only reason, inspector. I do care about you."

"Do you?" he asked softly.

All I could do was nod. I was not about to reveal the strength of my feelings for him.

CHAPTER THIRTY-FIVE

THE TRUTH EMERGES

a RESTLESS NIGHT led to my telephoning Owen Clapham the following morning. "Please come," I said, "I need your assistance."

He asked no questions. Less than an hour later, he arrived at Worthington Manor.

"Me granddaughter?" he asked, an anxious look on his face.

"She's safe, Mister Clapham." I'd heard no different, so I clung to that belief. "I want to talk to the Brightwell Mansion maid, and I need your Scotland Yard expertise to do that. Would you be willing to help?"

Visibly relieved, he said, "Whatever you need, Miss Worthington, I'm at your service."

I'd called the Duchess of Brightwell to request a meeting with Mary Seward and been referred to Mister Hughes, the duke's secretary I'd met at the ball. After informing me the duchess was indisposed, he assured me an interview with the maid would not be a problem.

Upon our arrival at Brightwell Mansion, we were welcomed by Mister Hughes who offered the duchess's apologies for not personally receiving us. Although I strongly suspected what ailed her, I made no comment other than I wished her return to good health. He then guided us to the drawing room on the first floor by way of the stairs where Lord Wakefield had been found. A shiver ran down my spine as I recalled the last time I'd been here. I suppressed the horror of that memory for I had a more important task to perform. I requested and received approval to draw a quick sketch of the area. Once that was done, we headed up the staircase to the drawing room.

After we entered it, Mister Hughes informed us tea had been requested by the duchess herself. It and the maid, Mary Seward, would be along presently. And then he bowed and quit the room.

A few minutes later the tea service arrived, followed shortly by Mary Seward. As I noted at the inquest, she was a slip of a thing, barely eighteen if that, and appeared quite nervous. But then she had a lot to answer for.

"Please take a seat, Miss Seward." I pointed to a chair across from the settee I was occupying. Once she'd done so, I introduced myself, "I'm Catherine Worthington, and this is Owen Clapham. He's a former inspector from Scotland Yard."

She startled at the mention of his occupation, and her gaze darted back to the door. Looking for an escape, most likely.

"Would you like some tea or biscuits, Miss Seward?" Regardless of her status, it was impolite not to offer them to her.

"No, thank 'ee," she said, in a trembling voice.

"How about you, Mister Clapham?"

"No, thank you." He stood ramrod straight next to me, his gaze firmly fixed on Miss Seward. On the way here, I'd explained his role. Basically, he was here to put the fear of God into her. He was doing a magnificent job.

"Very well." I retrieved my journal from my purse and opened it to the notes I'd written at the inquest. "Miss Seward, I'd like to go over your observations the night of Lord Wakefield's death. Is that amenable to you?"

"Amen . . . amen?" she asked, a confused expression on her face.

"My apologies. Would you be willing to do so?"

A barely perceptible nod.

"Splendid." Needing her cooperation, I offered her my best smile. "Now at the inquest, you testified you had been asked to bring refreshments to this very drawing room."

"Yes, miss," she said in a small voice.

"But when you went to the servants' stairs, you discovered two guests doing something" —I glanced at my notes— "untoward. Is that correct?"

Blushing, she nodded again.

"So, you had to come around to the family's stairs, as you called it, to deliver the tray."

"Yes, miss." Her shoulders were no longer hunched over. She was starting to trust me.

"The space that leads to the family's stairs on the ground floor was closed off that night, wasn't it?"

"Yes, miss. The family did not want the guests wandering into this section, so they'd shut the doors."

"You needed to have someone open them, did you not?"

"Yes, a footman. Once I passed through, he shut them behind me."

"Very good." I noted that in my journal. "So how many

feet do you think there are between the doors and the bottom of the stairs?"

She glanced up, scrunched her mouth, and finally said, "About twenty would be my guess."

"Very good, Miss Seward. You are just about right. It's twenty-five. We asked Mister Hughes."

She smiled. "He knows everything there is to know about Brightwell Mansion."

Not quite, I wanted to say.

"Now as you approached the stairs, did you see anything or notice anyone?"

"No, miss," she said in a quivering tone.

"How far were you from Lord Wakefield when you noticed him?"

"When I got to the stairs?" It was a question, not a statement.

"Really? It would seem he'd be clearly visible from the doors."

"He wasn't. He wasn't! It was dark." Her voice rose with emotion.

"May I show you a sketch, Miss Seward?" I retrieved the drawing I'd done of the vestibule from the double doors to the bottom of the stairs.

"Yes." She caught her bottom lip between her teeth.

Joining her on the settee, I presented it to her. "As you can see, two chandeliers light the space, one by the doors and the other at the bottom of the staircase. Additionally, no less than four sconces are situated along the wall on either side. So, there is more than enough illumination to see the entire area, don't you think?"

"Yes." Poor thing was almost in tears.

I almost felt sorry for her, but I didn't. The stakes were too high. "Miss Seward. What did you see at the bottom of the stairs that night? And please don't lie to me."

"At first—at first, I was busy balancing the tray. It was awfully heavy."

"I can imagine."

"So, I didn't notice nothing wrong until" — she gulped— "until I was halfway there."

"To the staircase?"

She nodded. "She stood with her back to me, a great big, powdered wig on her head, like those ladies of old. The skirts were so wide, I couldn't see past her."

"She didn't hear you come in?"

"Not at first. But then the cups rattled, and she twisted around quick like, so fast the wig fell right off. That's when I saw a gentleman's legs. On the ground. Not moving."

"Did she say anything?"

Her chin bobbed up and down. "She asked me what I was doing there. A silly question, I thought. The tray with the food and tea service were plain as a pikestaff. But she didn't wait for my answer."

"What did she do?"

"She walked toward me, slow, like one of those big cats. She was holding something in her hand. A white stone streaked with red and grey. Her eyes—blue and brown they were—they shone with a weird light. I was that afraid, Miss."

"You noticed the color of her eyes through her mask?"

"She wasn't wearing one, Miss." She gulped again. "When she got close enough, she grabbed my arm. The tray was rattling something awful by then. And then she said, *'If you tell anybody you saw me here, I'll arrange for your death, and it won't be quick. Do you understand?'* I told her I did. And then she grabbed the wig and climbed the stairs. She dropped that stone at the top." She let out a shuddering breath. "I didn't see her no more after that."

"When did the tray you were carrying fall?"

"After she was gone, I walked up to the gentleman,

thinking he needed help. But he was lying ever so still. And then I saw his head. It had been bashed in, Miss. I dropped the tray then and screamed and screamed and screamed."

"Would you recognize the woman if you saw her again?"

"I don't think I will ever forget her face. I dream about it every night. Oh, Miss. You don't think she'll have me killed now that I told you?"

"She won't hurt you, Mary. The police are searching for her high and low. They'll find her too. Won't they, Mister Clapham."

"As sure as I'm standing here. Miss Seward needs to come with us, so she can tell Scotland Yard what she knows."

Rather than take objection, Miss Seward seemed to approve. "Will I see that inspector bloke again?" A dreamy expression bloomed across her face. "Blimey, he's ever so handsome."

I bit back a smile. "His name is Inspector Crawford, and I pretty much guarantee you will."

CHAPTER THIRTY-SIX

A MURDERER IS CAUGHT

*A*FTER INFORMING MISTER HUGHES of our plans to bring Miss Seward with us, Mister Clapham and I bundled her into the Rolls and headed toward Scotland Yard. Time being of the essence, we didn't stop at Worthington Manor to tell them our news. So, it was a surprise to arrive at police headquarters to discover Abigail Morgan had been caught trying to board a train and was being interrogated by Inspector Crawford.

"Pen him a note, Miss Worthington," Owen Clapham urged. "He needs to hear Miss Seward's account." He cast a glance toward the maid who was happily consuming a full spread right in the lobby of Scotland Yard.

On the way to police headquarters, she'd remarked she was feeling peckish due to her missing her tea. Never mind I'd offered refreshments to her. Rather than deal with a hungry witness who might not be willing to cooperate, we'd acquired a boxed meal along with a jug of ale at a pub.

Following his suggestion, I tore a blank page from my journal and penned a quick missive to Inspector Crawford. The desk sergeant, however, balked at interrupting an interrogation. So, I had no recourse but to ask for Chief Inspector Bolton. Not only had I aided him in a previous investigation, but he'd recommended Owen Clapham. Once we were shown to his office and I'd told him about Mary Seward's revelations, he took my note and personally delivered it to Inspector Crawford. Within minutes, Owen Clapham and I were shown to his office while Mary Seward remained under the watchful eye of the Chief Inspector.

Once I explained in excruciating detail what Mary Seward said, Inspector Crawford had her escorted into his chamber so he could question her.

She was nervous at first. But between him and me, we made her as comfortable as we could. Once she relaxed, the words fairly streamed out of her.

"So, you observed the lady standing over Lord Wakefield's body with a white stone in her hand?" Inspector Crawford asked.

"Yes, sir. I did."

"But you didn't see her actually strike Lord Wakefield with it?"

She shook her head. "I did not."

"And you would recognize her if you saw her again?"

"Yes, sir, I would."

He came to his feet. "Come with me then."

Her nerves made themselves known. "Wh-where are we going?"

"We have a suspect in custody. I'll need you to tell me if that's who you saw."

Now that she faced the reality of identifying the suspect, she seemed to shrink on herself. "Oh, sir. I don't know. She threatened to kill me, she did!"

I placed my arm across her shoulders. "Mary. If you say that's who you saw, she will be kept in jail and tried for the murder of Lord Wakefield. She can't harm you."

"Truly?" Her gaze desperately sought assurance.

I glanced at Inspector Crawford for confirmation.

After a moment's hesitation, he nodded. "Yes."

I knew why he'd paused. Miss Seward hadn't seen Miss Morgan strike the blow, so she could say she'd come across the body or, more likely, simply deny the whole thing. It would be her word against Mary Seward.

"Can Miss Worthington come with us?" Miss Seward asked.

"Of course," Inspector Crawford flashed one of his devastating smiles, and she sighed. I didn't blame her. I barely stopped myself from doing the same.

He escorted us to one of the lower floors which was comprised of dark hallways and even darker rooms.

"Ready?" he asked of Mary before he opened one of the doors.

When she tensed, I squeezed her hand. Together, we walked into what seemed to be an anteroom of the interrogation area. Through a glass, we could see Abigail Morgan seated on a wooden chair, handcuffed hands clenched on the table in front of her. An officer stood watch in the corner. The harsh light from a lamp shone brightly on her face. I imagine she couldn't see much beyond that. Certainly not us, as we stood in the dark.

"Blimey, she looks a proper sight," Mary Seward exclaimed.

"She certainly does," I concurred. The left side of Abigail Morgan's face was mottled with purple bruises, and something wasn't quite right about her jaw.

Mary Seward's gaze bounced to Inspector Crawford. "Did the coppers do that to her?"

"No, I did," I said with a certain amount of satisfaction.

"Miss." Admiration glowed in her eyes.

"She poisoned a dear friend of mine."

"Is your friend all right?"

"Yes, but she almost died."

Compassion shown clear in Mary Seward's gaze.

"Is that the woman you saw at the bottom of the stairs standing over Lord Wakefield's body, Miss Seward?" Inspector Crawford asked.

She squared her shoulders, stared right at Abigail Morgan, and said, "Yes, it was. You can't miss those loony eyes. Give me a fright, they do."

"Very well," Inspector Crawford said. "Mister Clapham, would you please escort Miss Seward back to my office and take very good care of her."

"It will be my pleasure, inspector," Owen Clapham replied.

Mary Seward fluttered her eyelashes at Inspector Crawford. "Thank 'ee kindly, sir."

He offered her a small bow. "No, thank you, Miss Seward. You've done the crown a great service."

"'Coo."

After she and Mister Clapham left, I said, "Seems you have an admirer, Inspector Crawford."

An arched brow was all I got in return.

"So, what's next? I assume you kept me here for a purpose."

"How very perspicacious of you, Miss Worthington."

"Cut line, inspector. What do you wish of me?"

He lost that charming smile of his. "As you probably guessed, Miss Seward's testimony won't be enough to convict Abigail Morgan. She'll simply deny it. If we are to charge her with Lord Wakefield's murder, she must be made to confess."

I blew out a whooshed breath. "That's quite a challenge."

"Indeed."

"You think I can help?"

"I do."

"How?"

He rubbed a hand across his brow. "Consumed as I was with the drug trafficking investigation, I didn't envision her as a suspect." He glanced directly at me. "But you did. You've studied her, so you know her better than I do. She has an Achilles heel. Everyone does. Find it and get her to admit to the murder."

I glanced through the glass into the room where Abigail Morgan sat, head held high, glancing away from the light. She did have an Achilles heel, and I knew what it was. But would it be enough for her to acknowledge her guilt? I didn't know. But I would have to try. Newcastle's life hanged in the balance.

But first there was a serious matter to consider. "Won't you get into trouble involving me in an interrogation?"

"Maybe in another one. But not this one. She's ruined countless lives by illegally importing cocaine. People have died after ingesting the drug. No one in Scotland Yard will whisper a word of censure."

"Very well. I'll do my best. Take me to her."

He pushed open the door between the antechamber and the interrogation room. Blinded by the light as she was, it took Abigail Morgan a few moments to identify me. "You!" She hissed. Her reaction was not totally unexpected.

"Good afternoon, Miss Morgan. How are you feeling?"

"Dandy." The word seemed to strain out of her.

"Can we fetch you some tea or something to eat?"

Her eyes blazed with fury. "Can't chew."

"I imagine speech might be difficult as well. If you don't mind, I'll do most of the talking."

I received no response in return.

"We have two matters to address. One is the drug trafficking. The other Lord Wakefield's murder. Witnesses have implicated you in both."

A choked sound escaped her.

"A witness saw and heard you discussing the formation of the Calypso Shipping Consortium with Lord Wakefield."

"Who?" she spit out.

"The name is not important. Just be assured every word of your conversations was heard. And then, of course, there's your brother who you implicated in your drug importation scheme. I'm sure he'll testify against you. After all, he's innocent of the scheme. The only role he played was to sign the papers you placed in front of him. He knew nothing of your plans to import cocaine. That won't help him avoid imprisonment as it was his signature on all the documents, though. Isn't that correct, Inspector Crawford?"

"Most certainly. Not only that, but the Crown will seize all illegally acquired funds."

"You'll need to find it first," she managed to say.

He relaxed into his chair. "We already have, Miss Morgan."

I had no idea if that was true, but I nodded in agreement. "If you harbored any hope of benefitting from your ill-gotten gains, you'd be sadly mistaken." I allowed that to sink in before I continued. "In the matter of Lord Wakefield's murder, another witness has also come forward."

"What" —she mumbled something— "she say?"

"I didn't say it was a she, Miss Morgan."

Her gaze narrowed with loathing.

"You were observed standing over the body of Lord Wakefield, a bloodied stone in your hand. The witness identified you just now." I pointed to the glass behind us.

"You b—" She came off her chair to charge me.

But the officer standing behind her clamped his hands on her shoulders and held her down. "Now, Miss, there's no call to do that. Let's do this easy like."

Twisting, she snarled at him. The effort must have hurt because a whimper escaped her.

Leaning into Inspector Crawford, I whispered, "Can't she be given something for the pain?"

"She refused a physician," he murmured back. "We can't force her to take anything she doesn't want."

Which meant I would need to hurry this along. As much as I abhorred the woman, I did not wish to see her suffer. "Miss Morgan, the longer you refuse to admit your responsibility for the drug trafficking enterprise and Lord Wakefield's murder, the longer you will be in agony."

"Go to—" Animal sounds escaped her as she collapsed on the table, mindless with pain.

My gaze bounced to Inspector Crawford. "We have to stop."

Somehow, she rallied long enough to say, "No." She blinked, clearly exhausted, and pointed to me. "You" —she took a breath— "write. I'll sign. I want" —she mumbled— "no pain."

"Fetch the physician, officer." Turning to me, he said, "How fast can you write?"

"Fast enough."

He dictated what was necessary while I wrote it all down. After the statement was read to her, she signed the document in the presence of the doctor and a clerk who'd been asked to witness the signing. Only after that was done, did she accept the blessed relief that laudanum offered.

Once she'd been led away, half comatose, I asked, "Will the statement hold up in court at the drug trafficking trial?"

"I believe so. Public sentiment is bound to turn against her for the damage she's caused. We not only have her confession, but testimony from Mrs. Pennyworth and her own brother. No judge will be brave enough to declare her statement was coerced."

"What about Lord Wakefield's murder? Is there enough evidence to charge her?"

"Yes. The maid's account will go a long way to do so. A conviction might not be possible, though."

"Why not?"

"It's her word against Mary Seward's. We have no motive that we can prove."

"You need to get the Duchess of Brightwell to admit Lord Wakefield was providing cocaine to her."

"I just received word this morning. She's been admitted to a clinic near Bath for a recuperative cure. She's unreachable, Catherine."

Mister Hughes had said she was indisposed. He hadn't lied. He'd just failed to mention she was not at Brightwell Mansion. "Will you release Newcastle?"

"It will be up to the Commissioner to decide."

I returned home dejected. We'd tried so hard to discover the evidence, worked through every clue. Abigail Morgan had confessed. And yet, in the end, it might not be enough to save Newcastle. But I would not give up. After a good night's sleep, I would craft up a new scheme to obtain the evidence Inspector Crawford needed, even if I had to break into that Bath clinic to get it.

But as it turned out, I needed to do nothing at all.

At her arraignment a few days later, Abigail Morgan willingly admitted to being the true head of the shipping consortium and Lord Wakefield's murderer. When asked by the judge why she'd killed him, she confirmed what I'd deduced. Lord Wakefield was doling out cocaine like it was sweets to persons of high stature. Apparently, the Duchess of Brightwell was not the only one. She'd been afraid he would be found out and would reveal her role to save himself. She had no recourse but to kill him to prevent that from happening. How ironic that in the end it was her own actions that ruined her.

Taking ownership of her role in the shipping consortium stemmed from the smidgen of love she felt for her brother. Her Achilles heel, if you will, which I'd observed during my conversations with them. In court, she swore he knew nothing about the importation of cocaine. He was innocent and, therefore, should not be blamed. With his title preserved and the fortune he would earn from his latest invention, I expected Archibald Morgan's life would proceed as if nothing had happened. But, of course, time would be the final arbiter of that.

When the news hit the papers, it was a scandal of prodigious proportions. It was all anybody could talk about. Archibald Morgan and Newcastle were freed and welcomed back into their respective worlds. Inspector Crawford was roundly praised for his actions in both investigations. I'd asked him to keep my contribution to himself. The last thing I wanted was more notoriety. But, of course, word got out, and I was once again swarmed with requests to accept private inquiries. Maybe this time I would do something with them.

CHAPTER THIRTY-SEVEN

ALL'S WELL THAT ENDS WELL

*T*HE SUPPER TO CELEBRATE another successful conclusion to an investigation had been held. As was the custom, the ladies had retired to the drawing room while the men remained in the dining room to enjoy their cigars and port. Although Inspector Crawford had been invited, he'd declined claiming duty called. So, it was a surprise that I found myself the recipient of a note brought by Carlton. "From Inspector Crawford, Miss Worthington. With his compliments."

Its short message read, "Meet me on the terrace." What on earth?

Situated as it was in the rear of Worthington House, the terrace presided over our meticulously kept lush garden. It was not an unusual place for us to meet. We'd done it before at the conclusion of our previous investigation. At that time, he'd hinted it was the start of something between us. But then he'd been seconded to the case in Yorkshire, and everything had come to a halt. Did he wish to resume whatever had existed between us or put paid to it all? Well, there was only one way to find out.

With seemingly all eyes on me, I excused myself and headed toward the terrace where I found Inspector Crawford waiting for me. To my surprise, he was dressed in formal evening wear. I was not complaining as he was a sight to behold. But it did beg the question. Did he intend to join us after all? If so, why did he want to meet me here?

"Is something wrong?" I asked as soon as I saw him.

"No. Nothing's the matter."

"Then why the subterfuge?"

He gave me a pointed look which I found hard to interpret. But then it became crystal clear. "I went to see your father this afternoon."

"Oh." My heart took up a mad rhythm as I realized the import of those words.

"I asked his permission to offer for you."

"And what did he say?" I asked, almost breathless.

"He said he had no objection. That it was up to you to decide. And then he reminded me of the many proposals you've turned down."

I couldn't help but smile. "He would do that. He has a sense of humor, you know."

"Yes, well. I didn't quite appreciate it at the time." He seemed nervous, a strange thing for I'd never seen him exhibit the slightest of nerves.

"Inspector Crawford, I—"

He held up his hand. "Before you say anything, please let me speak my piece."

"Very well." He deserved that and more.

"The last thing you want to do is marry."

"Yes."

"I understand the reason why. You're barely twenty-one,

and you have yet to do all the things you wish to do. You should do them."

Where was he going with this?

"One must come to a marriage with an eagerness to do so and a full commitment to the success of the union. You are not there yet."

"No."

"I understand all of that, but here's the thing." His gaze seared me. "I'm in love with you, Catherine."

My breath hitched. All these months hoping, wondering, only to finally hear him say it.

"I love your spirit, your courage, your kind heart. I would be honored if you consented to be my wife. But you're not ready for such a pledge. I don't know how long it will take, or if you ever will be. And I—"

I closed the distance between us, grabbed his lapels, and pulled him toward me. "Stop talking and kiss me."

His mouth claimed mine with passionate hunger, as his hands held me tightly to him. I wanted to sink into him and him into me and get lost in this madness together.

After he slowly ended the kiss, I rested my head against the strength of his chest and listened to the wild beating of his heart. "Oh, my." I hadn't known what to expect, certainly not the burning heat, the mad pleasure, the desperate ache for more.

He rested his head atop mine. "Exactly."

I glanced up at him. "I want this. I want you. I won't give this up." And then finally. "What are we going to do?"

He cupped my cheek. "Get engaged?"

Panic shot through me, and I broke apart. I didn't want to marry. At least not right away. I had things I wanted to do, and they required the freedom to do them. "No. That won't work."

His gaze dimmed. The change in him broke my heart. I'd devastated him.

"What if we have an understanding instead?" I rushed to say. That's what Ned and Lily had, even if their circumstances were different.

"Of what?"

"Of our feelings for each other."

"What are your feelings, Catherine?"

"I'm attracted to you, of course." It was more than that, but I was not ready to admit it. If I spoke the words, it would make things final.

"That's not enough. Not for me, anyway." He brushed a hand across his brow, glanced off into the distance, and then turned back to me. "I better go." He started to step away.

If I felt panic before, it was nothing to what I felt now. He was saying goodbye. I would never be this close to him again. Get lost in the magic of his kiss. Spar with him over an investigation. "Wait."

He gazed at me out of bleak eyes.

"Is there no other way?" Desperation tinged my voice.

"Afraid not. It's an engagement or nothing."

"Why?"

"Because it's the only way we can be together, Catherine. Surely, you see that."

"You could escort me to the theatre, or dancing, or wherever, without us being engaged."

"Other gentlemen could do so as well. And, of course, I'd be free to enjoy the company of other ladies. Is that what you wish?" He was dead serious.

I'd been wildly jealous when I thought his handkerchief had been the gift of a lady. And when I'd spotted him with Lady Cookson at Hollingsworth's lecture, I'd suffered for days. The thought of him being with another woman made me ill. The actuality would devastate me. "No. I don't."

It was my turn to put some distance between us and think things through. My hands clutched the balustrade, its rough surface biting into my hand. What he was asking of me seemed untenable, but the thought of not having him was too much to bear. I simply could not give him up, would not give him up. But if I were to promise myself to him, I had to do it my way. I swiveled toward him. "I won't be tied down."

"I wouldn't think of doing such a thing."

"We might disagree on a path I wish to take."

"More than likely. But I will bring up my point of view." When I sought to object, he stopped me. "Not so you adopt it, but that you may have an alternate opinion."

"Fair enough. What do we do now?"

That charming grin of his made an appearance. "We tell your family, of course."

I gulped. "Do we have to? I'll never hear the end of it." After turning down a myriad of proposals and affirming time and time again I had no wish to marry, they would definitely have something to say about my change of heart. But was it truly a change of heart? Or had it already been given to the man standing before me and I'd been too stupid to realize it?

"Afraid so." His commiserating smile felt like a caress. "If it's any consolation, they already know I was going to propose."

Of course, they did. Father would have told them.

"Would you do one thing for me?"

"Anything, dearest."

I let out a long-held breath. How could I not love such a man? "Would you properly propose? I'd like to have a story to tell our children." For there would be children at some point in the future. In the far, far, far off future.

"Of course." He captured my hand, got down on one knee, and gazed up at me. The way the moonlight shone brightly on his face revealed every ounce of emotion. It showed nothing but love. "You are the most maddening woman I've ever met."

Laughter escaped me. "That's a fine way to start a proposal."

He quirked a smile. "I'm not done."

"Very well. Go on."

"You're impetuous, foolhardy, reckless—"

"You're supposed to be romantic, not making a hash of it."

"—And I wouldn't have you any other way. You're perfect the way you are. And I'm madly, insanely, irrationally I might add, in love with you."

Tears filled my eyes. "Oh, Robert. I love you too."

"Catherine Louise Worthington, would you do me the great honor of becoming my wife?"

"Yes" was the only word I could get past the lump in my throat.

He came to his feet and kissed me again. And even though it was not thundering and lightning, I still felt the storm within.

CHAPTER THIRTY-EIGHT

AN ANNOUNCEMENT IS MADE

"*S*HALL WE GO TELL YOUR FAMILY?" Robert asked.

I nodded.

He must have noticed my less than enthusiastic response because he came to a sudden stop. "We don't have to do this, Catherine. If you're not absolutely sure, I can simply leave, and you can act as if nothing happened."

"But something has happened. You proposed, and I accepted."

"I haven't . . . forced you to do something you don't want?"

Laughter burst out of me. "As if you ever would. As if you ever could. No, Robert, you haven't. I only dread their reaction. After all, I've spent months telling everyone I had no wish to marry."

"Your family loves you, and your friends treasure you. They'll be happy for you."

283

"Well, there's nothing like the present to find out." I curled my hand around his elbow. "Lead on, Macduff."

From all his height, he glanced down at me, a grin on his lips. "Quoting from *Macbeth*? A tragedy?"

"If the shoe fits," I said with a teasing smile.

Not only was my family in the drawing room, but so were Sebastian and Lily. Lord Marlowe and Lady Emma. Newcastle and Lady Wakefield. Lords Hollingsworth and Rutledge. And Owen Clapham. In short, everyone who'd had anything to do with our lives in the last few months.

"Well?" Someone asked.

"She said yes," Robert exclaimed.

"Of course, I did. I'm not an idiot." I had to save face somehow.

Everyone swarmed in to congratulate us.

"I knew it!" Margaret hugged me before turning to Sebastian. "Didn't I say so, time and again?"

"So, you did, my love. My felicitations, Kitty, Inspector Crawford. May you be as happy as Megs and I are."

Lily hugged me next. "I'm so happy for you."

"Thank you. How are you feeling?" She'd bounced back from her ordeal with amazing alacrity. Proof of which were the roses on her cheeks. But it would be a long time before I stopped inquiring about her health.

"Fine. More than fine." She sent a loving glance toward Ned who approached us next.

"I wish you every happiness, my dear sister." He kissed my cheek before offering his hand to Robert. "Welcome to the family, Inspector."

"Thank you."

Hollingsworth stepped forward next. "Good luck, old man. You deserve nothing but the best." His gaze turned to me. "And you now have that."

"That's so kind of you to say so, Lord Hollingsworth," I said.

He crooked a grin. "Of course, she'll lead you a merry chase."

I narrowed my gaze at him.

Lady Wakefield, with Newcastle by her side, held my hands. "You'll have a fine marriage, you know. You're very well suited."

"Thank you," I said. "How is Lavender Rose?" As soon as Newcastle was freed, Lady Wakefield had gathered her daughter and taken her home to Wakefield House. But it was only temporary as she and Lavender Rose would shortly settle into one of Newcastle's country estates. After her year of mourning ended, Newcastle and Lady Wakefield were planning to wed.

"She spoke her first word."

"How wonderful. What was it?" I asked, expecting her to say Mama.

"Cat."

I burst into laughter.

She shared a loving glance with Newcastle. "Simon presented her with a kitten two days ago."

"Did you really, milord?"

"I did."

She curled her arm through his elbow. "And now he's become her favorite."

My gaze bounced between the two of them. "Oh, I think you're both her favorite."

Newcastle's face flushed with pleasure before he turned to Robert. "What can I say?"

"Wish us the best?" Robert suggested.

"That and much more."

When it was Lady Emma's turn, she heartily embraced me. "Congratulations."

"You're not shaking your head in despair?"

"How could I, dear Kitty? You've always been meant for each other."

I pressed her hand.

A wildly grinning Owen Clapham took his turn. "My heartiest felicitations and best wishes."

"Thank you, Mister Clapham. How is Bumble, or should I call her Eleanor?"

"Either would do. She's been safely delivered of a little girl that she named Ophelia."

"Oh." My gaze misted with tears. "I'm so happy for her and you."

"I would have never found her without you." Seemingly choked up with emotion, he merely nodded to Robert before walking away.

A hesitant Lord Marlowe stepped up. Rather than wish us the best, he spoke only three words, "Et tu, Brute."

"Oh, get on with you, man," Hollingsworth exclaimed. "'Tis time to congratulate them not enact a Shakespearean tragedy."

After we glanced at each other, laughter exploded out of Robert and me.

Father waited for our hilarity to subside before he approached. "You're not turning this one down?"

"No," was all I could manage.

"He's an excellent choice, Kitty. I heartily approve." After embracing me, Father shook Robert's hand. "Take good care of her, Son. She's very precious to me."

"I intend to, sir."

Sporting a wide grin, Lord Rutledge slapped Robert's back. "Congratulations, my boy."

"Thank you, milord."

He kissed me on the cheek. "You, my girl, should wear the pearls I gifted you on your wedding day."

"I'll be proud to do so, milord."

After everyone had their say, champagne was ordered to celebrate.

"When's the wedding?" Hollingsworth asked, a devilish glint in his gaze.

"As we have been engaged less than a minute, we have yet to consider it. Regardless, it will have to be after Margaret's, and she's not getting married until June." Which was a reprieve of sorts.

"Actually, we've moved up the date," Margaret said. "We're holding the ceremony at Wynchcombe Castle on Christmas Eve. Everyone here is invited by the way," she said, glancing around.

A sinking feeling hit my stomach, but somehow, I managed to smile. "How wonderful. Why the change?"

"Well, dear Lily will be making her debut in the spring," Margaret explained, "so Sebastian and I want to be here to smooth her way. By then, I'll be the Duchess of Wynchcombe, so I'll be able to sponsor her court presentation as well."

Margaret's kindness toward her future sister-in-law was truly admirable. It augured well for the success of her marriage to Sebastian. He was doing his best to make amends for the many years he and Lily had been cruelly kept apart by their grandfather.

"But what about Oxford?" I doubted she'd give up her goal of earning a degree from that august university, especially with only one year left to go.

"I've arranged matters with the warden of my college. After the Hilary term, I'll reside in London, although I'll still have to travel to Oxford one day a week to attend tutorials. My efforts on behalf of women's causes both now and in the spring will provide credit toward my degree. And, of course, I will still have to write papers on those subjects."

"If anybody can pull all that off, it would be you, Margaret."

Sebastian placed an arm around her waist and kissed her cheek. "I hope somewhere in there you'll find time for your husband."

"I'll keep Tuesdays and Thursdays open for you," she said with a wink.

"And all of your nights," he whispered sotto voce. They exchanged a look which spoke of promises made. They were so perfectly suited for each other.

"So now that my wedding date is settled, when will yours be?" Margaret asked, turning back to me.

"You'd make a beautiful June bride," Lily suggested.

My breath cut short. June was less than a year away. "Perhaps. Although autumn would be better. Such a beautiful time of year. Or maybe the following Christmas."

A laughing Robert folded me into his arms right in front of everyone. "At that rate, I'll be an old man before I can claim you as my bride."

"Claim?" I asked, arching a brow.

Hollingsworth dropped a hand on Robert's shoulder. "I'd quit while you're ahead."

The inspector shrugged him off. "I don't take advice from confirmed bachelors."

How could I not have seen the camaraderie they shared?

I led Robert away from the crowd toward a window where we could enjoy a bit of privacy. "We haven't talked about our wedding date as there's been no time. Would you mind awfully waiting a little while?"

He tweaked my chin. "Take all the time you need. I'll be right here waiting for you."

"You're very sure of your charms, Inspector." He thought to ensorcell me with the magic of his kisses and caresses. I didn't blame him. He was very good at it.

An enigmatic smile was his only response.

I glanced up to find Mother standing not far, tears in her eyes. Seemingly with one mind, Margaret and I rushed to embrace her.

"Two daughters engaged. My heart overflows with joy."

"One to a peer, and one to the wife of a Scotland Yard Inspector," I said, eager to let everyone know how very proud I was of my fiancé's status.

"Make that Chief Inspector," Robert said.

"You were promoted?" I asked.

"Yes. It will mean more responsibility."

"Which you will prove more than capable of handling, Robert," Mother said.

"Thank you, ma'am."

"Please call me Mildred. We're family now."

"So, we are."

Once the celebration dwindled and the guests departed, I accompanied Robert to the foyer.

He held my left hand as we stood by the front door. "We'll need to go shopping so you can choose an engagement ring."

I thought of the cost that would entail. "We don't have to."

A frown marred his brow. "You don't wish to wear one?"

"No, it's not that. It's just . . . the expense of it." I'd always wondered about his finances. His Eaton Square address, his high-end suits, his Rolex wristwatch all spoke of money, but I had no idea how flush he was. Not that it mattered. I would take him any way he came.

He stroked my cheek with his thumb. "That's something you need never worry about."

Ever curious, I had to ask, "Why?"

"It's not my secret to tell, Catherine. If it were, I would let you know. Be assured there are plenty of funds, and they're all under the management of Worthington & Son."

Well, that was a surprise. "Father's firm? How?"

"As soon as I'm at liberty to do so, I will share the information with you. Now about that visit to the jeweler. Tomorrow at two?"

"Yes."

He threaded his hands through mine. "So, once you're a married woman—"

"Which won't happen for some time."

"—you'll give up your investigations?" His half smile should have alerted me. But it didn't.

Instead, I yanked my hands free. "I certainly will not. Margaret does not intend to give up her work on women's causes. I most certainly will not relinquish my investigations. As a matter of fact, Lady Emma and I will be setting up our own enterprise. We're going to call it Ladies of Distinction Detective Agency."

"Lady Emma is joining you in this endeavor?"

"She doesn't wish to return home, and she's proven quite adept at sleuthing. Almost as good as me if I may add."

He gazed off into the distance, a wrinkle to his brow. "Well, that's certainly something to think about."

I squared my shoulders. "You must take me as I am, Inspector. Or leave me." Too late, I wished I could take back those last words.

He gazed at me with all the love in the world. "As if I ever could." He shook his head. "What am I going to do with you?"

I curled my arms around him and drew him close. "The more important question, Robert, is what are we going to do together? I, for one, can't wait to find out."

His response was everything I'd ever dreamed of and more.

* * *

FOLLOW the adventures of Kitty Worthington, Inspector Crawford, and Kitty's family and friends in the next book, **Murder at the Tower of London**, Book 4 in The Kitty Worthington Mysteries. Available from Amazon Murder at the Tower of London

After a royal prince is assassinated at the Tower of London, Kitty Worthington is asked to investigate. The murder seems to be the work of a madman who soon makes her his next target. Can she catch the killer before she loses her head as well?

London. 1923. Excited about her new direction in life, Kitty Worthington dashes about London in her spiffy new motorcar. Granted, searching for purloined poodles and lost labradors may not be what she envisioned, but they keep her busy enough. At least, there aren't any bodies dropping at her feet.

But then a royal dignitary loses his head at the Tower of London, and she finds herself embroiled in yet another murder investigation. The suspects are endless. Could it be the wastrel son? The betrayed wife? The devious cousin? The ghost of Anne Boleyn?

With the help of her ace team, comprised of lords and ladies, her maid and chauffeur, and Sir Winston, her ever flatulent Bassett Hound, she sets out to solve the mystery. But there's a fiend on the loose who's made her his next target. If she wants to catch the murderer before she loses her own head, she needs something more, someone who knows all about the royals. And that can be only one person, heaven help her, her mother.

Murder at the Tower of London, the fourth book in The Kitty Worthington Mysteries, is another frolicking, historical cozy mystery filled with cagey suspects, a duplicitous villain, and an intrepid heroine sure to win your heart. Available from Amazon Murder at the Tower of London

* * *

HAVE you read the first Kitty Worthington Mystery? **Murder on the Golden Arrow**, book 1 in the Kitty Worthington Mysteries, is available on Amazon Murder on the Golden Arrow

What's a bright young woman to do when her brother becomes the main suspect in a murder? Why, solve the case of course.

England. 1923. After a year away at finishing school where she learned etiquette, deportment, and the difference between a salad fork and a fish one, Kitty Worthington is eager to return home. But minutes after she and her brother Ned board the Golden Arrow, the unthinkable happens. A woman with a mysterious connection to her brother is poisoned, and the murderer can only be someone aboard the train.

When Scotland Yard hones on Ned as the main suspect, Kitty sets out to investigate. Not an easy thing to do while juggling the demands of her debut season and a mother intent on finding a suitable, aristocratic husband for her.

With the aid of her maid, two noble beaus, and a flatulent Basset Hound named Sir Winston, Kitty treads a fearless path through the glamorous world of high society and London's dark underbelly to find the murderer. For if she fails, the insufferable Inspector Crawford will most surely hang a noose around her brother's neck.

A frolicking historical cozy mystery filled with dodgy suspects, a dastardly villain, and an intrepid heroine sure to win your heart. Available on Amazon and Kindle Unlimited Murder on the Golden Arrow

ISBN-13: (EBook) 978-1-943321-14-8

ISBN-13: (Print) 978-1-943321-17-9

Hearts Afire Publishing First Edition: June 2022

CAST OF CHARACTERS

Kitty Worthington - Our amateur sleuth

The Family
    Mildred Worthington - Kitty's mother
    Edward Worthington - Kitty's father
    Ned Worthington - Kitty's oldest brother
    Richard Worthington - Kitty's next older brother, in Egypt
    Margaret Worthington - Kitty's older sister

The Worthington Household
    Betsy - Kitty's maid
    Mr. Carlton - the family butler
    Mrs. Simpson - the family housekeeper
    Neville - the family chauffeur and Betsy's beau
    Cook - Betsy's aunt
    Sir Winston - the family's Bassett Hound

The Wynchcombe Family

Sebastian Dalrymple - the Duke of Wynchcombe and Margaret's fiancé

Lady Lily Dalrymple - Sebastian's sister

Duke of Wynchcombe Household

Mr. Temple - the Wynchcombe House butler

Other Notable Characters

Detective Inspector Robert Crawford

Owen Clapham - former Scotland Yard detective inspector, now Kitty's tutor

Lord Marlowe - an Earl

Lord Newcastle - another Earl and Ned's friend

Lady Emma Carlyle - debutante

Lord Wakefield - an earl

Lady Wakefield - Lord Wakefield's wife

Lord Hollingsworth - explorer and adventurer

Lady Cookson - friend of detective inspector Crawford

Duchess of Brightwell - Midsummer Masked Ball Hostess

Duke of Brightwell - Midsummer Masked Ball Host

Abigail Morgan- cousin to Lord Wakefield

Archibald Morgan- heir apparent to Lord Wakefield and Abigail's brother

Made in the USA
Monee, IL
19 June 2022